Readers Love
Shira Anthony

Stealing the Wind

“The fantastic world Mrs. Anthony has created motivates you even more to understand and learn about the characters…. I consider myself a hopeless fan from now on, awaiting for the next installment of the Mermen of Ea series.”

—Book Suburbia

“What a fantastic start to a new fantasy series. I was sucked in from the first page and am now waiting impatiently for the next book.”

—Gay List Book Reviews

“I recommend this one for any lover of fantasy stories, mermen, or to those who simply want to enjoy the adventure. I’m looking forward to reading more about these two in book two.”

—Hearts on Fire

The Melody Thief

“Awesome!!! I loved everything Shira Anthony brought to the story—the characters, the language, the music and the conflict. Every concept exceptionally written and enjoyable.”

—LeAnn’s Book Reviews

“I recommend this book to everyone with a romantic heart, like me, and a love for the magic of music, and of love’s ability to overcome any obstacle. Thanks, again, Shira, for reminding us that beauty lies in all of us and that music, like nothing else, will bring this to the surface.”

—Rainbow Books Reviews

By SHIRA ANTHONY

NOVELS
Blue Notes
Melody Thief
Aria
Prelude
Encore
Symphony in Blue

MERMEN OF EA
Stealing the Wind

With VENONA KEYES
The Trust

With EM LYNLEY
A DELECTABLE NOVEL
Lighting the Way Home

NOVELLAS
The Dream of a Thousand Nights

Published by DREAMSPINNER PRESS
http://www.dreamspinnerpress.com

Blue Notes

Shira Anthony

Dreamspinner Press

Published by
Dreamspinner Press
5032 Capital Circle SW
Suite 2, PMB# 279
Tallahassee, FL 32305-7886
USA
http://www.dreamspinnerpress.com/

ISBN: 978-1-62798-382-2
Digital ISBN: 978-1-62798-381-5

Printed in the United States of America
Second Edition
February 2014
First edition published by Dreamspinner Press, December 2011.

ACKNOWLEDGMENTS

To Jim, for all of the years that your musical voice joined with mine and for your friendship long after the Diva of Demington's retirement. I would like nothing more than to write you a happily-ever-after.

To Thea Nishimori, for your tireless work in helping me craft Jules and Jason's story.

And to my parents, Sheldon and Lucille, for giving me the gift of France. *Je vous remercie*.

CHAPTER 1

JASON GREENE leaned back against the headrest and watched the clouds beneath the wing of the airplane. Used to traveling business class, with all six foot three of him now wedged into the narrow coach seat, he cursed every aeronautical engineer who had ever suggested refitting wide-bodied jets to accommodate more passengers.

He eyed the center section of the cabin with longing, regretting that he'd chosen a window seat. Several college students with more foresight were already stretched out on the few empty seats in the back to sleep during the long flight from Philadelphia to Paris. In the final analysis, however (and, exceptional lawyer that he was, he *always* analyzed), it was his fault alone that he should suffer the indignities of traveling like an eighteen-year-old again; it was his foolhardy last-minute decision that had landed him here.

What the hell were you thinking?

The thought had run like an endless loop through his exhausted mind for the past three hours. He knew the answer, of course: he *hadn't* thought at all, he'd just reacted. He'd done a lot of that lately.

A female flight attendant—blonde, attractive, and in her midthirties—stopped at his row with a stack of plastic cups and a pitcher of water. "Something to drink?" she offered, her voice a sensual undertone. No doubt she appreciated the lone well-dressed man amidst the myriad students wired to iPods, iPads, and other devices.

He'd come to dismiss such attention; he'd long engendered this kind of response from women. With his wavy auburn hair, strong jaw, and bright-green eyes, he was, as his grandmother often reminded him, "quite a catch." Add to that a salary well into the six-figure range and his job as an equity partner at a large Philadelphia law firm, and Jason Greene had never had much trouble finding women to date. Except that he hadn't quite managed to keep the woman he'd fallen in love with happy.

"Yes, some water, please," he replied, offering the flight attendant the same pleasant, reassuring smile he'd offered his clients for the past ten years. The same smile he'd offered Diane upon his return home to their high-rise apartment each night, having missed dinner yet again. It was far more effective with the flight attendant.

She handed him a cup of water. "Business or pleasure?" Perhaps she mistook his politeness for something more like interest. (He wasn't interested—he'd had enough of women to last him a lifetime.)

"Neither," he answered, forestalling any further discussion. She responded with a slight chuckle, then moved on to the next row back.

He closed his eyes and pressed the button to recline his seat. It only moved about an inch. He looked around. He hadn't noticed his seat was right in front of an exit row. *Figures.* He shook his head. Resigned to his fate, he grabbed the extra pillow off the empty seat next to his and pushed up the armrest to give himself more room. He pulled the slippery blue polyester blanket over himself and shifted on an angle to tuck his long legs under the aisle seat in front of him. It wasn't comfortable, but it would do.

He looked out the window once more. It was dark now, and here, above the clouds, he saw stars. He closed his eyes and rearranged the pillows so that his head rested against the cool bulkhead. He drifted off into an uneasy sleep with the drone of the engines in his ears.

ONLY A day before, he'd been dressed in a charcoal-gray Armani suit with a yellow-striped Brooks Brothers tie, looking out a wall of windows at the thickening gray clouds over Philadelphia. The forecast called for snow. Again.

"You want *what*?" Scott Reston, the managing partner of Halwell, Richardson & Dailey, leaned back in his chair and gaped at Jason as though he were an alien.

"I'm taking a leave of absence," Jason repeated calmly. "Starting tomorrow."

"*Tomorrow*?" Scott's voice resonated with shock. "Jason, I know you're pissed that Diane—"

"I've worked my ass off for this firm," he countered before Scott could complete his sentence, all the while maintaining his calm resolve. His jaw tightened in spite of his control. "I've been pulling in enough billables to more than cover a few months off."

"*Months*?" The word came out in a half-strangled gasp. "You want months? Look, Jaz, if you need help, I can put the new kid—what's his name, Sanderson?—on some of your cases."

"It's not about the caseload. I haven't taken time off in years, except the trip with Diane to her sister's wedding. I need—"

"Then take a few weeks," Scott interrupted, no doubt hoping this settled the matter. "Go somewhere warm. You can use our apartment in Cancun if you want. Maybe you can pick up some cute Mexican babe while you're—"

"Two months, Scott." Jason lapsed into his commanding courtroom voice without a second thought. "The other partners won't question it if you're on board. Hell, if you want, I'll take a smaller draw this year." The rumble of Jason's deep baritone caused one of the paperweights on Scott's desk to vibrate.

"Hell, Jaz Man. It's *me*, remember? The guy you pulled all-nighters with in law school? That lawyer shit won't work here. And since when do you let a bitch like Diane—"

"Drop it." Jason knew his tone was colder than the icicles that hung on the eaves outside the building, but he didn't give a shit. This was one subject he wasn't going to get into with Scott—or anyone else, for that matter. "This wasn't her fault."

"The fuck! She *cheated* on you."

"I *said*, drop it. Whatever she did, she had her reasons."

Reason one: too many hours spent at the office. Reason two: too few hours spent at home. Both your fault.

"Jaz Man...." Scott groaned and leaned back in his chair with the same party-boy look Jason remembered from law school. "Jaz, you're killing me. I'm up to my neck in depos in the Alvarez case, and

TransAllied just sent me a class-action complaint in a race case out of Cleveland. You're the only one licensed up there."

"Nothing'll happen in the next two months on the Cleveland case, and you know it," he shot back. "I'll remove it to federal court, and one of your new hires can start on a motion for summary judgment and getting documents together for discovery. And if the judge wants a local guy in on the scheduling conference, you can call my buddy Phil Lane up there to handle it. He owes me one."

Scott's frown deepened. "I can't convince you that you're a crazy asshole, can I?"

"Unlikely," he replied with a self-deprecating laugh. "You've had more than ten years to try." He took a deep breath, allowed his shoulders to relax a bit, and made an attempt to soften his expression. "Look, Scotty… I need this. It'll only be for two months. I promise I'll come back and make it up to you. Just two months."

"Yeah, yeah." Scott exhaled, sounding a bit like a pipe releasing steam. "Fine. I'll take the heat from the big guns. With all the money you've been pulling in for the past few years, they'll squawk a little, but they'll be more worried about losing you for good."

"Thanks." Jason turned to leave.

"So where're you going? Backpacking in South America? Some desert island in the Caribbean?" Scott asked. "Buddhist retreat in Tibet?"

"Paris." Jason stopped at the door with his fingers curled around the handle.

"Paris in *January*?"

"Yeah."

"Cold as hell, I hear."

"Yeah. Something like that."

THE PLANE touched down at Charles de Gaulle Airport on time in a misting rain. Pulling his small suitcase behind him, headed for the line of taxis, Jason laughed to himself. It was considerably warmer here than in Philly. It had snowed in this part of France a few weeks before, but nothing remained of the drifts that had paralyzed the region.

A taxi pulled to the curb, and the driver got out and put Jason's bag in the trunk. "À 146 rue d'Assas," he told the driver.

"Oui, monsieur" came the curt response.

Jason leaned forward, elbow on one knee, and watched the dull procession of warehouses that stretched between the airport and the city. The scenery didn't look all that much different than the outskirts of Philly except for the tiny cars and French road signs announcing various autoroutes. It wasn't until he saw the white stone basilica of Sacré-Cœur perched high atop Montmartre that he relaxed back into the seat.

It's been too long.

The rain picked up as the taxi turned the corner onto rue d'Assas, affording a quick view of the grand fountain at the end of the Jardins du Luxembourg with its immense horses. The park looked gray, lifeless. He handed the driver a fifty-euro bill, pulled up the door code on his smartphone and entered it into the silver keypad, then walked into the tiled vestibule when the wooden door clicked open. After rummaging briefly in his pockets, he pulled out a set of keys and unlocked the door to the courtyard. As he pulled it, his suitcase clattered across the uneven flagstones toward yet another doorway. In spite of the cold, tiny vines of delicate yellow flowers climbed the side of the building. In spring, the entire courtyard would be full of colorful blooms tended by the building's various residents.

The second door opened without a key, and he walked a few more feet to an apartment door painted a bright shade of blue, almost turquoise. He tapped the automatic lights, illuminating the corridor, and plunged his key into the lock. The apartment was cold—colder even than outside. It had been unoccupied for months, and the frigid air from the courtyard leaked in through the ancient windows.

He left his suitcase by the front door and flipped a switch to light the entryway. A burst of color on the dining room table caught his eye as he turned up the thermostat. *Rosie*, he thought with a smile. She must have asked the building superintendent to set the flowers there for him.

The edges of his mouth turned up as he inhaled the sweet scent of the bouquet. Freesia and irises. There was an envelope propped against the vase, with a typewritten message inside:

Jason—

Looks like I'll be in Milan until late March. Call me on my cell when you get in. I'll take the TGV up for a weekend when you're ready for visitors. I've had Rémy stock the fridge for a few days. The place is yours for as long as you need it. Remember to relax!

Love you,

Rosalie

Three years older than he, his sister, Rosalie, had purchased the Paris apartment years ago, having done quite well in her work as a fashion designer. Jason had stayed here once, more than ten years before, between law school and his first job as an attorney.

She's right—you need to relax. That's what this is all about, isn't it?

He hopped into the shower to wash away the long flight and tried to clear his mind. He knew this trip was about more than needing time off to relax. He was running—running from everything wrong with his life: the long hours, the loving relationship that had slipped through his hands, the pain of betrayal, and the desire to do something with his life other than earn more money than he could ever spend. He hadn't taken the job because he'd wanted the money anyhow. He hadn't wanted to end things with Diane. But he hadn't done anything to change his life either. He'd just done what he'd been doing for years.

Until now.

He toweled off, then clicked the remote on Rosalie's sound system. Fifties jazz filled the apartment, and for the first time in weeks, he smiled.

For a half an hour, he lay on the couch, letting the music wash over him. At last, drawing inspiration from the music, he threw on a pair of jeans and a warm sweater, shoved his wallet and phone into his pocket, and grabbed his jacket and umbrella. With thoughts of a long walk, something to eat, and perhaps listening to some live music later on, he was out the door minutes later, uncombed hair and all.

"OY! HENRI!" Jules Bardon shouted over the din of clattering dishes. "You said you'd get your drums set up before you started working."

Blond hair flopping into his eyes and up to his arms in soapsuds, Henri shouted back, "You can do it for a change, you lazy ass! You want to get me fired? If I lose my job, you lose a place to sleep, remember?"

Jules scowled, walked over to the sinks, and planted himself behind Henri. "And whose fault is it you're so late getting to work? You spent the night with Pascal again, didn't you?"

"Is that a problem?" Henri retorted without looking up from his task. "Maybe you're just jealous. Since you dumped—" He paused for effect. "—what's his name…?"

"Philippe," Jules supplied.

"Right. Since you dumped Philippe, you haven't gotten any."

"Philippe was a shit," Jules countered, only half joking.

"I'm sure I could convince Pascal to let you join *us*, if you'd like." Henri smirked. A soap bubble rose from the sink, and Jules flicked an angry finger by Henri's face to pop it.

"Not interested. But if you're going to spend the whole night fucking, the least you could do is set an alarm. What the hell do I know about putting together a drum set?"

"You've watched me do it a hundred times," Henri shot back, laughing and plunking several plates down on the side of the sink. Tiny rivers of water ran from the counter down to the drain. More bubbles floated up toward the ceiling. The place reeked of grease, cigarette smoke, and soap.

"Maurice doesn't let us play here very often." Jules was half-tempted to throttle his roommate. They'd been waiting for a chance like this for nearly a year, since the last time some band had canceled at the last minute. "You have to take this seriously. You never know who might be listening."

Henri turned and put a soapy hand on Jules's shoulder. "Dreamer." He bit his cheek, then added, "Fine. I'll set up my drums if *you* finish the dishes."

"You got gloves somewhere?"

"Gloves?" Henri held up his bare hands and smirked. His fingers were puckered and white.

"If I do the dishes, my calluses will—"

"You're a fucking prima donna, Jules," Henri grumbled. He shrugged, turned back to the sink, and laughed again. "It's all right. There are gloves on the shelf to your left." He looked over his shoulder and winked.

Jules shook his head and reached for the gloves. He snapped the rubber menacingly at Henri before giving him a shove in the direction of the nightclub's stage, just beyond the kitchen.

THE NIGHT sky had begun to clear as Jason left the small café where he'd eaten dinner, and he wandered up toward Île de la Cité, hoping to catch a view of the Eiffel Tower. Crossing the Seine at ten o'clock, he watched as the tower was illuminated in a shower of sparkles. His sister had told him the Parisians had so enjoyed the lighting for the millennium that they'd insisted the special effects continue for the foreseeable future. Leaning against the wall that ran along the river's edge, Jason thought of nothing but the lights as he ignored the damp chill of the evening.

When the light show ended, Jason headed back down boulevard Saint-Michel in search of some of the jazz clubs he'd discovered hidden amongst the tiny streets years ago. Normally he'd have asked a friend for a recommendation or consulted a guidebook on his phone. But tonight he didn't do either. Other than hopping the plane to Paris, how long had it been since he'd done something spontaneous? Other than the night he'd walked in on Diane having sex with someone else, his entire life had become predictable. Boring.

Why not?

He had nowhere to go, nobody waiting for him, no deadlines to meet. He could sleep late. A few drinks and some good music would help him sleep a lot better anyhow. He grinned and walked onward, cold hands shoved into his pockets.

Why the hell not?

He spotted a club as he turned the corner—a small, grayish-looking dive with a purple neon sign above the entrance, nestled between a bakery and a store that sold Japanese manga. Inhaling the fragrance of pastries baking in the boulangerie, he walked over to peer inside. He couldn't see anything, but the sounds of modern jazz wafted onto the street. He glanced up and read the sign: "Le Loup-Garou." The Werewolf.

A fitting name for a hole like this. And just the kind of place where you'd expect to hear great music.

JULES GLANCED over at Henri and their pianist, David. David grinned and nodded as he caressed the keys of the upright piano, his touch so delicate that Jules could hear him breathe with each phrase. David complained that the instrument was out of tune and a "piece of shit," but the sound he managed to coax from it was astonishingly sweet. Henri's mellow brush strokes over the surface of the snare drum joined the soft piano, much like the sound of the rain on the city streets—understated yet insistent. Sexy.

Jules gripped the neck of his violin and tucked the instrument under his chin. There was a rough patch of skin there, a result of years of playing, that looked much like the mark of an overzealous lover. He drew his bow above the strings and allowed it to hover there for an instant before lightly catching the D string. The sound of the violin flickered like a candle flame blown by an unseen breeze, then grew and melded with the muted piano, sultry and inviting. Jules closed his eyes, letting the sound wash over him, responding to the slow harmonic progression on the piano, both instruments weaving the ghostly melody.

IN A dim alcove only a dozen or so feet from the musicians, Jason sat nursing his drink, transported by the sound of the violin. It wasn't jazz in its purest form—it was more of a hybrid, combining the traditional jazz rhythms of the fifties with a modern yet classical approach. But whatever you might call the music, he found it transcendent. Between pieces, Jason glanced around the room to discover the group's name but found no mention of it anywhere.

The set ended and the club erupted in applause. The musicians nodded, their manner casual, aloof, even a bit embarrassed. The violinist met Jason's eyes and, for a brief instant, lingered there. Jason's face heated. Breaking their eye contact to look down at his empty glass, he told himself that the heat in his cheeks was from the alcohol and the lack of sleep. He motioned to the lone waiter for a refill. When he turned back toward the stage, he found himself sitting face-to-face with the violinist.

"May I join you?" the violinist asked, a coy grin on his delicate lips. Jason figured that he might be nineteen, tops. As his companion brushed a stray lock of shoulder-length black hair from his eyes, Jason realized that he had one brown eye and one green. He was a waif of a kid, his face uniquely French, from the slightly pronounced nose to the sharper edge of his jaw. Even seated as he was, Jason could see that the kid's body swam in a large pair of jeans that hung low on his hips, exposing blue plaid boxers. On top, he wore a body-hugging black T-shirt with the word "Quoi?" splashed across the front in bright red.

"Be my guest," Jason replied in French, still unsure of what to think about the kid. "Seems as though you've already invited yourself."

"You're French-Canadian?" the newcomer inquired, grin widening.

"American." Jason noted the rough edges of the uneven tattoo on the kid's right forearm. Homemade, no doubt.

"Really? Your French is excellent."

"And your music's good," Jason countered playfully. "What's your trio called?"

"Dunno. We haven't named it yet—we don't play that much. Wouldn't have played tonight except the group Maurice booked canceled and he couldn't find a replacement. My roommate's the dishwasher here." He gestured at the drummer, who was watching them with interest from the edge of the small stage. "So, do you live in Paris?" he added after a moment's pause.

"Visiting."

The waiter deposited two drinks on the table and winked at the violinist.

"My name's Jules. Jules Bardon."

"Jason Greene."

"Enchanté." Jules took Jason's hand across the table. The gesture was far too friendly. Flirtatious. Jason pulled his hand away and raised an eyebrow. Jules appeared unfazed. "Here on business?"

"No."

"Pleasure, then?"

"No."

Jules laughed—a soft, almost girlish laugh. "Do I make you uncomfortable?" He fixed his gaze on Jason.

"No," lied Jason, finding Jules's gaze a bit too intense.

"I could *make* this a pleasure visit for you." Jules absentmindedly traced a long finger across his own lips.

"I don't bat for that team." Jason borrowed the American expression wholesale as his French failed him at last. It was not the first time he'd spoken the words, although it was the first time he'd spoken them in French. They were also not entirely true; it was simply that the right opportunity had never presented itself.

Jules looked at him for a moment, clearly uncomprehending, then laughed again.

"What's so funny?" Jason demanded, noting a hint of licorice on the air as his companion replaced his drink on the table.

"Oh," Jules said, "I understand." He laughed again. "Sorry. I've just never heard it put that way before. At first I thought you were asking me about baseball." He took a swig of his drink and shrugged. "Too bad. You looked like you could use a good—"

"Jules!"

"I have to go." Jules sighed and appeared disappointed. "Time for the next set. It was nice to meet you, Jason." He tripped over the name, and it came out sounding something like "Jah-sohn." Jason chuckled in spite of himself, reminded of the various ways in which his name had been mangled by French speakers through the years.

Jules sucked down the rest of his drink in one swallow and stood up. “If you change your mind…,” he began, but the drummer grabbed him by the arm and dragged him back toward the stage.

Not likely, kid. Jason chuckled again. He had enough shit to deal with.

IT WAS nearly two in the morning when Jason left the club—a full twenty-four hours since he’d really slept well. The rain had begun to fall again, this time in torrents. In spite of the downpour, Jason decided to walk. The Métro had stopped running nearly an hour before, and the rain and exercise helped clear his mind.

He headed down boulevard Saint-Germain, past the darkened storefronts and the few cafés that were still open. He crossed a side street, glancing to his left to see the impressive Panthéon with its white stone surface still lit. In that moment, he realized that he’d never taken the time to explore Paris as an adult—he’d chosen instead to get wasted and hang out in clubs rather than do any serious sightseeing. No, most of his memories of the city were those from his childhood when his parents had dragged him and Rosalie around to all the museums and tourist destinations.

He reached the corner of Saint-Michel and waited for the light to turn. On the other side of the street, he spotted a lone figure waiting at a bus stop. “Jules?” he called out as he stepped onto the other curb.

“Jason?” Jules appeared surprised but pleased to see him. Jason noticed he was shouldering a neon-green violin case with a few peeling Rolling Stones stickers. Jules had no umbrella and no jacket and was soaked to the skin, his dark hair plastered to his pale cheeks as he shivered. His lips were already slightly blue.

“I enjoyed the music,” was all Jason said. *Damn, but the kid looks young.* He reminded Jason of a street kid.

“Thanks,” Jules mumbled as he wiped the rain from his cheeks.

“Missed your bus?”

“Yeah. There’s another in about an hour. They don’t run often this time of night.”

"Have a good night." Jason offered Jules a sympathetic smile. He crossed the street and started back to his apartment as the rain began to fall even harder. Jason shivered and pulled his jacket a bit tighter around his neck.

He hummed one of the pieces Jules's trio had played, the splash of his feet against the sidewalk mimicking the rhythm of the music. Something about the music had lingered with him.

A crack of thunder brought him back to himself. His jacket was growing soggy from the rain. He saw the taxi near the corner of the next street and stepped over a small river of water to hail it.

"Where can I take you?" the driver asked as Jason slipped inside the cab.

Jason thought of Jules standing on the street corner, freezing. He'd walked into the Loup-Garou on a lark. He'd taken a chance, done something different. He could imagine Diane's voice in his mind: "Are you insane? Why would you even think about taking someone you just met home?" It probably *was* insane.

Why not?

He thought of a hundred reasons he shouldn't take the chance, including the way Jules had so openly flirted with him. But the hundred reasons morphed into the enticing sound of Jules's music and the way Jason had felt as he listened.

Why not? If he listened to his brain, he'd still be in Philadelphia now, poring over documents, wondering what he could have done differently in his life. Wishing he *had* done things differently. "Do it," his gut told him. "Take a chance. For once in your life, don't hesitate."

Why the hell not?

He gave the driver Rosie's address but added, "Take me to the corner first. By the bus stop. There's something I need to do."

Jules's face registered surprise as the cab stopped in front of the bus stop and Jason poked his head out. "Get in," Jason said.

"I… what?"

"I'll take you to your apartment."

Jules shook his head. "It's nearly an hour from here by car. I can't ask you to do that for me."

"You can't stay out here."

Jules shivered. "I'll be fine." He pushed his soaking hair from his face. A clap of thunder nearly made Jason jump.

Why the hell not?

"You can spend the night at my apartment," Jason said. "I've got a place nearby." He immediately regretted these words—what the hell was he doing, asking a kid who had been hitting on him just hours before to spend the night? But he'd had a lot to drink, he was too tired to think straight, and Jules looked terrible.

This is crazy. He ignored the voice—was it Diane's voice he heard again, or just his fear talking?

Why the hell not?

"In the guest bedroom," he added quickly to clarify the sleeping arrangements.

Jules's expression turned to one of astonishment. "I… I…," he stammered. "Sure." Then: "Hey, I thought you were visiting."

"It's a long story," Jason replied, motioning Jules into the taxi. "Maybe I'll tell you sometime."

"I'd like that." Jules pushed the hair out of his face. Jason said nothing as the cab took off down the street. "Oh, and Jason?"

"Yes?"

"Thanks."

"Yeah."

CHAPTER 2

JASON AWOKE to the enticing smell of strong French coffee and warm bread. He glanced at the clock on the nightstand—it was nearly noon. His first instinct was to curse himself for having slept in so late, but he realized he wasn't expected at work—or anywhere, for that matter. He couldn't remember the last time that he'd slept past 6:00 a.m., even on a weekend. He felt a bit guilty sleeping in so late. More guilty not working. He reminded himself he was supposed to be relaxing. This was a vacation, wasn't it? He stretched his arms over his head and fell back on the pillow, dozing a few minutes more.

The haze of sleep began to lift as his eyes adjusted to the bright sunshine streaming in through his bedroom window. The smell of the coffee was now a siren call, and he got out of bed and stumbled, naked, down the hallway to the bathroom. That was when it struck him: the coffee aroma was coming from the apartment kitchen. *Shit.* He'd forgotten about Jules. He turned around to grab his pants from the bedroom and came face-to-face with Jules. Jules grinned and bit his bottom lip, making no effort to turn (or look) away.

"Nice," he said, raking his gaze over Jason's body and fixing on his broad shoulders. For a moment they just stood there in the hallway. Jules was wearing only a pair of boxers. Without the baggy pants and T-shirt to get in the way, Jason saw that he had a youthful, well-defined body—the hint of a six-pack, a bit of definition at his shoulders, and a silver belly-button ring. Jason realized now that the tattoo he'd noticed in the club was a crude rendering of the logo from the Blue Note jazz club in Manhattan with its distinctive note set in the middle of the club's name. He stood nearly a head shorter than Jason, not so unusual for a Frenchman. Jason towered over most of them.

Jason had always been proud of his body, with his muscular physique and well-toned legs from years of getting up at the crack of dawn to run. Now, for the first time in his life, he was intensely uncomfortable in his own nakedness. He silently cursed himself for it, then turned back to the bathroom without saying a word and emerged a few minutes later wrapped in a robe.

Jules walked out of the kitchen, holding a tray laden with two coffee cups and hot milk. He placed the tray on the dining table, which had been set for two. There was a fresh baguette already lying there, along with a few croissants, jam, butter, and cheese.

"Hungry?" Jules asked, clearly basking in Jason's stunned expression.

"Where'd you get the bread?" Jason countered. He knew his sister hadn't left any bread or croissants in the refrigerator—day-old baked goods were, Rosalie always said, a crime against nature.

"Went out while you were sleeping," Jules replied with a bright grin.

"How did you get back into the apartment?"

"I used the code and borrowed your keys."

"How did you get the code for the front door?" Jason had a vague sensation that Jules was toying with him—teasing him—but he was too jet-lagged to think straight.

"I've got a good memory. I watched you last night."

Jason sighed. Jules was definitely a brat, and a sharp one at that.

The cell phone on the coffee table rang, and Jason picked it up. *Shit.* He'd forgotten to call Rosalie. He tapped the screen and said, "Hello?"

"Jason?"

"Hey, sorry," he replied. "I meant to call you, but…."

"No problem, Jaz" came her lilting voice through the phone. "I just wanted to be sure you made it in okay." It was good to hear her voice; she had become the calm in the midst of the storm that had raged about him for the past few weeks. She'd done what nobody else had done: she'd listened to him. Her only advice had been to take some time off to think things over.

"Thanks for the flowers," he said with a quick glance back at the table. The few blooms that had been closed when he arrived were now fully open. Jules was now seated, elbow on the table, his chin resting in his hand.

"I'm glad you like them. I figured you could use a little pick-me-up."

"Yeah." Throughout the conversation, Jules watched him with obvious interest, and Jason wondered how much English he knew.

"Heard anything else from Diane?" Rosalie asked.

"Diane? No," he replied, doing his best not to let her know he didn't appreciate the reminder of why he'd come to Paris in the first place. "Why?"

"She called me."

For a full minute, Jason said nothing. "What did she want?" he asked at last. An image flashed through his mind—of Diane and the other man, their naked bodies intertwined on his own bed, sheets twisted in knots. He pushed the vision from his thoughts and forced himself to focus on Rosalie's words.

"She feels bad. She wants to talk to you."

"There's nothing to talk about" was his steely response. At the table, Jules shifted in his seat and poured himself a cup of coffee. With heightened awareness of Jules's presence, Jason continued, "Rosie, it's over. We both fucked up."

"She said the same thing. I told her you needed time but that I'd tell you she'd called."

"Thanks."

"You know I'd be the last one to push you on this," she said. "After what she did to you—"

"Like I said," Jason interrupted, "we both fucked up."

"You're too hard on yourself, Jaz." There was sadness in his sister's voice. "Whatever you did, you would never have *cheated* on her."

It was true, and Jason knew it. The thought gave him no comfort.

"Look, Rosie," he said, the smell of the coffee now more than he could resist, "I gotta run. I'll call you in a few days, okay?"

"I'll let you off the hook for now." He knew she knew he was trying to get her off the phone. "I love you, Jaz."

"Love you too, Rosie." He tapped the phone and replaced it on the table and stared at it for a few seconds.

"Diane," Jules repeated between sips of his coffee. "Your wife?"

So Jules *did* understand English. Jason scowled at him.

"Tes oignons," he retorted, an expression he'd always loved. It meant literally "your onions," as in "take care of your own," and was the French equivalent of "mind your own business."

"Girlfriend, then."

"Fiancée."

Jules smirked. Then, changing the subject, he offered, "Du café?"

"Thanks." Jason's mouth watered. "Au lait, s'il te plaît."

Jules poured a bit of the dark liquid into one of the large cups, then filled the rest with hot milk. Jason took the cup from him, their fingers brushing lightly.

"Stop doing that."

"Doing what?" Jules countered, the now-familiar evil grin settling over his angelic features.

"You know damn well what I mean." Jason inhaled the scent of the coffee. "You're a—" His French failed him once more, and he struggled to find the word he was looking for. "—flirt."

"That bothers you? Are you a homophobe?" Neither prospect appeared to disturb Jules in the least.

"No. Of course not." Jason knew he sounded a bit more defensive than he'd intended.

"Your coffee's getting cold," Jules said. He lifted his own cup to his mouth, took a sip, and licked the froth from his lips.

Jason took a long drink, finding to his surprise that he was admiring the curve of Jules's Cupid's bow.

Jules picked up the plate with the cheese. Jason's stomach growled in response. "Comté, gruyère, and a Saint-Marcellin frais."

Jason grinned. "Saint-Marcellin. My favorite."

"You serious?"

“Ouais.” Jason used the slang pronunciation of the affirmative he’d learned as a child. “I lived in Grenoble for a few years when I was in high school. My parents loved cheese, and this one was made nearby.” He didn’t mention that he’d tried to get the fresh, unripened version of the cheese in the States without success until he’d paid a hefty premium for overnight shipping via FedEx. But Diane had never liked the stuff, and he’d stopped ordering it.

“So that’s why your French is so good. I wondered. You have a funny little accent—sometimes I don’t even notice it. That’s why I thought you were Canadian, Jason.”

“Call me Jaz,” Jason answered as Jules mangled his name once more.

“Jaz?”

“My nickname. It’s easier to pronounce.”

“Nice.” Jules picked up the baguette and tore a piece off, then handed it to Jason. “I like jazz.”

Jason snorted and shook his head. “You never give up, do you?”

“Why should I?” countered Jules. “You’re a very attractive man, Jas—Jaz.”

“How old are you, anyhow?” Jason spread the Saint-Marcellin on the hunk of bread.

“Twenty-two,” Jules replied. “Old enough, don’t you think?”

“Old enough for what?” In spite of Jules’s forward manner, Jason realized that he liked him—although not, he told himself, in the way Jules hoped he might.

“I could show you.” Jules batted his dark lashes at Jason. Jason ignored this—at least he tried to ignore it—taking a bite of his bread and cheese. They ate in companionable silence for a few more minutes. Then Jules asked, “So you really liked the music last night?” He leaned forward over the table and, for once, looked quite serious.

“Yes. I really did. Who writes your music?”

“I do.” Jules sat a bit straighter as he said this, clearly proud.

“It’s refreshing. Where did you learn to write like that?”

“I went to conservatory after lycée.” Jules used the French word for high school. “Classical.”

"Really? Then you're still in school?"

"No." Jules's lips tightened. "It just… didn't work out."

Jason knew he'd hit a nerve and didn't press it further. *We all have our secrets.* "I'm going over to Trocadéro this afternoon. You want to join me?" he asked, trying to keep his tone as casual as he could. He didn't want Jules to get the wrong idea.

"Sure," Jules answered between chews. "Why are you going there?"

"No reason. Just thought I'd play tourist for once and check out the Eiffel Tower. It's been a long time since I've been there. You ever been to the top?"

"No." Jules refilled his coffee. "But I've always wanted to. How much does it cost?"

Jason realized he hadn't considered that Jules might not have any money. "My treat," he said. "I hate sightseeing alone."

"You sure?"

"Sure." Jason nodded.

"I'd love to." Jason could see genuine excitement in Jules's eyes. It had never occurred to him that a Parisian might never have been to the top of the Eiffel Tower.

THE WEATHER was bright as they exited the Métro. Jules, whom Jason had nudged into borrowing one of Rosie's sweatshirts, had pulled his hair into a short ponytail, several shorter strands falling across his forehead. In daylight, the contrast between Jules's brown eye and green eye was striking.

"I've never met anyone with two different-colored eyes," Jason said as they climbed the steps to the platform overlooking the Seine and the Eiffel Tower beyond.

"My eyes are brown." Jules appeared pleased Jason had noticed. "I lost one of my contacts. I couldn't afford another pair, but Henri said he thought it looked cool, so I wear the single contact for the hell of it."

"I like brown eyes." It was true, especially when they were flecked with bits of amber like Jules's.

A couple of teenagers on skateboards descended the shallow steps nearby, and Jason thought wistfully of his old board sitting in his parents' attic in Ohio.

"You skate?" Jules asked.

"Used to. It's been a long time."

"I always wanted to try." Jules watched the skateboarders with fascination. "I couldn't afford to buy one."

"You grew up in the city?"

"Just outside. In Nanterre." Jason knew the area well—a troubled Parisian suburb with a lot of high-rise, low-cost housing, and the scene of the massacre of eight members of the town council in 2002.

"Your family still live there?"

"No." Jason sensed Jules's hesitation in answering the personal questions and let the subject drop.

They reached the top of the plaza. Below, the fountains were still, and across the Seine, the Eiffel Tower rose skyward. "I've always liked this view," Jason said, leaning on the stone wall. To their left, a few giggling Japanese girls in short skirts and berets were taking photographs. Jason offered (in English) to take a picture of the group, and the girls giggled some more, handing him their cameras and even asking Jason to pose with them. Jules watched all of this with obvious amusement.

Jason rejoined Jules by the wall a few minutes later. A man approached them, holding Eiffel Tower key rings in various colors. Jason was about to wave the man away but changed his mind and negotiated a good price on two—one in blue and one in green. Turning to Jules, he asked, "Blue or green?"

"Green." Jules took the key ring from Jason and clipped it onto one of his belt loops. "Merci."

They walked down the long steps and past the silent fountains. From time to time Jason got the impression that Jules was staring at him, as if Jules were trying to figure him out. An hour later, after a crowded ride up in the elevator (during which Jules managed to press his body as close to Jason's as humanly possible under the pretext of "making more space" for the other tourists), the two of them stood atop the Eiffel Tower, looking out over the city. Jules's face was flushed with excitement, and for just a moment, Jason remembered the first time his parents had brought him here. His younger self must have looked just like Jules.

"What do you think?" Jason asked as Jules leaned over the edge.

"It's incredible." Jules sounded breathless. "I've been to Montmartre, and the view there is impressive, but this…." He stopped speaking and just stared. Jason put his hand on Jules's shoulder without thinking, squeezing it lightly. He removed it a moment later as he realized this would only encourage Jules to flirt with him again. It wasn't as though the flirting bothered him all that much—Jules *was* attractive—but Jason didn't want to lead him on either.

The realization that he found Jules attractive left him feeling awkward and uncomfortable in his own skin. "I remember thinking the same thing once," he told Jules as he pushed the thought aside. Then, after a few more minutes had passed, he added, "Do you have to be somewhere today?"

"You mean like work?"

"Yes."

"No. I help Henri out at the club sometimes, but it's closed Mondays."

"Good. I've got something I want you to see."

A LITTLE over an hour later, they both stood atop one of Paris's ubiquitous Bateaux Mouches, or "Fly Boats," the low-slung boats whose glass windows recalled the multifaceted eyes on insects and transported tourists around the Seine. The cold wind whipped through Jules's hair as he leaned over the railing of the uppermost deck and watched the city slowly unfold before him. Everything looked so different from the water. It felt like an entirely different city than the one he knew. Quieter. Serene.

At first he'd hesitated to let Jason pay for his ticket. Not that he had much money—just enough for this week's bus fare and for some work he needed done on one of his violin bows. He already felt a little guilty for having stayed at Jason's the night before. But he quickly realized Jason enjoyed paying for him and that Jason enjoyed his company.

Out of the corner of his eye, he saw Jason smile. He liked that smile even more because he was pretty sure he'd helped put it there. When he'd first seen Jason in the club the night before, he hadn't been smiling. He'd looked sad. Even a bit lonely.

"I've never seen Notre Dame from this angle," Jules marveled as the boat floated past Île de la Cité. "Did you know the gargoyles are really the ends of pipes that carry water down from the roof?"

"I seem to remember hearing that."

"The church used gargoyles and chimeras in their architecture to frighten the common people into attending mass," Jules added. "Or at least, that's what they taught us in school. We studied Roman and Gothic architecture. It was one of my better subjects."

"Troisième." Jason appeared wistful. "I remember learning about the different types of arches. My French was still pretty rough—we hadn't been in France that long, but I remember the pictures of churches and aqueducts in the textbook. My parents dragged me to see the Roman structures in Arles and Nîmes," he added, shaking his head, "and about a hundred little churches on the way. I hated it. But now I realize I was lucky."

"You were lucky," Jules said as the boat left Notre Dame behind. He'd never been outside of Paris, even though he'd always wanted to travel. Maybe if he *had* traveled, he'd feel like Jason did.

"Why were your parents in France?" Jules waved at some of the tourists on the Pont Neuf, some of whom waved back as Jason chuckled.

"My dad was a university professor. He took a year's sabbatical from his position, and he and my mom liked France so much that they extended it for a second year."

"Cool."

"I hated it."

"Why?" Jules asked with genuine interest.

"I was a kid. I wanted to be back with my friends in the States." Jason paused and looked back over the water. "I was an idiot."

Jules laughed. He liked that Jason said things like that—unexpected things. He wondered whether it had to do with Jason being American or if it was just Jason who was like that. Maybe it was both. "It makes you sad to remember it, though." He wasn't sure why he said this, but he was quite sure he was right about it. Something in the way Jason's smile seemed to fade when he thought about his time spent in France made Jules wonder what Jason was thinking in that moment. Jason, however, said nothing. Jules guessed he wasn't ready to share anything that personal with someone he'd met less than twenty-four hours before.

"So, Jaz," Jules continued, "what do you do in the States?"

"I'm a lawyer."

Jules rolled his eyes.

"What's that look for?"

"It explains the fancy clothes," Jules said without really thinking. He'd noticed Jason's Diesel jeans and D&G shirt. The jeans probably cost more than he earned in three months.

Jason frowned, shifted from one foot to the other, then gazed back out at the city. "Yeah, I make a lot of money." He sounded defensive. "Does that bother you?"

Jules knew he'd touched on a sensitive topic. He hadn't really meant to. He honestly didn't mind the ratty jeans he'd been wearing at the club—they were probably a lot more comfortable than Jason's.

"Nah," he drawled in an effort not to show Jason that he cared that he'd offended him. "Just pointing it out, that's all. Seems like it bothers *you*, though." He inwardly kicked himself for having said this. He knew he had a way of pushing people's buttons, and he really hadn't intended to irritate Jason.

He faced Jason and smiled. Jason smiled back. Good. So he probably didn't get irritated that easily. He liked Jason. He was pretty sure Jason liked him too. And even though Jason had said he was straight, the way Jason looked at him when he thought he couldn't see made him wonder.

Nothing's going to happen if you don't make the first move. What harm was there in trying? If Jason wasn't interested, he'd say so. Jules sidled over to Jason and slipped a finger under the waistband of Jason's pants. "I like the clothes." He looked up at Jason, challenging him to respond.

Jason calmly extricated Jules's hand and brought it up between the two of them. "You don't quit, do you?" Jules saw the color in Jason's cheeks rise as he said this, although his expression remained controlled.

"Nah." Jules noted with some satisfaction that Jason still held his hand.

"Quitting's not my style."

BACK AT the apartment several hours later, Jason sat on the chaise portion of the sleek Italian sectional (another of Rosalie's sophisticated touches) and checked his e-mail while Jules prepared dinner in the kitchen. Jules had insisted on cooking, and Jason—knowing that Jules saw this as a way to thank him for his generosity—had obliged. They had stopped at a small supermarket on the way back, where Jason let Jules select the ingredients for their meal. Now, as the smell of butter and shallots wafted from the kitchen to the living room, Jason pondered whether he should ask Jules to spend the night again. He gazed out at the dark street.

It's already getting late. Tomorrow I'll send him on his way. As soon as he made the decision, he felt better: in control again, as he preferred to be.

DINNER WAS delicious and quite simple: chicken breasts in a delicate cream sauce, pureed vegetables, a leafy salad with Jules's homemade vinaigrette, and, of course, the obligatory bread and cheese to follow. For his part, Jason had purchased several bottles of wine, choosing the white Pouilly-Fumé with its dry, smoky flavor to pair with the chicken. John Coltrane's classic jazz album *Blue Train* played softly in the background. But for the fact that his companion was a man, Jason was reminded of the intimate dinners he and Diane had shared when they'd first dated.

He and Jules talked about less personal things this time—how Coltrane's style had changed after he'd quit drugs, trends in jazz and classical music, and the difference between French and American cuisines. Jules surprised Jason with his understanding of each subject and his wit. He'd grown up on the rough streets of the Paris suburbs, but he'd obviously transcended his difficult circumstances.

Over coffee, Jules asked Jason about the recent negotiations in the US Congress over the budget, easily comparing the American system of governance to the French parliamentary system. They discussed the latest French political sex scandal, terrorism in Iraq, and the legacy of Ronald Reagan.

During and even after dinner, Jules did not flirt with Jason, although Jason found it difficult to separate Jules's outgoing personality from some of his more flamboyant behavior. Agreeing with little comment that Jules would spend one more night in the guest bedroom, the two men cleared the table, Jason insisting on doing the dishes over Jules's vocal protests.

The dishes done, they returned to the living room, and Jason settled back onto the couch. Jules pulled out his neon violin case and asked, "Mind if I play a little?"

"You kidding? I'd love to hear you play."

Jules grinned and clicked open the fiberglass case, pulling his bow out first, tightening and rosining the hairs, then picking up the violin and planting it beneath his chin. He closed his eyes to tune the instrument and opened them again to ask, "What should I play for you?"

Jason hadn't been expecting the question. "I don't know. I guess something that you love to play."

"All right," replied Jules, his mismatched eyes glittering in anticipation. "Bach. Sonata No. 2 in A Minor."

The choice surprised Jason, but he said nothing, instead propping a pillow behind his head and leaning further back against the sofa.

Jules took a deep breath and closed his eyes once more, gently laying bow to string and beginning the opening phrases with their insistent, rhythmic repetition sounding below the melodic line. The simplicity of the piece was both stunning and heart wrenching. Each phrase built upon the next, rising in intensity and in pitch. It reminded Jason of a prayer, powerful in its stark beauty, and he heard Jules's soul poured out into every note. And then it was over and Jason was left sitting in silence, staring at Jules as he had in the club, transfixed.

"Well? What did you think?" Jules asked.

The words woke Jason from his reverie. "That was… beautiful, Jules." There were tears in his eyes, and yet he could not put into words why the music had so stirred his heart. In that moment, he saw the kid in a different light—no, "kid" definitely was *not* the right word. The look in Jules's eyes was anything but childlike.

What are you thinking, Greene? You're letting this get away from you.

Jules rested the violin and bow on the case and sat down next to Jason. He hesitated for a moment, watching Jason with uncomfortable intensity, then reached for Jason and brushed a single tear from his cheek. For Jason the touch was electric and his physical response unexpected.

"Bach always touches my soul," Jules half whispered. His fingers still rested against Jason's cheek. "He must have known great love, and great pain, to write something so powerful."

Jason realized that his own pain must be showing on his face, because Jules, too, looked sad.

"I've never been religious"—Jules's gaze never left Jason's—"but I played this piece in a tiny church once. It was like God was there with me, speaking through me."

When Jason remained silent, Jules leaned forward and kissed him lightly on the lips. Jason's breath stuttered and he grew hard from the gossamer touch. He wanted to laugh, to cry, to take Jules in his arms. In that brief instant, he wanted to let go. Let it *all* go. He wanted to keep feeling the way Jules's music had made him feel: alive and free. He didn't want it to end.

At a loss to explain the intense emotional and sexual response of his own body and equally unable to stop himself, Jason reached for Jules and returned the kiss. Jules's lips tasted of wine and musk, and Jason hungered for more.

What are you doing? With this thought, he pulled abruptly away from Jules, stared at him for a moment, then frowned and stood up. His heart pounded in his chest, and he felt dizzy.

"I'm sorry," he mumbled, his throat dry. "I shouldn't have… I'm tired. I'm going to sleep."

"Of course." Jules appeared to be just as stunned by their brief embrace as Jason was.

IT TOOK Jason nearly an hour to fall asleep, and even then his sleep was restless. He couldn't fathom his reaction to Jules's music, at first telling himself (as he had before) that his response could be blamed on alcohol and jet lag. And yet he knew that he was only denying the truth: he was attracted to Jules. In that moment, he'd *wanted* Jules. He'd wanted to feel Jules's body against his own. He'd wanted *all* of him.

It's not as if you've never considered what it might be like with a man.

The vague memory of a high school party and the drunken hand job in his friend's basement resurfaced. The first and only time he ever remembered wanting—really *wanting*—someone of the same sex that way. Until now. It had felt damn good, but it hadn't happened again. Jason had found it easier to be with women—they'd always been plentiful and eager. Still, he remembered the feel of his lips on Jules's and the scent of his skin.

Damn, he smelled good.

At last his mind slipped into sleep, succumbing to his body's deep exhaustion.

CHAPTER 3

THAT NIGHT he dreamed of Robbie Jansen, the kid from his childhood who knew everything. At least, that was how it always seemed to Jason when he was growing up. In retrospect, he realized there were a lot of things Robbie didn't understand. But the important stuff? Robbie knew that, and then some. It took Jason a hell of a lot longer to learn it for himself. A *lot* longer.

He met Robbie in middle school, in eighth grade. They only lived about a mile apart, but in the suburbs, you could go for years living that close by and never run into each other. Jason never ventured very far from his Cleveland Heights neighborhood on his bike, and he was in the next school district over from where Robbie lived, across the four-lane street that felt as though it divided two completely different universes.

Robbie was the kid everyone liked to make fun of. Looking back, Jason realized most of the kids were jealous of Robbie but just never admitted it to each other, let alone to themselves. At thirteen, Robbie wore his dark hair long, sported kohl eyeliner, black skinny jeans, a piercing in his right ear. His T-shirts changed depending upon his mood: Bob Marley and Jimi Hendrix for days when he was feeling particularly nonconformist, Kermit the Frog and Care Bears when he was feeling mellow, and T-shirts with geeky slogans like "Meh" or "NO" or "I'm with stupid" the rest of the time.

Teenagers love to categorize, and Jason was no exception; categorizing helped sort things into simple, neat boxes that were easy to understand. Jason categorized Robbie as a "goth" or "emo," although he honestly wasn't sure what those things meant. There were always the rumors that Robbie was "queer," a category Jason wasn't really sure about either, except that it was something he was sure as hell he didn't want to be. Later, Jason stopped categorizing, mostly because he decided he wasn't too happy with the category he always got lumped into: "geek."

Yeah, he was a geek. He could laugh about it now. Jason was the kid with straight As who spent his afterschool time at the piano, practicing. He was Jason Greene, the nebbishy Jewish kid whose bar mitzvah party was held in the social hall of Beth Israel Synagogue instead of a cool place like the skating rink or the bowling alley. They'd decorated the social hall in a *Star Wars* theme that was supposed to look like the inside of the Millennium Falcon. Total geekdom.

The first time Jason met Robbie, Robbie was wearing a T-shirt that read "Huh?" and he had his hair pulled back in a loose ponytail. Robbie was standing in front of him in line in the school cafeteria. Jason waited as the cafeteria lady spooned a heap of mashed potatoes on his plate when his stomach growled loudly enough for Robbie to hear. Robbie giggled. Normally Jason would have been mortified, but there was something about Robbie that made him laugh instead. Ten minutes later, seated at the same long table, they finally stopped their hysterical laughter.

"I'm Jason." He knew he was stating the obvious. They had shared the same homeroom for more than a month, even though they'd never spoken before.

"Yeah," Robbie replied with a smirk. "I kinda knew that."

"You're Robbie, right?"

"Yeah," Robbie answered. "I kinda knew that too." Jason wasn't sure whether to laugh at this or not, so he just attacked the mashed potatoes. They were covered in a thick layer of ketchup, which seemed to impress Robbie, because he added, "I like ketchup too."

Jason smiled. When you're thirteen, you're always afraid that what you're doing isn't cool enough to share with anyone except your closest friends. Jason was pretty sure covering your food with ketchup wasn't particularly cool, but Robbie seemed to think it was.

"Did you know that ketchup came from China originally? It was made from pickled fish and spices." Robbie made a face and laughed. "It wasn't made using tomatoes until the 1800s."

Jason didn't remember what they'd talked about that day other than ketchup, but afterward they said hello to each other in the halls and even made faces at each other when the principal droned on during morning announcements. But that was the extent of their friendship until Jason's bar mitzvah.

The party was supposed to go until midnight—Jason had fought with his parents to get the extra hour—and most of the "old folks" had gone home, leaving behind Jason's classmates and a few younger kids and their exhausted parents. The kids were having a great time dancing to the DJ, although Jason was pissed off that instead of playing the Stones, the guy was playing Duran Duran. Robbie must have felt the same way, because Jason found him seated in the corner of the high-ceilinged room, his feet up on a chair, listening to his Walkman.

"Whatcha listening to?" Jason asked, doing his best imitation of a cool kid.

"Little Feat," Robbie shouted back. He pulled the headphones from his ears and handed them to Jason. "The original. You know, back before '72. Legend has it that Little Feat formed after Frank Zappa fired Lowell George from the Mothers of Invention because he was too talented. Told him to form his own band."

Jason nodded, although he had no clue what Robbie was talking about. Still, for a kid who grew up on Chopin and Brahms played around the house, Jason loved any kind of music, and especially jazz, so in high school, the kids started calling him "Jaz" for short. Jason thought the music was cool and that Robbie was cool because he knew so much about it.

They listened for a while until Robbie suggested they go outside where it was quieter so they could listen some more. Jason agreed, and they snuck out the side exit. They sat down on the grass with their backs against the building.

It was early October and cool enough that you could see your breath on the air. Jason still remembered the smell of the leaves. They were seated shoulder to shoulder; the headphones made anything else difficult. A year later, Jason might have worried about what it "looked like," two boys sitting there, bodies close together. But at thirteen, he was pretty much clueless.

The cassette ended. "I really liked that," Jason told Robbie. "I wonder if I can get the sheet music for 'Willin'.'"

"What do you play?"

"Piano," Jason said after some hesitation. He didn't think piano counted as cool.

"Really? Damn, I wish I could play." Robbie's eyes were bright with interest. "What kind of stuff do you play?"

"Classical, mostly," Jason replied a bit less tentatively than before. "I also love jazz and rock."

"That's what Little Feat's all about." Robbie wore an earnest expression. "It's all about different kinds of music. Different styles."

"Yeah." It was why Jason liked Little Feat's music so much.

"I'm not a purist," Robbie announced. Jason wasn't really sure what that meant—he was smart enough to have an idea, but it wasn't exactly a word he would have bandied about at thirteen.

Jason thought Robbie was really smart. He also thought Robbie had the bluest eyes he'd ever seen. "No, definitely not."

Robbie smiled and chewed his lower lip. "I like you, Jason." Robbie tilted his head and put the Walkman down next to him. "Maybe you can play piano for me sometime."

"I'd like to."

"Did you know that the piano was invented because the clavichord was too quiet an instrument?" Robbie asked.

Jason nodded—he'd heard the story before.

"They figured out that the hammer needed to come off of the string to let it vibrate. With the clavichord, the hammer stayed on the string, so it dampened the sound. Pretty smart, huh?"

"Yeah," Jason agreed, thinking that *Robbie* was pretty smart.

For a few minutes neither of them spoke. Then Robbie did something that completely floored Jason. He leaned over and kissed him—right on the lips. For a moment Jason sat, dumbfounded. Then Robbie surprised Jason once again by asking, quite bluntly, "Did you like that?"

Jason was speechless.

"It's okay if you don't," Robbie continued, clearly unfazed by Jason's lack of response. "Different styles, you know." He winked, picked up the Walkman, and, with a quick look in Jason's direction, walked back into the synagogue.

Jason didn't really talk to Robbie after that. He filed the whole encounter—"The Kiss"—away in his "weird experiences" drawer. As a teenager, he had lots of those, of course. So Jason just went on with the business of being an eighth grader. It was easy. He talked to his friends about girls, even asked a few out. He liked girls. He liked making out with them. He even liked the way their bodies felt.

It wasn't until late spring that Jason really thought about Robbie and "The Kiss" again. Not consciously, but he dreamed about Robbie. Maybe he'd dreamed about Robbie before, but he remembered this particular dream clearly. He remembered Robbie's lips pressed against his own and the way Robbie smelled—a mixture of cinnamon gum and something uniquely his own.

Jason dreamed about kissing Robbie, smelling him, *touching* him. In the dream, Robbie wasn't wearing a T-shirt. The skin of his chest was soft, smooth. He remembered wanting to touch Robbie's skin, and then, like magic, Jason was gliding his fingers over it. Robbie winked at him, just like he had that night at the party. Jason awoke the next day to an embarrassing wet spot on the sheets and the front of his pajama bottoms. His first wet dream ever, and it was about another guy! Jason never told anyone about it.

Eighth grade ended, and Jason spent the summer at music camp up in Michigan. That fall was a milestone: he was now a ninth grader, almost fifteen years old, and he was starting *high school.* Cleveland Heights High School seemed enormous, and all the upperclassmen seemed so sophisticated. Jason felt like the geekiest of geeks.

The school was farther away from his parents' house than the middle school, so some days Jason would hang around the orchestra room and practice after classes. Mr. Forester, the conductor, tapped him to play the celesta at the winter concert, and he told Jason he was welcome to use the piano anytime the room was free.

About a month after school started, Jason was practicing some Brahms at school. It was one of his favorite pieces—a romantic, angsty thing that he adored but that he probably wouldn't have admitted to anyone his age that he liked. He'd just finished the piece when he heard clapping from behind him. He turned around to see Robbie sitting near the doorway, a big grin on his face.

"That was really good, Jason. Brahms, opus 118, no. 2, right?"

That was the moment Jason knew for sure that Robbie knew everything.

"Did you know that Thomas Edison recorded Brahms playing the first Hungarian Dance?"

Jason shook his head.

"It's just a shortened version, but you can actually hear him playing his own music."

"That's really cool," Jason said. He knew he sounded like a complete idiot.

"Would you play me some more?" Robbie asked, seemingly undeterred by Jason's lack of a coherent response.

"Okay." Jason was a bit surer of himself now. This was familiar territory. He knew something about the music, even if he had no idea about Thomas Edison. "How about some Bach?"

"Oh!" Robbie nearly shouted. "Some of the *Well-Tempered Clavier*?"

"Sure." Jason knew a few pieces from the work. "How about the Prelude and Fugue no. 8 in E Flat Minor?"

"I love that one," Robbie gushed.

Jason turned back to the piano and set to work, doing his best to remember the piece without the music. It was probably the first time he was really thankful that he had a really good memory for music. After he finished playing, Robbie applauded again. Jason blushed—he was always a little shy about praise, even more so because it came from Robbie.

Jason hadn't forgotten "The Kiss," of course. In fact, he was curious. The problem was that even though he was curious, he was now old enough to understand the implications of kissing another boy. "Gay" was one label he didn't want.

He didn't handle the encounter in the music room very well. Instead he said, "I've got to go home. Later." Jason's heart thudded uncontrollably against his ribs as he shoved his music into his backpack and all but ran out of the room, leaving Robbie behind. Flight instinct. Pure and simple. Having feelings for Robbie was inconvenient. Jason had created his own perfect teenage universe, and he was pretty content to live in it, such as it was.

That night when Jason jerked off, for the first time, he imagined it was Robbie's hand on him instead of his own. He gasped Robbie's name into the pillow as his body shook. But when Jason awoke the next morning, he resolved to forget about Robbie. It was just too complicated. And besides, he liked girls, didn't he?

"HEY, JAZ!" Aaron Jacobson was one of the kids in his honors trig class. He lived down the street from Jason.

"Hey," Jason answered as he looked up from his notebook. Jason had been working on a project for his Rebels in Literature class and was sitting on the big brick wall in front of the school, waiting for his sister to give him a ride home. "You racing this weekend?" Aaron's parents sailed on Lake Erie, and their families often met up on the water after participating in the weekend races. The Jacobsons' boat was bigger than Jason's family's and in a different racing class, so they never competed against each other. That was probably a good thing, since Aaron's dad was a pretty competitive captain.

"Yeah," Aaron said. "You guys?"

"Nah. My cousin's confirmation is this weekend at temple."

There was a honk from the street, and they looked up to see Aaron's mom waiting in the car. "Oh! Gotta run. See ya next weekend, maybe?"

"Yeah, maybe," Jason said as Aaron trotted off across the courtyard and got into the car.

"You sail?"

Jason's heart jumped into his throat. Robbie was standing right behind him. "Yeah," Jason managed to choke out. "We've got a little boat we sail weekends. A Mirror dinghy."

"Really?" Robbie's eyes grew wide. "A Mirror? Cool! I've always wanted to sail one of those. Did you know that the Mirror dinghy was named for the *Mirror*, the British newspaper?" Jason shook his head. "It was designed in the early '60s."

"You sail?"

"Well," Robbie admitted with a grin, "not really. But I've always wanted to."

"You could come with us," Jason heard himself offer. He immediately regretted it. It had nothing to do with what his dad would say, either—he was always happy to have one of Jason's friends sail with them—Jason was just, well, uncomfortable. That whole gay thing again. Categories. Labels.

Robbie eyed Jason carefully, then said, "Nah, but thanks, anyhow." Then he shot Jason a beautiful smile, waved, and disappeared back into the school.

Jason only realized later that Robbie really *had* wanted to go. But Robbie understood that Jason wasn't ready.

EARLY JUNE, and school was almost out for the summer. Jason didn't want school to end even though his friends were thrilled. Jason had just found out that his father was taking a sabbatical in France, and they'd be leaving in mid-July for Grenoble. An entire year away from home. Jason was *pissed.*

He shouted at his father in a typical fifteen-year-old display of emotion, "You don't *understand.* I *can't* leave. I *won't*! I just started high school. Do you *know* how hard that is? I *won't* do it all over again!"

Jason's father just gazed at him with his usual patient expression until it hit Jason—as it always did when he "lost it"—that he was acting like a kid. His dad was a very smart man. More than anything, Jason wanted to be treated like an adult. To *be* an adult. And by not treating Jason like a six-year-old and telling him he couldn't talk to his father like that, his father got him to realize he was acting like a kid. And once Jason realized he was acting like a kid, he stopped acting like one. It worked like a charm, for the most part.

But just because he wasn't screaming and yelling anymore didn't mean Jason was happy about leaving Cleveland. The thought of leaving his friends, his home for the past fifteen years, to go to a foreign country was the "most horrible thing ever."

So when Ronald Sharpe asked Jason to come to an impromptu party at his house (his folks were conveniently out of town), Jason didn't hesitate. There would be booze—Ronald had a bit of a rep as a wild kid—and that was just fine with Jason. He was angry, he was fifteen, and he was damn well going to drink beer. Somehow, in his hormone-addled, the world-is-mine-for-the-taking brain, that was the appropriate reaction.

Jason wore his best "bad boy" outfit to the party, a black T-shirt he'd bought just for the occasion with the money he'd saved from cutting the neighbors' lawns, and a pair of ripped Levi's. He'd grown a lot in ninth grade and was now nearly six feet tall. His acne had started to give up the ghost, and the girls had started to notice him. *Really* notice him. He still didn't think he was all that great to look at, but something had changed, and he suddenly had his pick of the girls in his class. For a fifteen-year-old boy, that was pretty nice. So, with his burgeoning self-confidence and his rebel anger, he headed off to Ronald's party to do some serious damage.

The party was just okay. Parties were like that: more hype than anything else. Everyone thought they were going to be really great, but they were just okay. The one thing that lived up to its billing was the amount of alcohol Ronald had managed to get his hands on.

Jason had tried beer before, but never more than just a sip of his dad's. His dad figured it was okay to let Jason taste the stuff. His parents were a bit new age. They were convinced that if they talked about alcohol, sex, and drugs, the subjects wouldn't be taboo. They even had a copy of *The Joy of Sex* in the basement where he and Rosie could see it and read it if they wanted to. And his folks were right, for the most part. Jason was pretty square and pretty responsible. Except that particular night, he was damn well going to get plastered. He'd made a pact with himself. He *deserved* it.

He was probably on beer number four or five when he wandered down to Ronald's basement. Some of the other kids had said there was some "cool stuff" down there, including stereo equipment, a laser-disc projector, and a large-screen TV, so he managed to wriggle out of some girl's grasp and head down there by himself.

He held on to the railing as he descended the steps—his head was a little fuzzy, and he was having trouble walking in a straight line. Once downstairs, he ran his palm lovingly over the top of the TV. At home, they had a tiny black-and-white model (his parents were the anti-TV, public broadcasting types who only watched *PBS NewsHour* or *Masterpiece Theatre*), so this really was "cool" beyond words.

"Did you know they're working on new technology for liquid crystal display and plasma?" a voice from behind him said. He turned to see Robbie grinning back at him. "Yeah. The wave of the future. This behemoth here"—Robbie walked over to the huge TV and patted it—"will be old tech soon."

"Cool," Jason said, sure that was the only word that ever came out of his mouth when Robbie blew him away with how he knew things.

"Yeah. They're talking about flat screens you can hang on the wall."

"Really?"

"Yeah. Really," Robbie replied.

Jason tried not to focus on Robbie's chest, but it wasn't easy. He kept remembering the dream and wondering what Robbie's skin would feel like. Would it be soft, like the girls' breasts he'd felt up, or something different? Hard like his own?

"How ya doin'?" Jason mumbled, keenly aware that his pants felt a little tight in the crotch and thankful his T-shirt was long enough to cover his boner.

"I'm good." Robbie flashed that smile, and Jason's heart nearly jumped out of his chest. "So whatcha up to this summer?" Robbie sat down on one of the couches near the TV and leaned his head back against the pillows.

"Nothing much." *Understatement of the century.* Jason was in denial, pure and simple.

"Oh," Robbie replied.

"You?"

"I leave for camp in a few weeks. Right now I'm working downtown at the zoo. I'm a docent."

"A what?" Jason didn't even try to guess at what a docent was, as drunk as he was.

"I take people around, answer questions, tell them about the animals," Robbie explained.

All Jason could think about was how the dimples around Robbie's mouth looked really cute. He told himself that it was a really gay thought, but he was past caring at this point. "That's interesting," Jason said. *A brilliant observation.*

Jason sat down next to Robbie. Their knees touched. Jason hadn't meant to sit so close to him. Or had he? Jason's pants got tighter, but he didn't move away.

"I like you, Jason." Robbie didn't seem at all embarrassed to say it, but Jason felt his face grow warm.

"Me too," Jason mumbled.

"Can I kiss you?"

Jason swallowed hard. "Sure." He wondered if it was really him answering. It felt like he was someone else pretending to be Jason.

Robbie's lips tasted just the way Jason remembered: cinnamon with a taste that he couldn't place. This time Robbie pressed his tongue past Jason's lips.

Jason knew what french kissing was. He'd done enough of it with the girls he dated. He was pretty good at it too. But somehow, when Robbie's tongue touched his, it was different. He moaned and then felt immediately embarrassed that he'd made any noise—it wasn't "cool," after all. But Robbie seemed to like the noise, and his hands, which had been holding Jason's face, now pulled him closer.

Robbie smelled so *good*. Jason *felt* good. Horny. And scared to death. The little part of him that wasn't totally sloshed kept telling him that this was weird—that he wasn't supposed to feel like this, not with *another guy*.

He pulled away.

"You okay?" Robbie asked.

Jason nodded.

Robbie smiled again and any lingering doubts Jason had were lost in a haze of alcohol and teenage hormones. This time, *Jason* was the one who kissed *Robbie*. Jason ran his fingers through Robbie's long hair and probed Robbie's mouth with his tongue. Robbie relaxed into the kiss, and their tongues tangled.

Jason slipped a hand under Robbie's shirt and caressed Robbie's chest. He was sure Robbie felt his heart pounding. He didn't care. All he knew was that it all felt so *good*. All thoughts of "gay" and "weird" and whatever else his teenage brain might have obsessed about were replaced by the need to feel Robbie.

The fabric of Robbie's well-worn T-shirt was soft, but his skin was softer still, smooth over the hard muscle.

"Pinch my nipple," Robbie whispered.

Jason did and was rewarded with a gasp. Jason played with the other nipple and Robbie moaned like Jason had a few minutes before. It was the most incredible sound Jason had ever heard.

"Can I touch you?" Robbie asked after a few minutes.

Jason nodded. The next thing he knew, Robbie put his hands in Jason's pants. Jason hadn't understood what Robbie had meant, but it felt so damn good that he was hardly going to complain.

Jason struggled to focus on Robbie. Part of him wanted to lean back and let Robbie do whatever he was doing and nothing else. But Jason had been with enough girls that he knew it would be selfish, so he continued to ghost his fingers over Robbie's chest and began to kiss his neck.

"Feels so good," Jason heard himself say. Robbie rubbed harder, until Jason felt that familiar, tantalizing tingle at the base of his spine and he had to stop himself from crying out.

For a few minutes, he just held on to Robbie, too stunned to move. Then they moved apart and Robbie smiled at him. Jason smiled back, then said, "I gotta clean up." He realized later how selfish of him that was. He should have reciprocated. But he was so stunned and terrified of what had just happened that he took off up the stairs after he had zipped up his pants.

Later, he'd remember looking at his face in the mirror and seeing the fear in his eyes. What the hell was he? What was wrong with him? What if his friends found out?

Jason stumbled out of the small bathroom a half an hour later. One of the other kids had been waiting outside. "Had to puke," he lied, trying to look really cool. The kid bought it too. He looked utterly impressed.

The basement was empty when Jason got back downstairs. He looked around the house for Robbie, but somebody told him he'd left. He tried to call Robbie about a week later, deciding that he needed to see him so that he could "figure things out." But Robbie's mother told him he'd already left for camp. He asked her to tell Robbie he'd called.

Jason never heard from Robbie after that. His family left for Europe before Robbie got back from camp. He knew it was a copout. Robbie didn't have e-mail (neither did Jason, for that matter), so the only way Jason could have contacted Robbie at camp was by writing a letter. But every time he started writing, he got stuck. What the hell was he supposed to say? "It felt really good but I'm not gay"? Or "I want to go out with you"? Or "I need time to figure things out"? Or "I really like you"?

He stopped complaining about leaving for France. Somehow, in his teenage brain, he'd convinced himself that leaving would make everything all right again. In France, he wouldn't have *those* feelings. He'd go back to dating girls because, of course, it was just Robbie who made him feel weird. And so they left. In France, he was normal Jason Greene, the American kid, the novelty.

CHAPTER 4

JASON AWOKE the next morning with the dawn. He hadn't slept well. After the dream about Robbie, the rest of his night had been filled with dreams of Jules. And when he finally woke, it was to a morning erection that refused to be ignored.

Determined not to repeat the free show he'd put on for Jules the day before, he grabbed his robe from the hook on the door and headed straight for the bathroom. He relieved himself with some effort, then stepped into the shower. The water felt good on his skin, the warmth penetrating the tightness in his shoulders. He absentmindedly hummed an Ella Fitzgerald tune as he lathered himself with soap and closed his eyes. Even here, within the sanctity of the shower walls, his mind wandered once more to his houseguest's enticing face—to the pink lips he had briefly kissed the night before and to Jules's compelling music.

Jason let his hand drift down to his chest, pausing briefly to lave the hard nipples there. He closed his eyes and traced a line lower down onto his belly, swirling the slippery bar of soap around until he reached the curls below. He washed the sensitive place between his legs, rubbed the distinct ridge that ran behind his balls and farther back to the small opening beyond, teasing it with the bubbles and finally running a hand down his hard shaft.

God. He groaned, careful to keep his voice down. He hadn't had a hard-on like this in months.

He soaped up his erection, then let the bar slip from his hands so he could wrap his fingers around himself. He pulled and rubbed, cupping his balls with his other hand, leaning back against the hard tile of the shower to get a better angle. He closed his eyes and his lips parted. Fresh water from the shower dribbled over his head and into his mouth in a sensual cascade.

That was when he realized it was *Jules's* face he imagined looking back at him when he moved his hand rhythmically up and down his shaft. In his mind, he saw those warm brown eyes, imagined Jules naked and soaking wet as the water ran over his lithe body, and pretended that Jules was pulling at his cock and slipping those graceful fingers back over his balls and between his cheeks.

He imagined what it would be like to explore Jules's body with his fingers. He wondered what Jules would taste like all over—not just his mouth but his graceful shoulders, the soft skin on the inside of his wrists, his taut abdomen. He imagined taking the belly-button ring into his mouth and pulling on it; he wondered if Jules would moan when he did. In his mind, he slipped his tongue into the indentation there and licked at the silver circle, then saw his hands reach around to clasp the tight globes of Jules's ass and pull him closer. He wondered what that ass would feel like in his hands. Soft? Smooth?

Oh God. It wasn't the thought of what Jules might feel like that sent him spiraling over the edge. No, it was the memory of Jules's lips pressed against his, the taste of the wine, and the echo of music through the small apartment.

He came with a low growl, splashing his belly and the wall of the shower, the orgasm fierce and satisfying. In its wake, his legs shook, and he gasped, taking in air as if he'd been holding his breath the entire time. Had he?

The water was, blessedly, still hot as he washed himself again—this time far more clinically, making sure to erase the evidence of his release from the shower walls as well as his body. The hot water relaxed his muscles, and the shaking in his legs ceased. He waited another minute or two until his breaths came uniformly once more, then shut off the water and toweled himself dry, tossed the robe back on, and knotted the belt at his waist.

He opened the bathroom door with newfound determination. *He needs to leave*. He walked down the hallway to the kitchen. *I need to tell him. Now.*

He heard movement—the sound of something frying on the stove, the smell of something like onions drifting out into the hallway. Jules, making breakfast. *Lunch.* It was too late for breakfast. He looked inside to find Jules, with an apron wrapped around his small waist and his hair pulled back from his face, using a wooden spoon to push something around in a pan.

"Jaz!" he exclaimed happily, his grin nearly as wide as his face. "Did you have a good shower?"

Jason's face grew warm, but he managed to answer with a "Yes, thank you." Then, steeling himself for what he knew he must do, he began, "Look, Jules, I—"

"I hope you like quiche," Jules interrupted with a smile that seemed to light up the entire room. "I'm pretty good at making it, and since it's lunchtime already, I figured why not."

"Jules," Jason said, determined to stay on task, "I really—"

"I used to make it for Henri sometimes," Jules continued, undaunted. "But since he's been spending so much time with Pascal lately, I haven't had anyone to cook it for."

Shit. Jules was positively glowing. *How the hell can you tell him to leave? What kind of crappy excuse could you even come up with? "I need you to leave because I'm having fantasies about you... about touching you... about fucking you"?*

"I wasn't sure what you liked in your quiche," Jules said, "so I decided to make two—one plain and one with spinach."

You are so *screwed. And you're definitely not cold enough to do this.* Jason sighed.

"Oh." Jules looked a bit crestfallen. "You don't like quiche, do you?"

Jason realized that he had misinterpreted the sigh for something else, and quickly answered, "Actually, I love quiche."

"Really?"

"Really," Jason repeated. "I was just…." He hesitated, then said quickly, "I was just thinking that I wasn't looking forward to sightseeing alone today. I was hoping you might be able to join me again."

Oh, that's just perfect! A minute ago you were trying to get rid of him, and now you're inviting him to join you. What the fuck are you thinking, Greene? There was, as expected, no legitimate answer.

Jules, however, brightened visibly and said, "I'd love that! Lunch will be ready in a little less than an hour. We can leave after that. Is that all right with you?"

"That'd be great," Jason answered with a forced smile.

It's just one more day. He headed back toward his bedroom to get dressed. *What's the harm in that, anyhow?*

BY THE time they'd finished the delicious quiche, it was nearly two. Jason suggested they spend the day visiting some of the famous churches in the city, so they started out at Notre Dame, which was only a half-hour walk from the apartment. The weather was beautifully clear; the damp heaviness in the air from the day before was gone. With its large windows lit with sun, the cathedral was beautiful, and they just sat in its center for the better part of an hour, taking in the high ceilings and vibrant colors of the glass.

After Notre Dame, they walked the few blocks to Sainte-Chapelle. From there, they took the Métro and walked the few blocks to the narrow steps that led up Montmartre. They visited the Sacré-Cœur basilica and ambled about the narrow streets, stopping for crêpes at a small restaurant before watching the artists on place du Tertre paint for the tourists. Jason bought a small watercolor of the Montmartre vineyard—the only vineyard in Paris—to take back to the States for his mother.

They'd been standing there, watching the artists paint, for about a half an hour when Jules slipped his hand into Jason's. Jason pulled away and shoved his hand into his pocket.

Jules appeared untroubled as he walked away to gawk at some souvenirs in a nearby store. Jason watched him, surprised to find himself wishing he hadn't rejected Jules's advance.

THAT NIGHT they ate dinner at a small restaurant off boulevard Saint-Germain. They talked more about music, about how Jules had started composing his own work three years before, about the other band members, David and Henri, and about Jules's hope that the group would have the opportunity to perform more often.

"It's difficult," Jules told Jason as he idly swirled the wine in his glass. "David and Henri are really talented, but they both have jobs. Sometimes weeks go by between rehearsals. And lately Henri's been staying over at Pascal's, so it's harder to get him to come early to the club. At least Maurice doesn't mind us practicing at the club during the day."

"How often do you play?" asked Jason, dipping a piece of baguette in the sauce on his plate.

"I've managed to get us three gigs in the past two months," Jules responded proudly. "Mostly private parties—you know, company-sponsored things. But we've gotten another gig at an art gallery from that."

"I don't understand why you don't play more at the Loup-Garou. You guys have to be better than most of the acts Maurice books."

Jules snorted and shook his head. "Maurice is old-school. He prefers traditional jazz to the newer stuff. He must think we're okay, or he wouldn't even let us fill in. But as far as booking us regularly, I'm not holding my breath. My stuff is just too different."

"What you're doing is great, but you need an agent," Jason said. "Someone to get your name out. And once more people hear you, I know you'll get plenty of gigs."

Jules laughed. "We need to decide on a name first."

"What are you thinking of?"

"I've got a few ideas," Jules replied. "I need to run them by Henri and David first, though."

"So you won't tell me?" Jason prodded with a good-natured grin.

"No." Jules grinned back. "But I promise you'll be the first to know."

"I'll hold you to that."

BACK AT the apartment, they listened to some of Rosalie's jazz recordings and sipped some brandy Jason found in the cabinet by the dining table. They spoke little, although Jules hummed along to a few of the songs in a smooth and melodic tenor that reminded Jason of Jules's violin.

Jason lay back on the couch, propped up on one arm, while Jules sat on the floor beneath him with his back against the cushions. In spite of the warmth from the brandy—or perhaps because of it—Jason was acutely aware of Jules's presence. Jules, however, did not take advantage of their physical closeness to flirt as he had done in the past, perhaps aware of Jason's conflicted feelings about him.

After a while, Jason yawned and looked at the clock on the mantle. Two in the morning. "I should really get some sleep, Jules," Jason said as Dinah Washington crooned through the speakers. "I'm still jet-lagged."

"Sure," Jules said. His eyes filled with obvious longing.

For a moment Jason hesitated, meeting those eyes directly, wanting more but not knowing how to respond. "Jules," he began, "I…."

Jules reached out and touched his fingers to Jason's jaw. "It's all right, Jaz," he whispered. "You don't have to explain."

"Good night, Jules."

"Good night, Jason."

"I had a great time today."

"I did too."

IT WAS still dark outside when Jason awoke, startled to discover Jules's arms wrapped around his waist.

"Shit!" he gasped. "What the hell are you doing?" His first reaction was that he ought to kick Jules out of his bed—and the apartment—immediately. But when he looked down at that beautiful face, he knew he would do neither.

"I know I shouldn't have." Jules pulled away, obviously having expected Jason's anger.

Jason could try to convince himself that it was a rebound kind of thing, that Jules was needy and so was he. But that would be a lie. He *wanted* this. God, but he wanted this!

"It's all right," Jason replied, his lips tight. "You can stay."

"Sure?" Jules's eyes widened and his mouth dropped open.

Jason answered by meeting Jules's lips with a gentle kiss that deepened as Jules pressed his body against Jason's. "I'm sure," he whispered as he reached again for Jules's mouth. This time he didn't hesitate but plunged his tongue deep inside, savoring the softness there and running his fingers through Jules's thick dark hair. Jules gasped as Jason pressed his hard cock against Jules's thigh, and he wrapped his arms tighter around Jason.

What now? Jason had never made love to a man before.

Perhaps sensing Jason's hesitation, Jules took the lead. He pushed off the covers and straddled Jason's hips, bending over and taking one of Jason's nipples between his teeth, causing Jason to hiss in response, but the combined sensation of pleasure and pain only served to arouse him more. Jules pulled his T-shirt over his head so that Jason's fingers touched the soft skin of his abdomen. Beneath, he felt Jules's hard muscles. He lingered over the belly-button ring with lustful curiosity. Jules's body felt nothing like a woman's, but Jason found it just as appealing. No. More so.

Moaning, Jules untied Jason's pajama bottoms. He looked up at Jason and smirked—no doubt he understood Jason had deliberately worn something to bed because of their awkward encounter two days before.

"Brat," Jason said in English, pushing Jules off and reclaiming his dominant position. He saw from Jules's expression that he didn't understand. "Gosse," he said in French. He didn't think the translation was spot-on, but it was good enough to fill the room with Jules's laughter. Jason hesitated for a second before mastering his insecurity and pulling down Jules's cotton boxers. When Jules looked up at him with smoldering, hungry eyes, Jason's self-doubt evaporated.

Jules's cock was hard. Unlike his own, it was uncut. Jason went with his instinct to touch it gently, then take it firmly in his hand when Jules did not protest. It was long and graceful, much like the body it belonged to. "I want to taste you," he heard himself say.

Jules's response was a long, deep sigh.

Jason touched the tip of Jules's erection gingerly, running his tongue around the crown and over the edge, making Jules groan and thrust his hips forward to meet Jason's mouth.

"Jaz," Jules panted.

Jason took Jules's cock in his mouth, hesitantly at first, unsure of what to do next. He was scared—scared of what his need to possess all of Jules meant and scared that he might not be doing what Jules wanted. But Jules's keening movements beneath him reassured him that he was on the right track, and he took more of Jules's length in his mouth, finally swallowing him down until the tip touched the back of his throat. He gagged and spluttered, then willed his muscles to relax. At last getting his bearings, he began to suck like he himself had always liked it: hard and demanding.

"Merde!" came Jules's strangled cry. He arched his back, pressing up toward Jason's mouth in rhythm with his movements. Tiny beads of sweat appeared on Jules's brow, and he closed his eyes. "God, that feels good," he whispered. At this, Jason increased the force of his suction and tasted Jules's precome—salty and slightly bitter.

"Wet your finger and put it inside of me," Jules directed. Jason felt his cock twitch at the mere thought, and he tentatively licked his right index finger and reached underneath, between the cheeks of Jules's ass, to feel the opening there. To begin with he rubbed it, feeling the tightness and hesitating to do more, but when Jules moaned in pleasure and pushed himself onto Jason's finger, the muscles there yielded and allowed his finger to slide inside.

"Another, please," Jules begged, eyes glazed, his breath coming in gulps.

Jason gazed up at him. "I don't want to hurt you."

"You won't hurt me. Please, put another finger inside. It feels so good."

Jason complied, also resuming his sucking and licking. After a while, at Jules's prompting, he inserted a third. Apparently this sensation was too much to resist, for Jason felt Jules's body tense with impending release.

"Stop!" Jules cried out. "I don't… I mean, I've been tested, but…."

It took a second for Jason to make sense of Jules's words. He had never even considered what it would mean to perform oral sex on another man, let alone all of the implications. Startled, he looked up at Jules.

"Jaz. This time, just use your hand. Please…."

Jason nodded dumbly and did as Jules requested. Within seconds, Jules's warmth spilled over his hand, and Jason relished how the muscles of his hole contracted against his fingers. Jules's transcendent expression was almost enough to make Jason spill all over himself too.

Jules licked his lips as Jason withdrew his fingers. "God," he moaned, "that was so good. I'm sorry, I didn't even think until…."

"Don't apologize," Jason answered. "That was the hottest thing I've ever… damn."

Jules grinned as he explained, "It's not that I didn't want it—it's only that you barely know me and I… I didn't want you to rush into it or do something that you weren't completely comfortable with."

Jason studied Jules for a moment before offering him a reassuring smile. "We can figure that part out later. For now, I was thinking—" He kissed Jules, following the line of Jules's jaw to his neck before pausing. "—you could show me what else I've been missing."

"Really?" Jules bit his lower lip and, with a slightly abashed expression, reached under the pillow to pull out a condom. "I know I shouldn't have, but I hoped…."

"Gosse," laughed Jason as Jules ripped open the package and began to stroke Jason's length. It didn't take long for Jason's flagging erection to reassert itself with a tap to his belly.

Jules rolled the condom onto Jason and reared up on his knees so he could spit on his own fingers and push them inside himself, never taking his eyes off of Jason. He continued to stroke Jason while he worked his fingers in and out, moaning shamelessly.

Watching Jules, Jason wanted to bury himself inside that warm flesh as Jules withdrew his fingers. Jules guided him to his tight entrance, and the tip of Jason's cock met the resistance there.

In for a penny.... He laughed to himself at the utter absurdity of his grandmother's ancient expression in light of what he was about to do.

"More." Jules grabbed Jason's muscled forearms and squeezed them. "I want to feel you inside of me."

Jason pushed past Jules's clenched ring. "Fuck," he groaned, feeling the tightness against his cock, the sensation almost too intense. He slowed his progress, waiting until Jules had gradually taken him in to the base. After pausing to catch his breath, he began to move.

"Jaz." Jules gasped and pulled himself up against Jason's chest to sit on his lap, his breath hot against Jason's ear. "Jaz," he repeated, speaking the name like an incantation—the sexiest thing Jason had ever heard. Jason responded by putting his hands under Jules's ass, lifting him a bit, then lowering him so that Jules swallowed him inside once more. Acclimating to the narrow passage, Jason began to increase the tempo, but not too quickly—he wasn't ready for this new sensation to end too soon.

Jules groaned again. "I didn't think you'd be willing… but I wanted you so much."

Jason caught Jules's lips, biting playfully at them and tugging. In the dim light from the streetlamp outside the window, Jules's face looked like an angel's. Jason was suddenly reminded of the marble statue of Mercury attaching winged sandals to his feet, which he had seen years ago at the Louvre.

"Jules," he intoned, knowing he couldn't hold back any longer. "It's so good. I can't…." He bit his tongue to keep from crying out, his body shaking with release. He pulled his hands out from under Jules and wrapped them around his agile body. They held each other while the tension in Jason's body eased.

A few minutes later, Jason got up and tossed the condom, then wiped them both off with a washcloth before slipping back into bed. He sighed as he pulled Jules against him and closed his eyes. Jules rolled over to encircle his waist and rested his head on his chest. They fell asleep, legs intertwined.

CHAPTER 5

JASON AWOKE alone. Rubbing his eyes, he wondered for a split second if he had dreamed the night before. When he glanced to his left, the indentation on the extra pillow told him otherwise, but he found no other sign of Jules in the room. He stood up and did a few stretches, promising himself he'd go for a run before the day was out. The night spent with Jules had left him a bit stiff in the shoulders as well as the thighs.

"Jules?" He walked into the hallway and looked around the apartment. The guest room was empty, the bed made up well enough to make his mother proud. There was no sign of the neon-green violin case. He was alone.

What did you expect? That he'd have breakfast waiting again?

The answer was yes, he had expected just that. He kicked himself for caring enough that it even bothered him. He took a deep breath, rubbed his eyes again, relieved himself in the bathroom, then walked back to his room. It was already past noon. He debated making coffee but decided to drink a glass of water and go running instead. Sitting around the apartment and wondering why he'd been sure Jules would be there when he woke up wasn't going to change anything. Especially if there was nobody to eat with, breakfast could wait.

THE AIR outside was damp, the skies gray and threatening. He walked over to the Jardins du Luxembourg and opened the iron gate at the entrance, then paused by the fountain to stretch and tighten the laces on his running shoes before taking off down the gravel walkway deeper into the park. Despite the overcast skies, he saw Sacré-Cœur in the distance. The gardens were mostly empty—it was Tuesday, and the few people not at work or in school were unlikely to congregate on the wet park benches that lined the paths.

In spite of the chill that hung in the air, running felt good. Jason had come to rely on a morning run to start his day, often waking up as early as five so he could get to the office by seven. He enjoyed the relative peace and quiet of the early morning city to help clear his mind. Today, of course, it was no longer morning, but the steady sound of gravel crunching beneath his shoes had the same meditative effect. And today more than any other day before in his life, he needed to think.

He wasn't sure *what* to think. He certainly hadn't intended to have sex with Jules. But he couldn't deny the effect Jules's music had on him. Still, he'd been attracted to more than just Jules's music. He genuinely liked Jules; he enjoyed his company. Was it because Jules was male that the entire experience was so mystifying?

Jason had never lacked for lovers in the past. Secretly, he'd hoped to meet some sexy Frenchwoman and spend half of his days in the sack—not that it would have made him forget Diane, but it would have done some good to his bruised ego. Instead, he had allowed himself to be seduced, and now the seducer had vanished. But then again, he hadn't really been seduced, had he?

No. You wanted him.

He stopped by one of the benches and stretched out a hamstring, which had tightened up.

Face it. You wanted him to be there this morning. You wanted to spend more time with him.

He reached the pool in front of the Palais du Luxembourg. The last time he was here, it had been late summer, and the grass had been a deep green. Couples had sat on blankets, kissing, children had scurried about, floating miniature boats in the pool, and the birds had been singing.

Stop sulking. You had a good time with him, didn't you? Let it go. Move on.

"Story of my life," he murmured to himself, frightening away a pigeon that had strayed too close. He stretched out his shoulders and headed back toward the apartment. He'd call Rosalie and ask her to join him for the weekend; he knew she'd never let him sulk. She also had a few friends in the city. He'd ask her to fix him up on a date or two, and he'd hit a few more jazz clubs and take in a few more of the sights.

BY THE time he returned to the apartment, having stopped at the boulangerie to pick up a fresh ficelle, a thin and crusty baguette, Jason felt far better about the next few months. He was disappointed that Jules had cut and run, but he'd get over it. He punched the code into the keypad and pushed open the door. Standing there, violin case slung over his back and a small rucksack at his feet, was Jules.

"I KNOW it's asking a lot," Jules said a few minutes later as he poured them both coffee and set the cups on the table by the couch.

Jason stared at Jules. "You leave without saying a word, then come back and ask if you can *live* with me? What kind of an idiot do you think I am?"

Jules paled. "I left you a note." He picked up a piece of paper that had fallen to the floor and handed it to Jason. Jason took it from him and read it over.

> *Jason—*
>
> *I didn't want to wake you. I'm going back to my apartment to get a clean change of clothes. I also need to pick up my second bow on the way back. I had it rehaired.*
>
> *There's a half a baguette left from last night. Not a great breakfast, but I promise I'll make us some lunch when I get back.*
>
> *Last night was wonderful. All of it.*
>
> *—Jules*

Jason felt like a complete jerk. "I didn't see this," he said. "I'm sorry."

To his surprise, Jules's face lit up. "*I* get it. You woke up this morning and thought I was gone for good." Jason said nothing. "That's it, isn't it?"

Damn brat.

"Something like that," Jason replied at last, running a hand through his hair, still wet from sweat and rain. "Not that I expected anything more, but…." Jules's kiss silenced him.

Here we go again.

"You missed me, didn't you?" Jules asked as the kiss broke.

"You were only gone a few hours." Jason was on the defensive now.

"But you were sad when you thought I wasn't coming back."

"I'm not sure I'd put it that way."

Jules grinned. "So can I stay with you? Just for a little while. A few days, maybe a week?"

"Tell me again why I should say yes," Jason countered, his gentle tone belying the harshness of his words. The minute he'd seen Jules again, he'd been looking for some way to ask Jules to stay.

"Henri's moving in with his boyfriend. He was the one paying the rent at our apartment. I was just sort of staying there."

"So you have nowhere to go." Jason looked at Jules's small rucksack. Had Jules fit all his worldly possessions into that one bag?

"There are other places I could go." Jules chewed on his lower lip. "But I'd rather stay here with you. Besides, you said you hate sightseeing alone. I could be your companion, show you Paris."

"I already know Paris," Jason deadpanned. Jules's face fell, and Jason realized he'd pushed it a bit too far. He smiled at Jules and added, "But I'd like the company, all the same."

"Then we're agreed." Jules's expression brightened once again. "I'll keep you company and cook for you, and you'll let me stay here until I can find another place to live." At that moment, it occurred to Jason that Jules had just played him nearly as well as the violin. Of course he'd known that Jason would want him to stay, but the puppy-dog eyes were added insurance.

"Speaking of cooking." Jason stood up and pulled off his sweatshirt, ignoring the look of lust he saw flash in Jules's eyes. "I haven't had anything to eat since last night. Why don't you throw something together while I take a shower? You can start earning your keep."

"I could help you in the shower." Jules smirked.

"I'm sure you could. But if I don't eat something soon, I'm going to fall over. I'll keep the offer in mind, though." He turned and walked down the hallway to the bathroom.

"I'll hold you to that!" he heard Jules say as he closed the door.

"COFFEE?"

"You have to ask?"

His hair still wet after his shower, Jason joined Jules at the dining table. He felt far better than he had right after his run. He wondered if part of the reason he felt so good was that Jules had turned up again. That and the heady smell of coffee and bread, of course.

Handing him a cup of café au lait, Jules sipped his own coffee and watched him.

"What?"

"Nothing." The dimples on Jules's cheeks deepened.

"You're looking at me like I just grew another head."

Jules snorted. "Another American expression? I like that one. Cute."

"You obviously want me to say something."

"Was it good? Last night?" Jules's gaze was once again intense, although Jason thought he saw something like insecurity flicker in Jules's eyes.

"Yes," Jason said without hesitation. "It was."

"And?"

Jason inhaled. "And nothing. It was good. What more do you want me to say?"

Jules's expression reminded Jason of the proverbial cat who'd caught the mouse. *He's damn cute when he gloats.* He looked down at his coffee to avoid Jules's stare. Instead of the image of Mercury, Jason now imagined Jules as a cherub, face full of mischief, aiming his bow.

"I was your first, wasn't I?"

"First man?" Jason he knew full well what Jules was asking. Jules nodded. "Yeah. Does that make you happy?"

"Yes. I've never been anyone else's first." Jules's expression had changed to one of wonder; it was almost as though he couldn't fathom why Jason would have wanted *him* to be the first. Jason realized he'd needed to hear the words.

Maybe I'm being too hard on him.

Jules handed Jason the plate of cheese. Jason broke off a piece of the ficelle and smeared some of the Saint-Marcellin on it.

"So," Jules said, "where are we going today?"

"*We*?" Jason teased before taking a bite of his bread.

"We agreed, right? I'll keep you company when you go sightseeing, and cook for you, and you let me stay here."

"That's all you want from the deal? Just a place to stay?" Jason took another sip of his coffee but never took his eyes off of Jules.

Jules grinned. "Big American lawyer," he said, feigning awe, "I'm at your mercy." He bowed his head and put his right hand over his heart. "But there is something I want. Maybe you want it too?" Jules bit his lower lip.

Jason put down his coffee, then stood up and walked around the table to stand behind Jules. "I don't know what you're talking about." When Jules giggled, he guessed his French had fallen short of the mark once again.

"Oh, I think you do." Jules took Jason's hand and began to kiss his palm, tiny feathered kisses that zinged up Jason's spine.

Holy fuck. He was so hard it hurt.

Jules licked Jason's hand, and Jason pressed two fingers between Jules's lips. Jules sucked on them suggestively, and Jason's cock strained against his jeans. Jason's persistent thought—*What the fuck am I doing?*—gave way to physical need. He pulled Jules's shirt over his head and pinched his nipples. Jason couldn't make excuses this time—no music, no alcohol. He wanted Jules again, and he wanted him *now*.

"Dessert after breakfast?" Jules stood up and looked into Jason's face. He was about five inches shorter than Jason, who had to lean down to capture his lips. Jason thrust his tongue between those full lips with their tantalizing Cupid's bow. Jules tasted like coffee, cheese, and bread, but it only served to turn Jason on more. "Show me what you want," he said after he released Jules's mouth.

"I'll need to take my clothes off." Jules grinned.

"Then take your clothes off."

Jules stepped back and, eyes still fixed on Jason, proceeded to unbutton the fly of his jeans. Slowly. *Very* slowly. The jeans were so baggy that when he unzipped them, they fell about his knees in a puddle.

"*All* of your clothes," Jason ordered, finding Jules's submissive stance irresistible.

Jules lifted an eyebrow as he pulled his boxers down. *Definitely Mercury*. There was nothing cherubic about the lithe body or the jutting erection, which Jules proudly displayed.

"Now turn around."

Jules obliged with a wicked grin. It was the first time Jason had seen Jules naked; he'd caught only glimpses in the darkness the night before. Appraising Jules's body now, he wanted nothing more than to pound him from behind, but he held back. Last night had been a first in many years—someone showing *him* how to do something sexual. Today would be different. Sure, he'd be happy to learn what he might not already know, but first he would be himself. Confident. In charge.

Starting at Jules's shoulders, Jason massaged the hard muscle, digging his fingertips in as he worked. Jules's moans told him what he needed to know: Jules liked it a little rough. He was strong. Jason had always liked strong women, and he wondered if he hadn't just been seeking a more masculine partner. Had he been waiting for this all along?

He skated his hands down Jules's back, pausing from time to time to reach around and tweak one of his nipples or tease the belly-button ring. "Hands on the table."

Jules obeyed, leaning over the table as the muscles in his thighs and ass tightened visibly in anticipation. Jason knew full well what Jules wanted, but instead, he threaded his arms through Jules's, leaning over so that his chest was against Jules's back and placing his own hands next to Jules's on the table. Pushing away Jules's long hair with his chin, Jason licked the tender skin beneath Jules's left ear and felt the gooseflesh rise.

"Please," Jules whispered.

"Please? Please what?"

"Please fuck me."

The throbbing between his own legs now painful, Jason extricated one hand and palmed the condom he'd had the presence of mind to shove into his back pocket when he'd dressed after his shower. He unbuttoned his jeans, freeing himself from the tight confines of the fabric, and donned the rubber before pressing his hard cock between Jules's tight cheeks. From this angle, he saw what was left of their breakfast on the table: the plate of cheese, strawberry jam, and the slab of room-temperature butter. Inspiration struck. He reached over to the butter, took a large handful in his fist, and rubbed it in his palms until it was almost a liquid.

"What are you doing?" Jules asked as Jason began to rub the butter over Jules's tight hole.

"I'm improvising."

Jules giggled. "You going to eat me?"

"Damn straight," Jason answered in English, eliciting both a laugh and moan from Jules as he shoved a slippery finger inside. "Last night might have been a first for me," he continued, all the while inserting a second finger, then a third, "but I know enough to realize that spit isn't the best lube."

"Brilliant," Jules whispered, too far gone to do much more than pant. Jason pulled his fingers out, and Jules groaned with disappointment.

"Don't worry." Jason rubbed the butter over his erection. "I'm going to give you what you want." Then, grasping his cock in his right hand, he parted Jules's white globes and pushed against the tight muscle between, feeling it give.

"Ahh." Jules hissed as his body trembled. "Yes… more… please…."

Jason pressed past the second set of interior muscles, reaching around Jules and grabbing his erection with slippery fingers. Jules whimpered, and Jason bit his tongue to keep from crying out. It felt tight and warm inside. He pushed further until Jules had swallowed him all the way.

For a moment he was still, content just to experience the heat of Jules's body. Then he began to move, at the same time squeezing and stroking Jules's hard length, mimicking his thrusts with the movement of his hand. He'd never experienced anything so intense; even the night before hadn't been as satisfying. Something about *seeing* Jules react to his touch was intensely erotic. Shifting one foot to get a better grip on Jules, he heard him moan in pleasure.

Interesting. He repeated the movement. Jules keened beneath him, and Jason smiled as the realization hit him. *So there's a sweet spot.* He pulled out slightly and then rammed back in at the same angle.

"Oh… yes! Right… there," Jules panted. Jason was thrilled to be the cause of Jules's stuttered cries, but those same cries also brought him to the limit of his endurance. He felt as though his entire being were about to explode.

"Yes! Jaz," Jules cried. "*Yes*!"

Jason's strangled cry joined Jules's as he shuddered his release. Warm, sticky come coated his fingers as Jules collapsed onto the table, shaking.

"I think we have an agreement," he whispered before trailing his lips over Jules's sweaty neck.

CHAPTER 6

THE NEXT morning Jason awoke before Jules. He stared at Jules sleeping so peacefully beside him. Fighting the urge to stroke the soft, full lips, he watched as the dim light of early morning illuminated Jules's beautiful face. The enormity of the events of his first week in Paris weighed heavily on him as he lay there and struggled to make sense of his scattered thoughts.

First thought: *You really like him.* Followed in quick succession by: *What the* fuck *are you doing, getting attached to someone this quickly after Diane?* And finally*: If sex with another guy is so mind-blowing, why did it take you so long to try it?*

Jason was still wide-awake half an hour later when he sat up in the bed, careful not to wake Jules. There was *one* thing that he was pretty sure of: he knew what would happen if he stayed in bed watching Jules. No, he'd go for a run and clear his head. There would be time for sex later. He scribbled Jules a note telling him he'd be back in about an hour, then headed outside.

The weather cooperated this time. It was chilly, but the sun was rising and the sky looked clear.

Take it as a positive sign. The universe is okay with your insanity... or something like that.

As he had the day before, he ran through the park and took a few extra loops around the pool for good measure. Afterward he stopped at the boulangerie and paused over the glass display to see what goodies the baker had to offer.

"I'll take two chaussons," he said, grinning to see the flaky apple-filled turnovers that he had adored as a kid, "two pains au chocolat, and a ficelle, please." He felt fifteen years old again.

The woman behind the counter smiled at him and handed him a small bag with his purchases. He thanked her, then walked the short block back to the apartment. "Rise and shine, gosse," he said brightly as he strode down the hallway toward the bedroom, "or I'll have to come in there and—"

"And what?" said a familiar female voice from the living room.

Shit. He dropped the bag he was holding on the kitchen counter. "Rosie?"

"Jaz!" She launched herself into his arms and hugged him tightly. His sister was a tiny thing, the top of her head barely reaching his chin, and he picked her an inch or two off the floor with his embrace. Seeing her now, he understood how much he'd missed her energy and warmth, and how much better it was to see her in person than simply talking to her over the phone.

"Hey, Rosie," he said in English, noting the (thankfully) fully clothed Jules on the couch next to where his sister had been sitting. "It's so good to see you! I thought you were coming in next weekend."

"I gathered." She pursed her lips as she'd always done when they were kids and she caught him getting into trouble. "Jules was just telling me that you two planned to go sightseeing today."

"Oh, he was, was he?" Jason wondered exactly how much Jules had told her.

"We've been having a great time chatting. His English is excellent." She looked back at Jules and winked conspiratorially. Her shoulder-length bob was a natural bright red, not the more muted auburn of Jason's hair, and tiny freckles still dotted her cheeks, making her look far younger than her thirty-eight years. She wore a short black dress with an asymmetrical hem—her design, no doubt—with brightly patterned tights and clunky black Dr. Martens on her small feet.

"And her French is very good," Jules added in nearly flawless English.

Jason looked at Jules and mouthed the equivalent of "you are so dead" in French.

Jules just grinned back.

"Rosie's fluent in at least five languages, last time I checked." Jason scowled at Jules, continuing to speak in English.

"I think I'll make us some breakfast." Jules walked past them into the small kitchen. Jason heard the glass door to the kitchen close and realized Jules was giving them time to speak—in private.

"Rosie," Jason began, "I—"

"Sit down, Jaz." She took a seat on the couch and tapped the spot beside her. "And relax, for God's sake. You look like you're going to pass out."

"Jules got kicked out of his apartment," Jason began, sitting stiff-backed on the couch, legs crossed and arms over his chest. "I met him at a jazz club off of Saint-Germain a few days ago."

Rosalie laughed and took his hand in hers. "Stop," she said, her voice gentle. "You're a grown man, and you know I'd be the last person to question your judgment."

Jason stared at her. He'd forgotten how much she put him at ease. So why the hell was he acting like a kid with his hand caught in the cookie jar?

"He's a sweetheart," she finished.

"Thanks. I should've known you'd understand."

"I figured it wouldn't take you too long to hook up with someone once you were out of Philly."

"I haven't hooked—" he began, but she put her fingers to his lips to silence him.

"Jason Matthew Greene. I saw the look of panic on your face. And he's obviously totally infatuated with you. This is *me*, remember. Rosie—the 'wild child'? I'd know that look anywhere. You're smitten."

Jason swallowed and relaxed a bit. *Smitten.* Yes, that was a good way to describe how he felt about Jules.

"I don't know how it happened, Rosie." He leaned forward on the couch, not willing to look her in the eyes. "I said I'd had it with women after what happened with Diane, but I never thought…. I can't explain it. He's an amazing musician. When I heard him play, it just… got to me. It was like a part of me I'd never realized was there just… appeared."

"I'm glad." She squeezed his hand. "And I'm glad to see you making more spontaneous decisions for a change. Thank God you're away from that law firm! You seem so much happier than when you were with Diane."

Am I happier? The thought hadn't occurred to him. He only knew he felt uneasy, even a little scared.

The door to the kitchen opened with an extra rattle—a polite heads-up that they were no longer alone. Jules walked into the living room and set a breakfast tray on the dining table.

"The coffee smells divine, Jules," Rosalie purred. She'd slipped back into French and was watching Jules with interest. "I can see why Jaz asked you to stick around."

Jules blushed charmingly as Jason helped his sister up and pulled a chair out for her at the table.

"He's a gentleman, your brother," Jules said. "Café au lait, Rosie?" Jason silently marveled at how quickly Jules and Rosie had hit it off; they acted like old friends.

That's my Rosie. The thought warmed him.

Rosalie smiled. "Oui, merci." Jules poured three cups. "So, Jules," she began while adding a few lumps of raw sugar cubes to her cup, "Jaz tells me that you're quite the musician."

"He's too kind." Jules blushed again and did his best to appear modest, but the compliment obviously pleased him.

"So when do I get to hear you play?" Rosalie pulled a chausson apart with brightly painted fingers and popped a small piece in her mouth.

"We don't have any gigs for a few more months," Jules said, "but we're supposed to rehearse late this afternoon at the club. You're welcome to listen, if you want."

Rosalie glanced at Jason, who nodded. "I'd love that, Jules. Maybe you can get my brother here to join you while you're at it."

Jason nearly choked on his croissant.

"*Join* us?" Jules stared at Jason with a mix of astonishment and playful irritation.

"Didn't he tell you?" Rosalie ignored Jason's scowl and leaned over to Jules. "He's a pianist. He even applied to the Curtis Institute in Philadelphia."

Except I wasn't good enough to get in. Jason fought the urge to strangle his sister.

Jules, who hadn't taken his eyes off of Jason, now grinned. "So you're a musician…."

"Was," corrected Jason. "I haven't played in years."

"He was a damned good pianist too," Rosalie added. Jason knew she'd always enjoyed watching him squirm, and she sure as hell wasn't going to let him off the hook easily now. "I guess he didn't tell you that he spent two years studying at the Conservatoire de Grenoble, either, did he?" This time, Jules's mouth dropped open. "No, of course he didn't," she concluded with a frown aimed at Jason.

"That part of my life's over." Jason hoped to foreclose the conversation. *What the hell is she doing, anyway, bringing this up now?* He'd tried hard to forget about that part of his life—damn, it had taken him years to get to the point where he could just *listen* to music without dredging up the pain of having given it up!

"So you say." She appeared unfazed. "I know you miss it."

Jason stood up as calmly as he could and took his empty plate to the kitchen. He ignored Jules's startled expression while glaring openly at Rosalie. He wasn't angry with her, but the topic was unsettling.

Although there were only five dishes in the sink, he began to wash them. He needed a few minutes alone to think. However, he hadn't expected Jules to follow him and wrap his arms around his waist.

"Why didn't you tell me?" Jules pressed a cheek against Jason's back.

"What difference does it make?" Without thinking, Jason turned on the water so fast that it splashed over the metal sink and onto his face. His shoulders and neck felt tight.

"It makes a *lot* of difference to me," Jules gently answered. "It means even more that my music touched you, knowing that you're a musician too."

Jason said nothing but wiped his face with the back of one hand.

"The memory gives you pain." It was not a question.

Even now, fifteen years later, the pain of loss still made Jason's stomach clench. It hurt even more than Diane's betrayal, although he hadn't realized it until just now.

"Yes," Jason admitted.

"I understand. When I had to leave school…." His voice broke, and Jason felt Jules's body tense against his own.

Hesitating, unsure of how to respond to Jules's admission and his obvious emotion, Jason stood and watched the water run down the drain. After a minute or two of awkward silence, he turned to put his arms around Jules and pulled him against his chest. There had been a time when he'd also worn his heart on his sleeve, and he considered what a contradiction Jules was: at once a flirt, a brat, and a sweet man shouldering his own share of pain. Jason wanted to ask him what had happened—why he'd quit school—but he sensed that Jules would tell him about it when he was ready.

What is it about him that makes me want to protect him?

He ruffled Jules's dark hair. "Let's go out," he suggested. "Rosie won't want to hang out at the apartment all day, and you've got a while before you need to be at the club."

"We could just stay here." Jules's face flushed as he took the opportunity to plant a shameless kiss on Jason's lips.

"And give Rosie more ammunition?" Jason scoffed. "Not on your life."

IT WAS Rosalie who made the final decision as to how they would spend the afternoon.

"We're taking Jules shopping," she announced as she wiped up the table.

"Shopping?" Jules was mortified. He barely had enough money to buy recycled jeans at the thrift store near his apartment. "But I don't need—"

"Don't worry, mon petit," Rosalie said with a grin, "it's my treat. And you desperately need some new clothing if you're serious about a career in music."

"I can't let you do that." Jules looked to Jason for support, but Jason just shrugged.

"She's got a few connections," Jason told him. Jules wasn't sure what that meant. He didn't want anyone buying him things; he already owed Jason more than he could ever repay. He'd spent most of his life so far watching every expense, spending only what he needed to survive. Rehairing his bow had already set him back far more than he'd wanted. He'd have to beg Maurice for more hours bartending at the Loup-Garou just to make up for that. But clothing?

"I'm a designer," Rosalie explained as she put a reassuring hand on his shoulder. "I sell my designs to a few boutiques in Paris. I help them; they help me. Unless, of course, you prefer high school grunge"—she used the American word here—"to euro chic."

"No, not at all." Jules didn't want to offend her. "I like your style, Rosie. But I wouldn't want—"

"I don't have to pay anything for the clothes, and it'll make me happy to do it." She turned to Jason and added in English, "And we'll get *you* a few new things too, Jaz." She ignored his offended expression and added, "You know, less uptight. Less… *Diane*."

Jason scowled, but Jules got the impression that he was actually looking forward to changing things up a bit. And even though Jason's wardrobe was expensive, Jules didn't think it suited Jason very well. "Fine," Jason answered, also in English. "I'll let you play dress-up with me like you used to."

Jules sniggered.

"He looked cute in my homemade dresses when we were kids," Rosalie told Jules, her green eyes sparkling with mischief. This time, it was Jason who blushed.

AS THEY walked out of the apartment a few minutes later, Jason turned to Jules. Speaking in French once more, he said, with a look of admonishment, "Time to come clean, gosse. Why is your English so good?"

Although they were side by side on the sidewalk, Jason caught the wistful expression on Jules's face. "I always had a good ear," Jules explained, "and I studied hard. I dreamed about going to the United States." Jules said this in an offhanded manner, but Jason detected the longing in Jules's voice.

"Is that why you got the tattoo?" Jason asked.

Jules appeared both embarrassed and pleased that Jason had noticed. "Yeah. When I was a kid, I always wanted to go to the Blue Note. I used to imagine what it must have been like to hear someone like Miles Davis or John Coltrane play there."

"I went there once or twice. I hope you get to see it someday."

But after Diane and I got together, I never went again. She hadn't liked jazz. He was starting to wonder what he'd ever seen in Diane; they seemed to have so little in common. Strange how he'd never really noticed it before.

IT WAS noon when they emerged from the Métro not far from Montmartre. Rosalie led them around the confusing neighborhood and up a steep set of stairs to a small street in the shadow of Sacré-Cœur. A work crew was digging at the top of the steps, and the old cobblestones could be seen beneath the asphalt. "This way," she said as they descended yet another set of steps before finally stopping at a small boutique near the next corner. She opened the door for the two men and waved at a tall blonde near the back of the store.

"Rosie!" the woman cried, rushing over to kiss Rosalie on both cheeks. "Where have you been hiding?"

"Milan," Rosalie answered. "Stefano and I are opening a store there."

"Really? That's wonderful!"

Rosalie turned and gestured to the two men. "Sylvette Gilman," she said, "this is Jules Bardon."

"Enchanté," Jules replied as they kissed on both cheeks.

"And this," Rosalie said, her smile nearly as wide as her face as she put her arm on Jason's, "is my little brother, Jason."

"He's not so little." Sylvette's long, straight hair swung about her as she took Jason's hand and added, "And he is gorgeous." Jason had expected the bises, as she'd done with Rosalie and Jules, but Sylvette had other ideas. She brushed the top of his hand with her thumb in a sensual gesture, as if she were drinking him in and savoring every moment of it.

"My pleasure," Jason said, putting his other hand on top of hers and taking the compliment in stride. In the periphery of his vision, he noticed Jules shift his balance from one foot to another. *He's jealous.* Jason did his best not to chuckle.

"So, handsome gentlemen," Sylvette said, releasing Jason's hand and stepping back to look at both of them, "how may I help you?"

"I was hoping that you could help Jules find a more sophisticated look." Rosalie took charge as she loved to do. "He's a jazz musician. Oh, and while you're at it, maybe we can find my brother something that doesn't scream 'American' quite so loudly."

Sylvette's blue eyes lit up at the prospect. "I'm sure we can handle that," she tittered. "Your designs would be a perfect choice for Jules here, don't you think? He has just the right kind of body. And for your brother…." She paused for a moment and sized Jason up again. "I'm thinking something Italian."

Rosalie clapped her hands. "Perfect!" Then, no doubt seeing the fear on Jules's and Jason's faces, she added, "Good Lord, boys, don't look so intimidated! I promise you'll both be pleased when we get through with you." Jason offered Jules a look of skeptical resignation, but the two women just ignored both men and walked to the back of the store, catching up on the latest industry gossip and discussing the upcoming summer merchandise.

FOUR HOURS later, Rosalie and the two men emerged from the store with armfuls of bags. Jules had warmed to Sylvette after realizing that she was married and had no real designs on Jason, and allowed her to dress him in the latest Paris styles. At Rosalie's insistence, he'd tossed his baggy jeans into the garbage behind the store. Instead, he now wore a pair of super-skinny jeans and a zippered double-breasted jacket in deep ivory wool with a black T-shirt underneath. His new wardrobe also included a dark-blue "ultra fit" suit with narrow pants and a matching narrow tie. At first he'd protested the choice, saying that he had no need for a suit (especially such an expensive one), but after

Jason and both of the women had insisted that it would be perfect for his club gigs, he'd given in and accepted it with gratitude.

Jason had been a more difficult customer. After vehement protests that Rosie's choices were a bit out of his comfort zone, he'd settled on a new pair of jeans, a pair of trendy plaid pants and black cashmere sweater, and a black leather jacket with metal trim that he laughingly insisted was a cross between a 1950s greaser and a 1980s pop star. "Or a cubist painter," Jules said, adding that the modern jacket was very sexy and made Jason look hot. Or the French equivalent, which Jason didn't understand the first time Jules said it.

By the time they dropped the bags off at the apartment and picked up Jules's violin, they had just enough time to walk to the club for the rehearsal. When they arrived at five o'clock, however, neither David nor Henri were around.

"They're always late." Jules shook his head and pressed his lips together, clearly irritated. "I'm the only one who takes this seriously, I think."

"How about something to drink?" Jason pulled a chair out from one of the tables for Rosalie. This suggestion elicited a grin from Jules, who walked behind the bar and made them all coffee, operating the enormous espresso machine with ease.

"I fill in as bartender sometimes," he told them as he placed three tiny, fragrant cups on their table. As they drank, Rosalie glanced at the upright piano on the stage.

"Maybe you can play something for us while we're waiting," Jules suggested to Jason. From the playful look Jason saw in his eyes, Jules clearly knew he was pressing his luck.

"Nah," Jason responded, more composed than before, determined not to let himself get rattled again.

"Come on, Jaz," Rosalie said. "It's just us, right?"

Another coffee and fifteen minutes of begging, pleading, and cajoling later, Jason finally relented. This surprised him even more than it did Jules or Rosalie. "Just this once," he warned them, having reassured himself that the club was empty. Jules's face lit up as he followed Jason over to the piano.

"What do you want me to play?" Jason asked. He used the same words Jules had spoken only a few nights before.

"Something you love," Jules answered with a broad smile. Their eyes met for a brief instant, and Jason knew Jules had remembered as well.

"Brahms, then. opus 118, no. 2."

Jason settled in on the piano bench, which wobbled and squeaked under his large frame. He was astonished at how easily it came back to him—the feel of the keys beneath his fingers, the way the instrument became a part of him, how the notes seemed to have been etched into his consciousness. He'd adored this piece from the time he was a child; his mother had often played it for him. And although Jason had never considered himself to *be* a romantic, he adored playing romantic music more than any other. It just seemed easier to express that sort of feeling through his playing.

He'd only picked piano back up at ten, an age far older than the typical conservatory student. He knew he had talent, so he'd told himself he'd failed to earn a spot at Curtis because of his lack of technique. He could have applied to other schools, his mother had reminded him when she found him tearing up the rejection letter, but he'd told himself that it was Curtis or nothing. He'd been young; the rebuff had hurt.

That was a very long time ago.

For several moments after the music ended, nobody spoke. At last Jules exhaled—he seemed to have been holding his breath for the last few measures of the piece. "Jaz," he said, "you're a wonderful musician."

Rosalie wore an expression Jason knew well—she knew how much giving up his music had wounded him. "You haven't lost your touch." She walked over to the piano and leaned against it. "I've always loved that piece."

"Thanks," Jason murmured. He looked down at the keys. His face felt hot, and his palms were sweaty. His hands were trembling almost imperceptibly. He rested them lightly on the keys so Rosalie wouldn't see. Or worse, Jules.

"Play something with me, Jaz," Jules suggested.

Jason shot a scathing look at Rosalie.

"Sorry. I told him you also play jazz." She didn't appear remorseful in the least.

"All right," Jason sighed. In spite of the ache in his chest, he realized that now that he'd started, he *wanted* to play more. *Maybe it's been long enough.*

Jules didn't hide his excitement but stood by the piano and leaned over to Jason. "What will we play?"

"How about the first piece you played at the club, the night I met you," Jason suggested.

Jules's eyebrows shot up. "Really? You think you can?" When Jason nodded, Jules's expression became wide-eyed and childlike. "I would love to!"

As Jules went to retrieve his instrument, Jason depressed the A key and used the pedal to sustain the pitch, then tapped it again as Jules tuned the violin.

Rosalie grinned, leaned on the piano, and rested her head in her hands. Jason smiled back at her and remembered all the times she'd done the same thing when he'd practiced at home. He'd loved to play for her. She'd always been the one looking out for him when he was a kid, but when he played for her, he felt as though he were the older sibling.

"E-flat minor?"

"How did you…?" Jules began. His eyes had grown wider, and his mouth was open in the shape of an O.

"I have perfect pitch," Jason said. He'd never thought much of it before—he figured it was just the way he was wired—but the admission usually garnered the same response.

"So if I sing you a note, you can tell me what pitch it is without finding it on the piano?"

"Yes," Jason said. "Of course, it means that this out-of-tune piano is also pretty painful."

"I think it's painful to anyone with an ear," laughed Jules. "David never stops complaining about it."

"I'm waiting," Rosalie said with more than a hint of impatience. "I want to hear this piece."

"Jules wrote it." Jason nodded at Jules. "I think you'll like it." Jules's cheeks pinked a little at the compliment.

Jason looked down at the keys for a moment, then inhaled with deliberation and laid his hands on them.

Jules's expression became one of silent awe as Jason began the opening phrases of the piece. The notes were identical to those David had played only days before, although his phrasing was different—more intense, more haunting. It was something Jason had felt when he'd heard the piece.

As he continued to play, the ache in Jason's chest deepened. The depth of his emotion frightened him, and he was relieved when Jules's violin joined the piano and his was no longer the only musical voice speaking. He recalled Jules's words about Bach: "He must have known great love, and great pain, to write something so powerful." He looked at Jules—at the faraway expression on his face—and wondered what pain he might find in Jules's heart.

Rosalie's face was tear-streaked by the time they finished. Never one embarrassed to share her feelings, she hugged first Jules, then Jason, who was still seated at the piano. She stroked Jason's hair for a moment, and he saw the fierce pride shining in her eyes.

"Jules," she said, looking back at him, "that was so incredibly *amazing*!"

Jason smiled at his sister's over-the-top reaction, and he loved her even more for it.

"You think so? Really?" Jules looked relieved.

"I think my brother may have some issues with women, but he sure knows how to pick his men," she replied with a straight face. "Do you think I can hire you to play my Milan show at the end of this month? I'm serious! I'll make sure you have a place to stay, plane tickets, and enough money to make it worth your while. Your music would be *so* much better than the recording I had planned on using, and Stefano will eat you up!"

"I… I…," Jules stammered and looked to Jason for help, but Jason just laughed.

"She's always been like this," he told Jules. "Just tell her yes. You can work out the details later with Henri and David."

Jules blinked. "Yes," he said. "Yes, I… *we* would love to!"

THEY ARRIVED back at the apartment past midnight after staying to listen to another band performing once Jules's trio finished rehearsing. The three of them downed nearly a bottle of wine each, so they were all a bit tipsy by the time they stumbled into the living room.

"I'll take the couch tonight," Jules offered, self-conscious for the first time that day. He wasn't sure how much Jason had told Rosalie about them, although he guessed Jason must have said something about whatever it was he and Jason were to each other. Still, he didn't want to offend her or make her feel uncomfortable.

"The *couch*?" Rosalie giggled as she hung her jacket on the coat-tree in the hallway and tossed her shoes across the living room. "Don't be stupid, Jules. I've already told my brother—" She hiccupped softly, then giggled again. "—that I know what you two are doing and that it's—" Another hiccup. "—fine with me. Really. I'm taking the guest bed. You two stay put."

Jason, probably too buzzed to argue, just shrugged and headed to the master bedroom. Jules hesitated and turned back to Rosalie.

"Come here," she ordered. She sank down in front of the couch and patted the spot next to her. When Jules joined her, she brushed a small hand over his dark hair and, stifling another yawn, declared, "Listen to me: I don't know what you're doing to my brother, but don't you *dare* stop." This time it was Jules who was tempted to giggle. "I'm not kidding! I haven't seen him this happy in… well, probably *ever*."

"I'm happy too," Jules said, drawing his knees to his chest and hugging them tightly. "But I worry—"

"Don't!" Rosalie interrupted. "God knows Jason will do enough of that for both of you. Just be there for him. He needs someone like you."

Jules said nothing but leaned his head on his knees and grinned at her. He liked the idea of being there for Jason. He knew it had only been a few days since they'd first met, but he understood enough about

Jason to know that whatever had brought him to Paris, he was feeling a little rough.

"I realize you two just met a few days ago," she said as if she'd read his mind, "but I know my brother. He really cares about you." Rosalie's tone was matter-of-fact, and it took a moment for her words to register in Jules's mind.

"I…," Jules began, unsure of what to say. He hadn't even considered the possibility that Jason might think of this as more than just a fling. Not that he minded the idea, but he certainly hadn't seen anything like that in Jason.

"Be patient with him." Rosalie patted his head and yawned. "Sometimes he can be a bit dense. And he's usually the last one to admit what he's feeling." She pulled herself up and left Jules sitting there, her words hovering around him like the gentle warmth of the wine.

As he lay in bed later, spooned in Jason's arms, he considered her pronouncement and found himself smiling again. He knew that Jason would have to return to the States in a few months' time, but he could live with that. Until then, he would work hard to keep Jason happy. And maybe he'd even find a little happiness for himself too.

CHAPTER 7

JULES HUMMED along to a Lou Reed tune on the stereo as he cooked. The kitchen smelled of butter, shallots, and gruyère cheese. His hair was tied back in a ragged ponytail at the nape of his neck, the kohl eyeliner he'd worn to the club the night before was now smudged around his eyes, and he wore a blue apron over his plaid boxers—Jason had laughingly told him he looked like a grunge housewife.

Rosalie had left the night before, reassured that Jason was in good hands. Jules was already looking forward to seeing her again in Milan in two weeks' time—he was so excited about the gig he could hardly think straight. He'd never traveled outside of Paris, let alone outside of France (or on an airplane, for that matter). Henri and David had agreed to additional practices in the meantime, and Jason had jokingly agreed to go with them as a "chaperone."

Some chaperone.

Jules laughed, his mind straying to what they'd done after Rosalie left. He and Jason had finished off the last inch or so of a bottle of Courvoisier, and he'd given Jason a neck massage. This, of course, had ended in Jason nearly pinning him to the floor and having his way with him. The memory alone made Jules shiver with anticipation of what might happen after they ate. Their planned trip to the Louvre could wait for a few more hours.

"I'm out of here!" he heard Jason call as he headed out for his morning run. "Back in half an hour." The door to the apartment opened and closed. For a moment Jules just leaned against the counter and grinned. He could get used to this.

Making music, making love, making quiche.

It didn't matter that he knew Jason would be going home in seven weeks; he would enjoy their time together and deal with the emotional fallout later. He was used to dealing with fallout; he'd had enough of it in his short life.

Jules went back to sautéing vegetables for the quiche. Not that quiche was a typical French breakfast food, but since they'd slept in late, he figured he'd call it lunch and the purists couldn't fault him for it. He was looking forward to surprising Jason with something other than a simple breakfast of bread and croissants and had told Jason to skip the pastries today because he was making them something special. Jason had looked at Jules with unbridled lust and made some off-color comment about how he liked surprises.

Jules finished assembling the quiche, adding the sautéed leeks and the egg mixture to the empty crust. It would take about an hour to bake. He placed the uncooked quiche in the oven. He imagined feeding it to Jason… or maybe the other way around.

The apartment phone rang. He walked into the living room but let the answering machine pick up since he still wasn't quite comfortable answering calls, even though Jason had told him that he was welcome to give out the number.

"What if it's your mother?" he'd pointed out. For his part, Jason had just laughed and told Jules not to worry, that his parents were far more open-minded than most Americans when it came to same-sex relationships. Still, he was pretty sure Jason's parents knew nothing about their son's exploits in Paris, and he preferred to play it safe.

"Jules?" Henri's voice came through the speaker. "Oy, Jules, pick up the phone. I know you told me to call you only if it was an emergency—"

Jules picked up the receiver. "Henri?" Something in Henri's voice made his heart pound. "Henri, what's the matter?"

"Jules," Henri began, sounding a bit breathless, "it's about your brother…."

JASON WALKED into the apartment, covered in sweat and carrying the usual baguette in one hand. The apartment smelled wonderful, the scent of leeks and cheese making his stomach growl in appreciation.

Rosie was right. He's good for me.

"So what's this special meal you promised?" he asked, poking his head into the kitchen. Not finding Jules, he glanced in the living room, then in the bathroom and the bedroom—Jules's clothes and violin were still there. He checked the guest bedroom and the toilet. Still no Jules.

He probably went out to get something for the breakfast. Jules's coat, keys, and wallet were gone from their usual places. Jason decided to take a quick shower—at least he wouldn't keep Jules waiting when he returned.

"I'm ready for the surprise." He opened the bathroom door a few minutes later to clear the steam. The hallway outside of the kitchen was starting to fill with smoke. "Shit!" With just a towel around his waist, he ran to the kitchen and waved his hands to clear the air. The oven was on, and whatever was inside was now burning. He quickly turned it off and opened the small window by the stove.

Now he *was* worried. However much of an enigma Jules still was to him, he wouldn't have left something cooking in the oven unless he'd planned on being back in time to pull it out. *Something's happened.* Jason was sure of it now. Leaving whatever had burned in the oven where it was, he closed the kitchen door.

Where are you, Jules?

He swapped his towel for a pair of sweats and went around the apartment opening the large windows to air the place out. He also looked for any more clues as to where Jules might have gone, but nothing seemed out of place or unusual. Jason noticed for the first time that the dining table was already set and that there was a tiny bud vase in its center with some yellow flowers, which he recognized from the courtyard. His stomach muscles tightened when he saw how much care Jules had taken.

He kicked himself for not having bought Jules a cell phone, though Jules had refused because he hadn't wanted Jason to spend the money. "If you need to reach me at the club," Jules had said, "you can always call Henri."

Henri.

He'd call Henri and see if he had any idea where Jules might have gone. He walked over to the small table where the phone sat to look for the number Jules had scribbled down a few days before. The light on the answering machine was flashing. He pressed the button.

"*Jules? Oy, Jules, pick up the phone. I know you told me only to call you if it was an emergency....*"

Shit.

Jason picked up the receiver and scrolled through the caller ID, then pressed Redial at the most recent entry.

"Allô?" The voice was hoarse, and Jason guessed Henri had been sleeping.

"Henri?"

"Ouais?"

"This is Jason—Jason Greene, Jules's friend. We met last week at the Loup-Garou."

"Jason. Of course. How are you?"

"I'm fine, Henri," Jason replied quickly. "You have any idea where Jules is?"

"Jules?"

"Yeah. Jules."

Not sleeping. Just dense.

Henri yawned. "Ouais. I just spoke with him a little while ago. His brother got into some trouble last night, and—"

"Where can I find him?" Jason pressed, unwilling to wait for an explanation.

"Who? Guy?"

Really dense.

"Is that Jules's brother's name?"

"Yeah. Jules said he was going to find Guy."

I'm sleeping with him, and I didn't even know he had *a brother. Who's the dense one here?*

Jason closed his eyes and fought the urge to hit the phone on the table hard enough to get Henri's full attention. "So where are they?" he demanded. He'd had witnesses in court who were this dense, but now—when the answer mattered to him personally—he was without patience.

"The police station in Nanterre," Henri replied.

JULES SAT on an uncomfortable bench against the cold, white wall. Guy had been moved from the police station to a holding area in the social services building next door. The building was an archetypal French government building built in the 1960s: sterile and utilitarian. The hallway was brightly lit with fluorescent fixtures, and the walls were bare. Jules hated places like this—they reminded him too much of his childhood, and not the good parts. The place smelled of disinfectant; the janitor had been by an hour before to mop down the linoleum. Jules had smiled at the old man, lifting his feet so he could mop underneath the bench.

He'd now been waiting more than four hours to see his brother. He pulled the tie out of his hair and tried to smooth the ragged ponytail. Since he'd left the apartment so quickly, he hadn't even thought to brush it until one of the workers he'd spoken to had looked at him as though *he* was the one who needed help and not his brother. He pressed his lips tightly together and tried to relax. He'd spent more time than he cared to remember in places just like this, trying to cajole his mother into cooperating with her caseworkers. A few times he'd even been hauled in himself for some stupid prank he'd helped his friends pull off. If he hadn't had his music, he guessed that he'd have been a more regular customer.

"Monsieur Bardon?"

"Yes, that's me." He stood up and offered the woman his right hand, self-conscious about how he must look to her.

"My name is Charlotte Devieux." She was middle-aged, dressed in a wrinkled navy suit, with dark circles under her eyes.

Night shift.

She took his hand and shook it. At least she hadn't refused it. Her palm was cold and damp; he caught a whiff of stale cigarette and perfume. "I'm your brother's caseworker. Are you Guy's guardian?"

"No." Jules swallowed hard and tried his best not to look nervous.

"Guy told me he has a mother—Dominique Bardon?"

"Yes," Jules answered.

"She's not here?"

"No. I don't know where she is. I tried to call her, but...." *She's probably out in the street somewhere, drunk or high. Nothing new.*

"It's all right, Monsieur Bardon," the woman said, a faint glimmer of understanding in her eyes. "Guy mentioned that there've been problems at home. Do you know how I can reach his father?"

"I don't know who his father is," Jules admitted awkwardly. His mother hadn't told either of them. "We're half brothers." There was sympathy in the caseworker's expression. *God, I hate it when they pity us.* "Can I speak with Guy?" His knees shook as he waited for her answer.

"Only the parent or guardian is permitted—"

"Please, Madame," Jules interrupted. He was trying not to piss her off, but he was desperate to speak to his brother. "I'm all he's got." His mouth felt dry and his eyes burned.

Charlotte Devieux pressed her lips together, then, shrugging, relented. "Okay. But only for a few minutes."

"Thank you so much." Jules remembered to breathe again. "Thank you!"

JULES EMERGED from the holding room a half hour later. What Guy told him hadn't improved his overall assessment of the situation. He'd hoped it would be something easy to explain, like trespassing or vandalism. Guy's history of hanging out with what Jules called "baby gangsters" had already landed the fourteen-year-old in trouble with the law. Guy had even spent a few nights in detention in the past. But this... this was far worse.

"It wasn't my stuff," Guy choked out when Jules confronted him with the drug charges. Guy looked thin, pale, and scared to death. He looked so young and vulnerable that it broke Jules's heart.

"Whose stuff was it, then?" Jules believed his brother, but he knew that unless Guy snitched on one of his friends, Guy would probably be the one doing jail time. No doubt Guy's friends—if you could call them that—had decided Guy had the least lengthy juvie record of the gang. And Guy, good-hearted (but misdirected) kid he was, was willing to take the fall. No amount of Jules's cajoling or reasoning had worked. To Guy, this was a point of honor. He would not betray his friends.

Damn her! He clenched his fists tightly at his sides. *I should never have listened to her when she said she was clean. I should have gotten him out of there.* His head hurt, and he rubbed his eyes with the palms of his hands.

He felt a strong hand on his shoulder and looked up; his mouth dropped open as he realized whose hand it was. For a moment he almost hadn't recognized Jason. Dressed in a well-cut suit and a blue silk tie, Jason had tamed his wavy hair with a bit of gel and wore a pair of glasses that made him look older than his thirty-four years. Jules guessed it was no accident that Jason chose not to wear his contacts. Jules couldn't remember when he'd ever been so glad to see someone. Not to mention the fact that Jason looked amazing. Even as lousy as Jules felt, it was hard not to notice.

"You should have called me," Jason told him. There was no recrimination in his tone, and he looked relieved to have found Jules.

"I… I…," Jules stammered. He fought back tears. "I didn't want you to… this isn't your…."

"It's okay." Jason squeezed Jules's shoulder in a reassuring manner. Jules fought the urge to collapse against Jason and those powerful arms. "It's going to be okay. I've got your back."

"What do you know?" Jules asked. He realized now how stupid he'd been to run out without saying anything or even leaving a note. He knew how he must have worried Jason. He'd been so panicked, he hadn't thought at all.

"Just about everything," Jason replied. "I did a little homework before coming after you, or I'd have been here a lot sooner."

"He didn't do it, Jason. I know how it looks, but Guy's not a bad kid. He doesn't deal. He's just covering for those assholes he hangs out with."

"Where's the caseworker?"

"Her office is right over there." Jules gestured down the hall. "She wanted to know where our mother is. She said only his guardian can—"

"Relax. Let me handle this for you." And when Jules looked up at him, about to protest, Jason added, "Please, Jules. This is what I *do*."

Jules just nodded, glad someone was taking charge.

"Come on." Jason wrapped his arm around Jules's shoulder. "Let's go speak with her." As he led Jules down the hallway with a reassuring smile, he reminded him softly, "I've got your back, gosse."

"MONSIEUR GREENE," Charlotte Devieux said moments later as she shook Jason's hand. "Enchantée. Are you Guy's lawyer?"

"I'm a friend of the family," Jason replied smoothly.

"I'm afraid I need to speak with the mother," the woman reiterated. "I can't allow—"

"Mademoiselle Devieux," Jason interrupted. He smiled at the woman and took off his glasses to reveal his stunning green eyes. "May I call you Charlotte?"

The woman nodded, and despite his overwhelming concern for his little brother, Jules almost laughed to hear Jason turn on the charm.

"Thank you. *Charlotte*." The woman's face softened as Jason repeated her name, and this time Jules swore that Jason's slight American accent was more pronounced. The effect was rather charming. And very, *very* sexy.

"Charlotte," Jason continued with supreme confidence, "I understand that in this kind of situation, your policy is to share information only with the child's guardian."

Charlotte Devieux nodded again; the expression on her face now had a dreamlike quality to it. She was clearly enamored of Jason.

"I think if you do a little research"—Jason's voice was self-assured but decidedly unthreatening—"you'll find that the boy's mother has been in and out of trouble with the law herself. In fact, I understand that she'd been receiving in-patient treatment at a drug clinic until a few months ago. Her caseworker hasn't been able to locate her."

"I didn't know that," the woman answered. Her voice sounded small, and Jules realized Charlotte Devieux *should* have known all of this but hadn't even read the file when she'd been handed Guy's case. He knew that the juvenile caseworkers were overworked, but it still infuriated him that his brother was at their mercy. Jason glanced over and shot him a reassuring look that said, *I know. Just let me handle this.*

"I'm sure you understand that this is a very difficult situation for Jules and his brother," Jason continued. His expression was sympathetic, caring. "Jules is the only real constant in Guy's life."

"I have to admit, I had a hard time believing that the boy was dealing drugs," the counselor told Jason, as if she were confiding in a friend. Her entire demeanor had changed since Jason began speaking to her. "He seemed like a pretty good kid. But Monsieur Greene, he told the officers the drugs were his. Unless he's willing to tell us who they belong to, with his record—"

There was a knock on the door. "Yes?" Charlotte said.

"Madame," said a young woman Jules guessed was an office assistant, "Madame Juliette Chanay is here to see you." The assistant appeared awestruck, as if she wasn't sure why the visitor was there at all.

Jason stood up. "We can leave if you'd like," he told the caseworker. Jason's expression was unreadable, but Jules was sure Jason was enjoying this new development immensely. The name sounded vaguely familiar to Jules, although he couldn't remember where he'd heard it.

"No, no" came a brusque female voice from outside. "I'm here at Monsieur Greene's request." The assistant stepped aside, and a tall woman peered into the office. Her dark hair was pulled into a tight bun at the nape of her neck, and her high cheekbones and long nose gave Jules the impression of a bird of prey.

"Madame Chanay," Charlotte Devieux said with a slight tremor in her voice, "please come inside."

Jason turned and held out his hand to the newcomer. "Nice to meet you," he said.

"And you, Monsieur Greene," Juliette Chanay replied as she shook Jason's hand. She was taller than Jules, dressed in an impeccable wool suit, and carried a satchel in her left hand. "I have to say, I was surprised when Jeremy called to say that a friend of his needed me for a juvenile matter." She smiled appreciatively at Jason. "But when he told me who his friend was…."

"Thank you for coming so quickly," Jason said. "This is Mademoiselle Devieux, the counselor assigned to Guy's case." He flashed another charming smile at the caseworker. Jules knew only too well how that smile could disarm.

"It's an honor to meet you, Madame," Charlotte Devieux gushed. "I've read about your cases in the newspaper."

"Enchantée." Juliette shook the caseworker's hand quickly. "And this must be Monsieur Bardon," she said as she took Jules's hand and smiled reassuringly at him.

"I don't understand," Jules put in. He looked up at Jason for an explanation.

"Juliette is going to handle your brother's case," Jason replied. Charlotte gasped at information.

"But—" Jules protested.

"But nothing." Juliette put her briefcase down on the social worker's desk and pulled out a stack of papers. "Let me speak with Madame Devieux about your brother's case for a few minutes. Why don't I meet you outside afterward—we can talk then."

"Thank you," Jason said. He led the stunned Jules out of the small office and back into the hallway, adding, "And thank *you* so much, Mademoiselle Devieux," before shutting the door behind them.

"You were incredible," Jules told Jason, awestruck.

"Like I said," Jason responded as he brushed his thumb against Jules's pale cheek, "this is my job."

"I can't thank you enough." He looked Jason over once more, as if to convince himself that this was the same Jason with whom he'd spent the past week. "But Guy can't afford…. *I* can't afford…," he continued, overwhelmed. He'd finally remembered where he'd heard of the woman: she'd recently handled a criminal case against a high-ranking official in the French government and won. It had been all over the papers—something about a flight attendant and sexual harassment—and Jules figured she must charge a fortune.

"There's nothing to afford," Jason explained. "I've got a buddy who does international law outside of DC. He owed me a favor, and

Juliette loved the idea of handling a juvenile case for a change—I think she's sick of the political crap. She's taking the case pro bono; she's not charging anything for it."

"I can't believe you'd do this for me." Jules looked down at the floor and shifted uncomfortably on his feet. "I mean, I didn't call you, I didn't even want you to know…."

"I guessed as much," Jason replied. "When we get back home, I'll figure out how to punish you." Jason's eyes were lit with lust, hinting at what sort of price he might exact from Jules. Heat rose in his groin.

"But my mother…," Jules forced himself back to the reality of the situation. "How did you know all that?"

"I did a little research." Jason sat down on the bench and motioned for Jules to join him. "And I guessed at some of it. Once I got in touch with Juliette, she was able to pull your brother's social services file."

"I didn't want to involve you in this," Jules moaned as he took a seat next to Jason. "You, of all people."

"This is what I *do*," Jason reassured him. "If I can't do it to help the people I care about, what good is it? Hell, if I were licensed to practice here, I'd have taken the case myself."

When Jules said nothing in response, Jason put an arm around his shoulder. "Jules," he said, cupping Jules's chin with his left hand. "Let me do this for you. Please."

IT WAS late when they got back to the apartment. Juliette had managed to get the judge to agree to continue Guy's case off the court's overburdened docket. Guy would spend the night in juvenile custody, but at least there would be time to figure things out before the case would be heard.

"Give him time, Jules," Jason said on the long cab ride back from the police station. "He'll do the right thing."

They sat on the couch to relax after Jason changed out of his suit into a comfortable pair of jeans. Jules was shirtless and happily snuggled against Jason's broad chest when his stomach growled loudly enough for both of them to hear.

"You've barely eaten all day, Jules. How about I get us something?" Jason's offer reminded Jules of cooking, and he cursed as he remembered the quiche he'd left in the oven. Jason just laughed. "I wasn't going to offer *that*." He pulled Jules back against his chest. "But you know," he added with a wink, "it smelled really good until the smoke started pouring out of the oven."

"I'm sorry—" began Jules.

Jason didn't let him get the words out of his mouth. Instead, he kissed Jules's lips. It was a tender and reassuring kiss. Just what Jules needed. "Skip the apologies. I'll let you try cooking breakfast again tomorrow. Then we can get this thing with Guy settled. Juliette thinks the judge will agree to six months at a special residential school, even if Guy doesn't give up his friends to the police."

"Six months?"

"It's better than jail. Given Guy's record—" This time it was Jules who kissed Jason. "What was *that* for?" Jason asked when their lips finally parted.

"I was thinking he'd end up with a year in jail. Six months at a school—away from my mother—that would be *so* much better!"

Jason grinned and kissed the top of Jules's head.

"So," Jules began, "why don't you let *me* make us something to eat instead. I could make us a frittata, if you're hungry."

Jason ran a single finger over Jules's lips. "There's still the little matter of your punishment," he teased with a cockeyed grin.

Jules licked Jason's finger and did his best to look demure. Not an easy accomplishment. "I'm ready," he replied, then ran his tongue around it wantonly.

"Suck me off."

Jules grinned at the playful look in Jason's eyes. "I think I can handle that." He tried to appear contrite but was pretty sure Jason wasn't buying any of it. If it hadn't been for Guy's precarious situation, Jules would have been hard-pressed to keep his hands off of Jason earlier—he'd looked so amazing in his lawyer getup.

Jason laughed as Jules got up from the couch, kneeled on the floor, pushed Jason's knees apart, and unzipped his fly. Then, grinning like a fool as he freed Jason's already hard cock from the confines of his jeans and boxers, Jules added, "Although I'm not sure *you* can handle it."

Jules's mouth on Jason's sensitive tip cut short Jason's feeble protests. He traced his tongue along the line of the slit, then around the crown until Jason lapsed into English. "Fuck," he gasped as he leaned farther back against the pillows.

"That's the idea." Jules giggled. He held the base of Jason's erection and ran his teeth around the head.

"God, that's good," Jason moaned as Jules took him deep inside his mouth. Jules reached underneath Jason's ass and squeezed, then began to tug Jason's pants downward. With a little help from Jason, Jules brought Jason's jeans and boxers down around his ankles.

"I've been a bad boy, Jaz," Jules admitted somberly as he released Jason from his mouth for a moment.

"I like bad," Jason managed to say before Jules swallowed him again.

Jules grabbed Jason's ass and scraped his fingernails across the hard muscle there as he teased the opening between his cheeks. Jason tensed and Jules guessed he'd never had someone touch him like that before. Jules was pretty sure Jason liked it, though, because he pressed against Jules's finger, begging silently for more.

Jules caught Jason's eye and pressed the tip of his forefinger inside. "Fuck!" Jason cried out. Jules knew he was fighting the urge to come right then and there. "You really *are* bad, aren't you?"

Jules just nodded. He had no intention of releasing Jason's cock from his mouth; he was enjoying this far too much to talk. Jason smelled of musk and sweat with a hint of come, turning Jules on with an intensity that he'd only experienced a few times before. He pressed his finger further inside Jason's ass and grinned as he coaxed a bit more precome from Jason's slit. There was something about knowing that he could make a powerful man like Jason writhe beneath him, just with his touch, that Jules found breathtaking. He imagined Jason as he'd been that afternoon—dressed for battle—which made him desire Jason all the more.

He felt Jason teetering on the edge. *Not so soon.* He released Jason completely, licking underneath the shaft and sucking on his balls until he felt that large body tense with need.

"Gosse," rasped Jason, his voice ragged. Jules pushed a second finger inside of Jason and took Jason back in his mouth. "Oh.... God...," Jason moaned. Jules sensed he was holding back, determined not to come yet.

Jules brushed strands of hair from his eyes, smiling up at Jason. He knew *exactly* what he was doing, and he was loving it. "I've been *really* bad," he repeated as he came up for air and moved his fingers in and out of Jason's ass. "Really, *really* bad."

Jules could tell Jason could barely contain himself, so when Jason pushed Jules off of him with a growl, Jules was half expecting it. That didn't mean he wasn't disappointed.

"Don't worry," Jason laughed, "change of plans. You're enjoying this far too much. Stand up and come here."

Jules complied, but he made a point of licking his slightly swollen lips. Jason's expression was perfection—he parted his mouth and his eyes went dark with lust. Who needed food with such a willing partner?

Jason unbuttoned Jules's pants and pulled his boxers down along with them so that Jules was naked from the waist down. "Now lean against the couch."

Jules did as he was told. He liked it when Jason took charge.

"Farther over," Jason commanded. Jules threw his head back and laughed, his hair flying about his face, ass pointing upward.

Jules grinned when he saw Jason grab a tube of lube and a condom from his discarded jeans. Sex was even better knowing Jason had wanted it all along.

Jason's swat on Jules's bare ass brought Jules back to the here and now. "Oui!" Jules cried. "Merde!"

"You like that?" Jason rumbled. He slapped Jules again, then slicked his fingers and pushed one inside his hole.

"Mmm," groaned Jules. "Yes."

Jason's hand felt incredible, stretching him. He wriggled, and Jason nipped playfully at his asscheeks, inserting a second and a third finger, scissoring them to Jules's keening cries. He withdrew his fingers and spanked Jules once more before slipping the rubber over his cock and pressing without hesitation into the ring of pink muscle.

"Jules." Jason's voice was impossibly low and resonant. "Too warm, too tight."

"Fuck, yes," Jules gasped, turned on as much by Jason's words as feeling Jason's cock in his ass. "I love it."

Jason swatted Jules again for good measure, then reached around and rubbed Jules's cock.

"Yes… Jaz.… Fuck me… harder!"

Jason complied as he stroked Jules's erection vigorously, using his other hand to steady himself against Jules's hips. With each thrust, Jules moved to meet him. Their bodies slapped against each other until Jason came with a cry as he clutched Jules close.

"Jaz." Jules looked back at Jason. "It's so good… Jaz.…"

"Jules," Jason moaned as Jules climaxed a moment later. "You're so beautiful." Jason gathered Jules in his arms as Jules tried to catch his breath. Jason's legs still shook with exertion as Jules shivered against his broad chest. Jules blinked back tears.

"Jaz… Jaz… Je… je t'aime," he whispered.

Jason rubbed his chin against Jules's cheek and Jules closed his eyes.

What did I just say? Jules shivered again. If his words disturbed Jason, Jason wasn't showing it. In fact, Jason held him a bit tighter. Jules figured that was a good thing.

CHAPTER 8

AS HE had done often since his arrival in Paris, Jason lay awake in bed for several hours, unable to sleep. Jules slept with his chest pressed against Jason's back and his arms around his waist, allowing Jason to feel the soft rise and fall of Jules's chest with each breath.

It felt good like this. Jason tried to recall a time when he'd felt as peaceful in someone else's arms, but came up empty. Sure, Diane had been affectionate in her own way, but it had been different.

He needs me. Diane never did.

Need. Jason once told himself that he appreciated Diane's crisp, no-nonsense approach to life and love. Ask for what you want, but don't ask for too much. Don't take: taking is weakness. Diane had never been weak. Jason had lived his life and she hers. Their busy schedules gave them little time together, but hell, they didn't *need* it. They could enjoy those rare moments that they *did* have together, and it would all be just fine. That was the plan. Only it hadn't been fine at all.

Jules shifted and murmured in his sleep—a vulnerable sound that made Jason's chest ache. He put his hand over Jules's smaller one and felt the arms that held him tighten just a bit. He remembered Jules's embarrassment, how he'd wanted to keep the situation with Guy to himself.

"Just keep driving," Diane once said as they passed a stray dog on the side of the freeway one morning. Jason had thought about the dog all day. That evening, he'd even driven back just to see if the dog was still there. It hadn't been, but he'd wondered if the dog was all right. He'd never told Diane; he knew she would have laughed at him.

He *liked* feeling needed.

"Je t'aime." Three little words in English, but a bit more complicated in French, Jason mused. Add "bien" at the end of the sentence and it could mean "I like you a lot." But he knew exactly what Jules meant, and it scared him more than he was willing to admit.

I love you. He'd only said those words once to Diane and really meant them—on the day she'd accepted his marriage proposal. That day, he'd honestly believed *she* needed *him*. He realized now that he'd never really understood the significance of those three words.

He hadn't responded to Jules's confession in kind. Sure, he had *lots* of excuses as to why. It all seemed to come down to the fact that he had strong feelings for Jules, but he just wasn't sure what they were. *Like?* Definitely. *Attraction?* You bet your ass. *Admiration?* How could he *not* admire Jules's determination?

But I'm so much older....

He'd worried about that, even more so after his performance at the police station. He'd breezed in, taken charge, and held Jules's hand. Of *course* Jules would tell him that he loved him, especially after that.

Shit. Why am I doing this to myself? I'm here for six more weeks. We'll go our separate ways, and when we're old and gray, we'll look back on this and smile.

What was it that Rosie always said? "If you understand, things are just as they are; if you do not understand, things are just as they are." It wouldn't matter if he didn't make sense of it tonight. It wouldn't matter if he never made sense of it at all.

Another hour passed, and he lay staring out the window at the moonlit sky. He forced himself to focus on the sleeping man beside him—on the feel of Jules's body warm against his own and the endearing way Jules pressed his cheek against his back. At last he drifted off to sleep with Jules's gentle breath on his neck.

JULES PRESSED the phone to his ear, caught Jason's eye, and flashed him a brilliant smile. Jason wasn't sure which looked better: lunch or the sight of Jules in just his boxers.

"Wonderful," Jules said, bouncing on the balls of his feet in obvious excitement. "That's great news, Madame Chanay." He paused for a moment, then said, “All right. Juliette.” Jason saw Jules’s cheeks pink a bit as he said her first name. “I can’t thank you enough, Juliette.” He replaced the receiver as Jason encircled his waist.

“Good news?” Jason kissed Jules’s cheek.

“The best. The judge agreed to our proposal. They’ll transfer Guy this afternoon.”

“Terrific!” They’d expected this, but he knew Jules still worried that something might go wrong.

“I won’t be able to see him before he leaves,” Jules added in a wistful voice, “but I can visit him at the school in a few months as long as things are going well. And I can call him once a week when he’s settled in. Madame Chanay—I mean Juliette—gave me the number.”

Jason was happy to see Jules back to his usual self. And if Jules was having second thoughts about confessing his love to Jason the night before, it didn’t show.

“So how do I thank you?” Jules’s eyes hid nothing—he most definitely had an idea of how he should thank Jason.

“I’ve got a few ideas,” Jason deadpanned. He sat down at the table while Jules cut the quiche. “But first I was thinking that we should get out and do something today. You did agree to go sightseeing with me, right?”

Jules nodded and poured their coffee. “Where are we going?”

“I thought we’d go to the Marais. We can walk around the neighborhood, then head over to rue des Rosiers for a late lunch. Ever been there?”

“No.” Jules watched as Jason took a bite of the quiche, and waited for Jason’s reaction.

“I think this is your best yet,” Jason said, his mouth still half-full of quiche.

“Really?” Jules beamed.

“*Really*,” Jason repeated as he wiped his mouth with a napkin. “Where’d you learn to cook like this?”

“My grandmother.” Jules grinned widely. “She took care of me when I was little. She taught me to cook a few things after school.” His expression turned wistful as he explained, “We lived with her in Versailles after Guy was born.”

“She taught you well.” Jason swallowed another piece of quiche with obvious relish.

“Yeah. She used to take us to the Château sometimes. I’d dream about living there. I didn’t realize how lucky I was, living with Mémé.” Jules’s voice grew softer, and he blinked a few times. “I only wish Guy remembered her. After she died….” He took a deep breath, regaining his composure. “More quiche?” he asked.

Jason put his hand on top of Jules’s. “I’d love some. But you don’t have to change the subject, you know.”

“Thanks.” Jules pulled his hand away from Jason’s. Jason thought he looked uncomfortable once again. Maybe he worried that he was imposing on Jason’s sympathy and goodwill.

From the file he’d read on Jules’s mother and brother, he could only guess at how difficult Jules’s childhood must have been. In a way, he’d been relieved not to find anything personal about Jules in the file—if he was going to learn anything like that about Jules, he’d much rather learn it from Jules himself.

Jason waited expectantly, but Jules did not open up any more about his family. *Still, it’s progress.* Jules had opened the door, if only a tiny bit.

“So, Jaz,” Jules began anew as he took a bit of quiche on his fork, “what’s to see in the Marais? I’ve heard about a few gay bars over there, but I’ve never been.”

Jason laughed. “I hadn’t been thinking about the bars. But they have the best falafel outside of New York City.” *I didn’t even realize it was a gay hangout.*

“Falafel?”

“Fried chickpeas,” Jason explained. “It’s usually served with flatbread, salad, and sauce.”

“Sounds interesting.”

“When Rosie became a vegetarian, she used to make falafel all the time. I never got sick of it, although my parents probably did.”

Jules laughed and a wave of affection warmed Jason’s chest.

"There are a few museums in the area I wouldn't mind visiting too," Jason continued.

Keep talking or you're going to end up spending the entire day in the apartment. It was a tempting thought. Still, he knew that it would do them both good to get out and about, and the weather looked promising.

"Which museums?" Jules asked brightly.

"I'd like to check out the Musée d'art et d'histoire du Judaïsme," Jason answered. "The Marais may be gay friendly, but it's also the Jewish quarter. After that, maybe the Victor Hugo museum if there's time."

"Are you Jewish?" Jules asked between sips of coffee.

The question made Jason uncomfortable, and he hesitated. Even in twenty-first-century France, plenty of people still disliked Jews. In fact, four people had died in the firebombing of a synagogue in Paris as recently as 1980.

"Yes," he finally replied.

"Cool" was Jules's unhesitating response. "I studied Jewish folk music at the conservatory. There's some incredible stuff for violin."

Jason relaxed. He wasn't ashamed of his heritage; in fact, he embraced it. Still, the thought that Jules might not be accepting of it—and the realization that he *cared* about what Jules thought—had taken him by surprise.

I should have trusted my instincts. Then again, maybe he was doing that for the first time in his life.

THE LARGE square outside of the Hôtel de Ville wasn't crowded. The air smelled fresh, as if spring were finally on its way, and the sun was warm enough on Jason's shoulders that he unzipped his leather jacket.

For the first time since he'd arrived in France, Jason didn't feel at all strange to be away from his office in the middle of the day. It hadn't been an easy transition, though, and he still regularly checked his e-mail on his phone.

"You miss being at the office?" Jules asked him as Jason glanced at the phone and tapped it several times.

"Actually, no." It was the truth, although it also surprised Jason to say it.

"You check your e-mail a lot."

Brat.

"And?"

"Nothing." Jules smirked. "But sometimes you look disappointed, like maybe you wished there *was* a problem that only *you* could handle."

Jason frowned and shoved the phone back in the pocket of his jeans. "Anyone ever tell you that you're irritating sometimes?"

Jules bit his lower lip. "Yeah," he said. "All the time. Henri says it's cute."

Henri is right.

"So what kind of law do you do in Philadelphia?" Jules asked as they headed away from the square. He used the French pronunciation of the name—"la Philadelphie"—which made Jason smile.

"Employment law," Jason answered. "Discrimination cases, that sort of thing." It was surprisingly difficult to find the French words to describe his work, and so he shortened his answers. As good as his French was, he'd only been seventeen when he left France to move back to the States. There were some words he simply hadn't learned yet.

"You mean like if someone is fired from their work because they're queer?"

Jason had been expecting a different question, and he hesitated. He'd never had any cases involving sexual orientation, but he could certainly imagine having to defend one. "Yes, like that. Although we mostly see cases about race and gender discrimination."

"So you make sure that the employer doesn't treat the employee badly," Jules concluded incorrectly, much to Jason's chagrin. "That's important work."

"No," Jason answered. "I represent the employers."

"Oh. I see."

Jason's shoulders tightened. "Employers need good lawyers too, Jules," he said. It was the first time in a long while that Jason found himself defending his choice of work.

"Of course."

From the tone of Jules's voice, Jason was sure that he had an opinion on the subject. Jason had had this discussion with Rosalie many times, and she hadn't been as willing to let it drop. She'd called it selling out, among other things. For once, he appreciated the fact that Jules did not always speak his mind.

"Do you like your work?" Jules asked a few minutes later when Jason remained silent.

"Sure." *Hardly a resounding endorsement.* He wasn't sure he had the answer, anyhow.

"You don't *sound* sure."

"Henri was right," Jason countered. "You *are* irritating."

Jules just smiled.

"WHAT DO Jews believe about homosexuality?" Jules asked as they walked through the exhibits at the Museum of Jewish Art and History a short time later. He was examining a series of modern menorahs for Chanukah, eyes wide at one made completely of Bic ballpoint pens.

"Depends on which Jew you ask," Jason answered with a chuckle. "My bubbe used to say, 'Ask five Jews for an opinion, and you'll get ten.'"

Jules laughed. "Bubbe?"

"Like your mémé—my grandmother," Jason explained. "But to answer your question, the more liberal movements of Judaism tend to be accepting. The orthodox are much less so. A fair number of synagogues in the States perform same-sex unions. The synagogue I went to was pretty open-minded."

"Did you go a lot, growing up—to synagogue?" Jules asked. Then, perhaps realizing he was firing off question after question, he quickly added, "If you don't want to answer, it's okay."

Jason laughed. "I don't mind. It's just funny, that's all."

"What's funny?"

"Just that when I was a kid, I was a little confused. We had a Christmas tree at the holidays, but we also celebrated Chanukah. We went to temple for High Holidays, but my dad's pretty much an atheist, so just my mother took us. After my bar mitzvah, we stopped going altogether. But then in college," Jason continued, "there was a small Jewish student association, and I attended Saturday morning services regularly. I even dusted off my Hebrew and chanted from the sacred scrolls. I haven't been since I graduated, though."

"Why not? You seem to be really interested in it."

"Once I met Diane, I stopped going. She wasn't Jewish, she wasn't interested in religion, and she wasn't interested in going with me. We had so little time together anyhow. I don't know.... It just became too difficult, I guess."

Jules said nothing; Jason guessed he wasn't sure whether to ask about Diane. That was fine with him—he wasn't sure he was ready to talk about her with Jules, or with anyone else.

IT WAS nearly two o'clock when they headed out of the museum and back toward rue des Rosiers. Most of the lunch crowd had thinned out, for which Jason was grateful—he'd made the mistake of trying to get lunch in the Marais on a Sunday the last time he'd been in Paris, and the crowds had been overwhelming.

"This way," he told Jules, pointing down a narrow street at a small restaurant called Chez Julianne. It looked from the outside to be a typical French restaurant with its red awning and ivy growing over the brick front, but the smells that wafted out onto the street were most definitely not French.

"Hungry?" he asked, noting the ravenous look on his companion's face.

"It smells wonderful," Jules replied as Jason held the door for him.

They sat in the back of the restaurant, which was still quite crowded despite the late hour. "Do you trust me?" Jason asked.

"Are we talking about food?" Jules shoved his hands in his pockets and chewed his lower lip.

"Yes," Jason pointedly replied, "I *was* talking about food. And need I remind you that you're still in the doghouse after yesterday?"

"Dog… house?" Jules giggled.

"You know what I mean."

"I'm happy to have you punish me *anytime*." Jules's brown eyes twinkled. "But to answer your question—yes, I trust you to order."

"By the way, what happened to the green contact since yesterday? I noticed your eyes are both brown." Jason had noticed it before, but he'd forgotten to ask.

"I figured I'd do better at the police station without it. Do you miss it?"

Jason had to wonder if Jules had taken the green contact out because he'd told Jules he liked brown eyes. "I thought I would," Jason said. "But you really *do* have beautiful eyes, you know. I like them this way."

"Thanks." Jules blushed pink and fidgeted.

"You're embarrassed, aren't you?" Jules's reaction surprised Jason. For a flirt, he seemed so shy at times.

"Me?" Jules's cheeks were still stained red. "Yeah, I guess so."

"Why? You have a beautiful face, Jules. And more than that… you have a beautiful body too."

Jules squirmed in his seat. "I guess I'm just not used to compliments. I mean, I sort of like it when I get compliments about my music. But that's different…."

Jason reached across the small table and took Jules's hand in his own. "You'll just have to get used to it," he said. "I told myself after—" He stopped himself, not wanting to bring Diane's name into this. "—after I lost someone important to me that I would tell the people I care about what I'm feeling, and not keep things to myself."

A hint of a smile danced at the corners of Jules's mouth. "Thanks, Jaz," he murmured.

THEY FEASTED on a lunch of a variety of mezes—small dishes like appetizers—to share between them. They were brought plates overflowing with falafel, kefta, hummus, sliced pastrami, tarama, feta cheese, grilled eggplant, olive tapenade, and eggplant caviar. Jason also ordered a large basket of bread with pita, rye, and dark pumpernickel, along with a bottle of hard cider to wash it all down. For dessert, they shared a piece of cheesecake.

Jules ate with surprising zeal, having seconds and even thirds of everything except the olive tapenade. Jason watched Jules's excitement and wonder as a newly discovered universe of tastes unfolded before him—which was even more enjoyable for Jason than the excellent food.

After lunch, they wandered around the Marais for a few hours, browsing some of the stores that sold Jewish merchandise. In one of the shops, Jason picked up a beautifully embroidered blue-and-green prayer shawl and held it up to the light. He caressed the soft silk lovingly. The colors reminded him of Lake Erie and the boat that he and his family had often sailed when he was a child. Lost in memory, he smiled.

"What is it?" asked Jules.

"It's a prayer shawl," Jason explained, "a tallit. In most synagogues, men and women wear them during the Saturday morning service. The shawl is supposed to remind Jews of the 613 commandments in the Torah—the holy scrolls. I like to think of using the shawl as a way to remind myself of the law… as if I'm wrapping myself in it."

"That's the perfect color for you, Jaz. You should buy it."

"I don't know. I don't really need—"

"You were the one who told me that you make too much money to spend, right?" Jules persisted. "What's it good for if you can't treat yourself to something beautiful from time to time?"

Jason ended up buying the shawl as well as a matching kippah, the ritual head covering, and he put his arm around Jules's shoulder as they left the store. "Thanks," he told Jules. "I'll always think of you when I wear them."

Not that I'd need any prompting to think of you, Jules.

"WE START rehearsing for Milan tomorrow," Jules announced while they rode the subway back to the apartment. "Will you come and listen? You know, give us some advice about which tunes to play? I know you're supposed to be on vacation, Jaz, but—"

"I'd love to." Jason squeezed Jules's hand. "It's not work to listen to your music. I'd gladly trade listening to you guys play for sitting in a hot courtroom anytime!"

"Thanks."

"No problem."

"Jaz?"

"Hmm?"

"What I said last night.... I know it's probably too soon, but... I meant it, you know."

Jason smiled warmly at Jules and pulled him against his chest, not caring if anyone else on the subway saw. "I know," he whispered in Jules's ear.

CHAPTER 9

HENRI GLARED at Jules over a quivering cymbal. "We've gone over this piece six times now," he growled as he gesticulated with a long drumstick. "It's not going to get any better. Besides, I've got to get the dishes put away before the club opens."

"Henri's right, Jules," David chimed in. He rested his hands on the piano keys and yawned openly. "It's getting late. Marie-Claire's waiting on me for dinner."

"Fine," snapped Jules. He pulled his violin out from under his chin and set it on his knee.

"Problems?" Jason asked as he walked in. He and Jules had spent the day at the Louvre, but he'd gone back to the apartment while Jules had headed directly to the club.

"Something's wrong with the bridge, but I can't figure it out." Jules scowled at the other two musicians.

"We've repeated it so many times," David complained, "my brain is starting to hurt." He wiggled his fingers. "Not to mention my hands."

"Which piece?" Jason settled into one of the chairs in front of the stage. "I didn't hear anything yesterday that sounded strange."

"Nuage Gris," Henri answered. "It's a new one—Jules wrote it a few days ago. He insists on playing it in Milan, but we can't seem to get through it without him stopping us."

"Let me hear it." Jason saw Jules's look of surprise. "I told you I didn't mind listening. Maybe I can help."

"Would you? I mean, I know you said… but would you really give us some suggestions?"

Jason laughed. "Of course. Hell, I'd rather make myself useful for a change."

"Great!" Jules beamed and nodded to David, signaling to the pianist to play.

It was a dark piece full of angst and dissonance, just as the title, "Gray Cloud," suggested. Jason immediately knew that Jules had written it after the incident with Guy; he heard it in the music. He closed his eyes, laced his hands behind his neck, and leaned back, allowing himself to be transported by the raw emotion of the piece.

An ethereal sound from the brushes against the drums joined the lone piano. There was no driving beat, just a whisper of movement from Henri's instrument that seemed to envelop the piano. It was nearly a minute into the piece before Jules tucked the violin beneath his chin and placed the bow to the strings.

Jules had muted the instrument so that the sound seemed to come from far away. From time to time, he plucked a string softly with his left hand. At first the plucks seemed random, but as Jason continued to listen, he began to appreciate that they were anything but—they had the effect of grounding the music in the way the drums would in a traditional piece.

Violin as rhythm section and melody. Jason felt the same tingling down his spine that he had when Jules had first played for him weeks before. *This song is brilliant.*

For some time after the group had finished playing, Jason sat there his eyes still closed. "Unbelievable," Jason whispered as he came back to himself. He ran a hand through his hair as he often did when he was deep in thought. "It was so—" He struggled for the word in French. "—captivating." It had been more than that, but Jason's high school vocabulary kept him from expressing it any better.

Jules's face was flushed, as if the music had reawakened the same emotions that had inspired him to write it. "Thanks," he murmured. He looked both embarrassed and pleased at the compliment, and Jason smiled.

"So, Jaz," Henri interjected, "what do you think about the bridge?"

"I hear what Jules is talking about." He nodded and rubbed his chin. Then he stood up and walked over to the piano, asking David, "Do you mind if I try something?"

"No problem." David hopped up from the bench.

Jason sat down and placed his fingers on the keyboard, closing his eyes and reproducing the difficult chord progressions of the bridge easily. He repeated one particular passage several times, frowning. When he opened his eyes, he saw David and Henri staring at him, mouths open and eyes wide.

"The problem's here," Jason told Jules as he played three chords in rapid progression, stressing the left hand, "and here. You're going for a dissonance, but the final chord isn't resolving in the same way you resolved the chords in the first section of the piece. I think if you use this chord"—he played a different inversion of the original chord—"you'll be able to resolve it like this." He played the final notes and nodded. "Yeah. That's it."

"Got it," David said, clearly awestruck. He took over his place at the piano from Jason. "Can we try that once more?"

Jason settled back into his chair, hands resting on his knees, fingers touching. By the time they were finished, Jules was beaming. "That's it!" he nearly shouted and popped up from his chair to run to Jason. He kissed him on the lips while still holding his violin and bow. "That's it! I can't believe you figured it out so quickly!"

"It's a lot easier when it's not your own composition, I think." Jason smiled as he watched Jules pack his violin away. "You guys sound great, you know," he added as Henri grinned at him and David came over to shake his hand.

"Nice to hear that," David said with a laugh, "what with Jules cracking his whip and all."

Jules swore under his breath, his grin belying the low growl.

"How about you both join us for dinner?" Jason offered. "My treat. Marie-Claire's welcome to come too. My sister told me about a new vegetarian restaurant near Étoile."

"*Vegetarian*?" Henri repeated with a skeptical frown. "I thought you Americans like your meat."

"Henri!" David shook his head and scowled at Henri.

"We do like our meat," Jason replied, unfazed. He'd come to see Henri's attitude as hiding something else—insecurity, perhaps?—and he'd decided he liked the man, even if he could be a bit dense at times. "But sometimes it's nice to try different things." Jason glanced at Jules and winked, making Jules grin lecherously.

"I'd love to go." David cuffed Henri's head. "And just ignore this idiot. If he's too good for vegetarian, let him starve."

"Fine." Henri pulled a cigarette out of his shirt pocket and proceeded to light it. "Is it okay if Pascal comes too? He's supposed to meet me here after I finish up in the kitchen."

"Of course," Jason answered. "Jules and I will go get some coffee, and we'll meet you all back here at eight." He put his arm over Jules's shoulder and steered him toward the door.

"You were great, Jaz," Jules said as they walked out onto the street, where the sun was setting in a vibrant display of orange and pink.

Jason stopped and pulled Jules closer, inhaling Jules's scent—a hint of citrus and musk. He could think of few things that smelled better. "Thanks, gosse."

Jules hugged him, then took his hand, lacing their fingers together. "Hey… Jaz…," he began tentatively, "I know this is a difficult subject, but…."

"Go on," Jason prompted, squeezing Jules's hand. "It's never stopped you before. I'll tell you if I don't want to answer."

Jules exhaled audibly. He looked at Jason and asked, "Why did you quit music?"

"Thought that might be what you were going to ask."

"If you don't want to talk about it…," Jules began, but Jason shook his head.

"It's fine, Jules. I don't know… maybe it's something about this place, or maybe it's something about you, but I think I can talk about it now." He ran a hand through his hair and looked down at Jules with a soft smile. Then, motioning to the café at the corner, he added, "Let's get something to drink, and I'll tell you—as best I can."

TEN MINUTES later, two steaming cups of coffee between them at the small table, Jason chuckled softly to see Jules looking back at him, attentive and serious. "Don't sweat it," he told Jules. "There's really not that much to tell. No major childhood traumas that I can remember, no big revelations."

Jules reached across the table and put his hand reassuringly atop Jason's. The gesture caused Jason to relax, if only a bit.

"My mom was a piano teacher, years ago," Jason explained. "So when I was about three, I asked her to teach me. At least, that's what they tell me—I really don't remember. I guess I was pretty good—for a little kid, that is. But when I got to middle school, I decided that music, piano especially, wasn't cool. So I quit."

He took a sip of coffee with his free hand before continuing. "I didn't take it back up again until I was in high school. By then, I'd missed about three years of training. I just wasn't good enough to get into the Curtis Institute."

It was nowhere near a full explanation, and he'd hoped it would suffice, but Jules was buying none of it. "Curtis was the only school you auditioned for?" he asked.

"Yeah. I told myself if I wasn't good enough to get in there, it wasn't meant to be." Jason knew how lame his excuse sounded. Back then, it had made sense. But now?

"Aren't there a lot of other schools where you could have studied? Like Juilliard in New York?" Jules asked.

"Yeah. My mom asked me the same thing. She and Rosie thought I was an idiot. They were probably right too."

"What's the answer, then? There's more to the story, isn't there?"

Jason chuckled. "You *are* damn cute when you're being annoying."

Jules just picked up his coffee cup and began to sip the thick liquid, his smirk obvious. But the determined glint in his eyes demanded a straight answer.

"Okay, okay." Jason held up his palms in defeat. "You got me. The answer is that I'm not sure."

"That's not much of an answer."

"Nope. It's not. Rosie says it's because I'm a perfectionist. Maybe she's right."

"You don't sound convinced."

"Pushing your luck?"

Jules laughed.

"Fine," Jason grumbled. "I had a bad experience when I was in high school."

Had he just admitted that? It was something that he hadn't shared with *anyone*, even Rosalie—something he'd tried very hard to forget.

"At the conservatory in Grenoble?"

"Yeah," Jason replied.

"What happened there?"

"I really don't want to talk about it." Jason clenched his fingers around his cup. "It was a long time ago."

"Maybe you should go back there."

"To Grenoble? What for?" Jason's hands suddenly grew cold and the tension rose in his neck, shoulders, and chest. He swallowed hard, but it had nothing to do with the coffee. And he realized, to his great surprise, that he was terrified of the prospect of going back to his childhood home.

What the hell am I scared of? That was years ago. Another lifetime.

"I don't know. Maybe just to think things through." Jules was studying him carefully, obviously gauging his reaction.

Jason considered the suggestion for a moment and forced himself not to dismiss it out of hand. "I guess I could."

"I'll go with you, if it'd help," Jules offered as he took Jason's hand. "I've never seen the Alps. My grandmother used to tell me how beautiful it was there. Have you ever been back?"

"No. Not to Grenoble." The warmth Jules's touch communicated somehow made him feel stronger. "But if you're willing to come…."

Did I just say that?

"What do you say in English?" A brilliant smile lit Jules's features. "I've got your back?"

Jason couldn't find the words to respond. Instead, he looked down at Jules's hand.

I need him too.

That thought frightened him even more than the prospect of a trip to Grenoble. He pulled his hand out from under Jules's, and for a moment, he thought he saw a hint of pain in Jules's warm brown eyes.

"Okay," he said at last, finding the prospect of disappointing Jules too difficult to bear. Jules's expression shifted to one of obvious relief. "We'll go to Grenoble after Milan." Immediately, Jason began to conceive of a dozen different ways in which he could justify not making the trip.

Then, before Jules could respond, he added, "We'd better get back to the club. It's time for dinner."

"JAZ?"

Jason looked up from the bench in the courtyard to see Jules poking his head out of the apartment. He'd been watching the stars flicker overhead and listening to the muted sounds of traffic coming from the boulevard. They'd returned from dinner about an hour before, and despite the good food and several glasses of wine, Jason felt uneasy. Nervous. He couldn't remember the last time he'd felt so….

Vulnerable?

"Hey," he answered, doing his best not to show his discomfort. "Good shower?"

"Yes. You coming inside?"

"Yeah." Jason stood up and walked back to where Jules was waiting at the door.

Jules's hair was wet, and he was wearing only a pair of Jason's sweatpants, which hung low on his narrow hips. Jason followed the muscles of Jules's abdomen down to the waistband of the pants. The faint line of hair running from Jules's chest disappeared almost obscenely beneath.

Jason kissed Jules passionately, all thoughts of Grenoble and childhood ghosts fleeing as he grew hard. Even now, more than two weeks after he'd first had sex with Jules, Jason couldn't believe how much Jules turned him on.

"What were you doing out there?" Jules asked after their lips parted. "It's cold."

"Then you'll just have to warm me up," Jason replied, avoiding the question and putting one arm around Jules to close the door behind him. Before they were halfway down the hallway, Jules had begun to pull Jason's T-shirt over his head.

"Merde," Jason cursed as Jules pushed him against the wall and ran his tongue over a hard nipple.

Jules looked up and bit his lower lip suggestively. Then he closed his mouth around the nipple once more, teasing it with his teeth. Making his way downward, he found the waist of Jason's jeans and popped open the buttons down the fly, freeing Jason's hard cock from the confines of the heavy fabric and reaching underneath to stroke Jason's balls as well as the sensitive skin behind.

Before Jason could suggest that they move to the living room, his pants were around his ankles and Jules had dropped to his knees and taken him into his mouth. "Jules. Oh God…." Jules's uncharacteristically aggressive approach left Jason breathless and struggling for words.

With his tongue, Jules traced the vein than ran underneath Jason's erection while he slid a wet finger between Jason's legs, teasing Jason's tight opening. Then he swallowed Jason so deeply that the auburn curls at the base of his cock tickled his lips. The sound of a saxophone filtered into the hallway from the living room stereo, mingling with Jason's heavy breaths. Jules hollowed his cheeks, sucked harder, and pressed his finger inside Jason.

"Shit!" Jason cried out as Jules hit his sweet spot. English now—he'd stopped fighting his need to be in control and had given himself over to the pure physicality of the contact.

Releasing Jason's cock from his mouth, Jules grabbed its base with his free hand and teased the tip with his tongue. Jason recognized the song on the stereo—Chick Corea's "Spain"—and when Jules began to hum along as he sucked, Jason nearly lost it.

"Jules." The vibrations from Jules's mouth brought Jason to the brink of orgasm. "Fuck. Oh fuck. Jules!"

"Not yet, Jaz," Jules murmured after sliding his lips free. "I want you inside of me. I want to feel you fill me up." He waited until Jason had managed to regain some semblance of control, then took Jason's hand and led him to the bedroom. Once inside, Jules ran his fingers through his own damp hair before grinning and pulling off his sweatpants. He was naked underneath.

"You really are beautiful." Jason hungrily took in the smooth skin over the lean muscle of Jules's chest, as well as the slight narrowing of his waist.

As expected, Jules appeared uneasy with the compliment. He took the hand that Jason was offering him, straddled Jason, and reached for the light switch.

"No, leave it on. I want to see your body." Jules shivered and whimpered as Jason stroked his shaft. His eyes still fixed on Jason's, Jules stood up on his knees and pressed a finger into himself.

Jason's lips parted. Transfixed, he watched as Jules pressed a second finger inside, then a third, before beginning to move up and down on them. "God, yes," he whispered, watching Jules's motions. "I could almost come just from watching you!"

At this, Jules removed his fingers and grabbed Jason's cock. He sheathed it, then picked up the bottle of lube from the nightstand. He warmed it briefly between his hands before rubbing it over both their cocks. "Please, Jaz," he whispered, "fuck me." He guided Jason's cock between his cheeks and pressed it against his hole.

Jason could never resist when Jules put it like that—and why should he? He grasped Jules's waist and pulled him down, feeling the brief pressure of the outer muscles as they softened to admit him. Ever so slowly, he pressed into Jules, feeling just a slight hitch this time as Jules settled down onto his hips. "Good?"

Jules nodded. "*Very* good!"

Jason lifted Jules and set him back down, pushing into his tightness. Jules continued to move up and down on Jason. Again and again the heat of Jules's body took him in. "I'm not going to last long," he gasped as Jules smiled and licked his lips, rubbing a hand over his cock as he steadied himself with his other hand on Jason's chest. "Oh God… Jules… you're… so… fucking… sexy… like… that." Jules's musical, carefree laugh sent Jason over the edge.

"Je t'aime, Jaz," Jules moaned in Jason's ear as he also came, the wet warmth spreading across Jason's abdomen.

THE NEXT day, Sunday, was almost entirely spent rehearsing for the Milan gig. By late afternoon, Jason had gone back to the apartment to do some work he claimed nobody else at the law firm could do. Jules had been sitting at the piano composing a new piece when he saw a shadowy figure near the doorway of the club.

"Maman?"

Jules's mouth went dry; his voice sounded tentative and childlike to his own ears. For a split second, he wondered if he were just imagining her—the petite dark-haired woman standing there, legs planted firmly as if prepared for a fight. She was dressed in jeans and a printed T-shirt, her hair pulled back into a rough ponytail.

Jules closed the piano and stood to face her.

"I am no longer your mother, not after what you've done," she replied as she walked toward him. Her voice was brittle and cold, with a knife's edge that cut him to the quick. She smelled of alcohol.

Jules noticed that the lines around her mouth and eyes had grown more pronounced since he'd last seen her two years before. Beneath her icy gaze, he felt ten years old. His hands trembled. He shoved them into his pockets and hoped she wouldn't see.

"How much do you want?"

"You worthless little—" she began, her face now contorted with rage. "You interfere in your brother's life and then you have the gall to insult *me*?"

"Where the *hell* were you when Guy needed you?" he snapped. A muscle in his cheek jumped involuntarily.

"I was busy." She appeared unconcerned. "Espèce de merde," she cursed under her breath. "Since when do you have any say over what happens to your brother? *You* were the one who left."

"*You* kicked *me* out, remember?" he hissed.

How could she have forgotten? He hadn't even been sixteen. If Henri's family hadn't let him crash on the floor, he'd still be sucking cock on the street. That or he'd be dead by now.

She slapped him across the cheek, forcing him to grab her wrist. "That's enough, Maman," he said under his breath.

"It's hardly enough." Her hollow laugh echoed pitifully through the empty club.

"Oy, Jules." Henri walked out of the kitchen, drying his hands on a towel. "Something the matter?" He saw Jules's mother—saw Jules holding on to her wrist—and stopped dead in his tracks. “Oh,” he muttered.

“It’s all right, Henri,” Jules reassured him. “I’ve got this under control.”

“You sure?” Henri asked. “Because if she’s bothering you, I’ll call the cops.”

Jules’s mother glared at Henri.

Better that I die on the street than find another home with Henri and his family.

“I’m sure,” was all Jules said aloud. He’d regained his self-control. “Give us a few minutes, okay, man?”

“Okay.” Henri appeared unconvinced but shrugged and walked back into the kitchen.

“Why are you here, Maman?” Jules’s face stung from her blow, but he tried to focus on the pain; it helped him from feeling anything other than anger toward her. He released his grip on her and took a few deep breaths.

“The rent’s due,” she said. He knew she was lying; she was probably living in some drug-addicted boyfriend’s apartment. She wanted money for drugs or booze.

“How much?”

“A thousand,” she answered.

A thousand euros? Shit. “I don’t have that kind of money,” he said calmly.

“What the fuck do you do all day? Play your music?” She spat on the floor and scowled. “At least you could play in the Métro and make it worth your while.”

He cringed; he’d thought of that at one point, but it had felt too much like begging. He was too proud.

“I’ve got a hundred, maybe two,” he told her. He wasn’t even sure he had that, but Henri might loan him a twenty. He waited for the threat that always came when she asked him for money.

“That caseworker called me,” she said.

Of course.

"What did she want?" Jules knew full well what his mother would say, and steeled himself against it.

"She wants my permission for Guy to stay over the summer at this *school*." She spoke the last word as if it were a horrible thing, as if she despised the idea.

Jules exhaled. "I'll get you the money." He had no idea where he'd get it from, but he'd figure something out. Maybe he could pick up some work from Henri's brother—he owned a garage near Nanterre.

She smiled. It was a charming smile and yet entirely devoid of any emotion. She reached for his face and caressed him on the chin. He forced himself not to pull away; it wouldn't help him or Guy to anger her again.

"Good boy, Jules," she said. "You were always such a sweet child. I'll be back tomorrow."

And with that she was gone, leaving him standing there. It was always like this. He was used to it.

"JAZ?"

"Hmm?"

Jason looked up from the couch to see Jules setting the table for dinner. Jules had made boeuf bourguignon, letting the stew simmer for most of the day while he was over at the Loup-Garou practicing with David and Henri. He'd insisted on making the dish after discovering that it was one of Jason's favorites, and the smell of the beef and Burgundy wine simmering on the stove had driven Jason to distraction. Almost as much as Jules drove him to distraction.

"Nah," Jules answered. "It's nothing."

"Come here." Jason reached a hand out to Jules and smiled. Jules walked over to the couch but didn't look Jason in the eye. "Something's up. I can tell."

"It's nothing," Jules repeated.

"Give it up, Jules." Jason pulled Jules against him and caught his lips. "God, you taste good, you know," he murmured a moment later. "I'd take you right here and now, but the look on your face tells me that something's eating you."

"Eating?"

Jason laughed. "Another American expression. You know what I mean."

Jules's usual smirk was strangely absent.

"So what's going on?" Jason had Jules in his arms now. "Tell me. Please."

"I need to borrow some money," Jules said. He avoided Jason's eyes as he spoke.

"Money? How much?"

"A few hundred Euros."

"A few *hundred*?" Jason was surprised—Jules had never asked him for money before, let alone that much.

"Yes," mumbled Jules. "But I understand if you can't…."

"What do you need it for?"

"It's not important."

Jason tightened his hold on Jules and planted a tender kiss on his neck. "I know it has to be something serious for you to ask me for money. Please tell me."

Jules wormed his way out of Jason's embrace. "It's okay," he said. "I really shouldn't even have asked! It's not a big deal, and I can take care of it myself." He stood and stalked over to the bedroom and slammed the door shut behind him.

Baffled, Jason followed him and leaned against the door. "Jules?"

The door opened abruptly, nearly knocking him off-balance.

Now wearing shoes and a sweater, Jules strode past Jason and grabbed his jacket off of the coat-tree. "I'm going out for a while," he said. "I'll be back late. Don't wait up for me."

"Jules?" Jason asked, paralyzed with shock.

"I'll be back late," Jules repeated and left the apartment.

CHAPTER 10

"HENRI?"

"Jaz, how's it going?" Henri grinned at Jason as he wiped a stray lock of hair from his forehead with a soapy hand.

The kitchen of the Loup-Garou smelled of frying oil, cigarettes, and dish soap. Jason found it somehow reassuring, a reminder that the entire universe hadn't come to a screeching halt just because Jules hadn't come home the night before.

"I'm fine," Jason answered. "Where's Jules?"

"He canceled today's practice," Henri explained as he worked on the dishes. "Said something came up that he had to take care of. Something about his violin. It's broken, I think."

"He seemed really upset about something last night," Jason prodded. "You sure this is about his violin?"

Henri shrugged. "His mother came by here yesterday. Never a good scene when that bi—" He glanced at Jason and corrected himself. "—when that *woman* stops by."

That explains it.

"Did Jules say when he'd be back?"

"Nah," Henri told him. "But with the Milan gig only two days away, we really need to be rehearsing. It's not like Jules to cancel—I'd expect that more from me or David, if you know what I mean."

Jason chuckled. "Thanks, Henri." He patted Henri on the back. "If you see Jules, don't mention that I was here, okay?"

"No problem, man," Henri said as Jason walked out of the kitchen.

A broken violin? Strange.

Once outside the club, Jason pulled his cell phone out of his pocket and tapped it a few times. “Juliette? It’s me, Jason Greene. Can I speak with you?”

AT NEARLY midnight, Jules unlocked the apartment door. Doing his best to be as quiet as possible, he pulled off his shoes and set them down by the door.

“I missed you.”

Jules froze. Jason was seated on the couch in the living room, his hands behind his head.

“Bonsoir,” Jules said. He tightened his jaw and tried his best to sound nonchalant. “I’m sorry—I didn’t mean for you to wait up for me.”

“I’m sure you didn’t.” There was no reproach in Jason’s words, just concern. Jules hoped Jason couldn’t see his face—he knew his eyes were red and swollen. He’d tried not to let it get to him, but he’d spent most of the evening on a park bench, trying to figure out how he’d be able to get his violin back in time for the Milan gig.

He looked away, not wanting to meet Jason’s gaze. That was when he saw the familiar neon-green case on the dining table.

“Missing something?”

“I…,” Jules stammered. “I…. Where did you find my violin?”

Jason stood up and took Jules in his arms. “You really are stubborn, aren’t you?” Jules said nothing, but he didn’t fight the gentle embrace either. “It’d be a little hard to play in Milan without a fiddle, you know.”

“How… how did you figure it out?” Jules tried to hold back his tears. He didn’t think he had any left to cry, but he’d been wrong.

“I’m a pretty observant guy. And you weren’t acting like yourself.” Jason held him tighter.

“I don’t want…,” Jules began. He relaxed against Jason’s chest. Why did Jason do things like that for him? He’d never wanted to involve Jason in his personal problems.

"Shhh." Jason rubbed Jules's head. It felt good. Reassuring. "It's all right. I'm not angry. I know why you did it. I understand. I knew the money wasn't for you.

"When you didn't come back," he continued, "I decided to go to the club and check up on you. I knew you had a rehearsal with David and Henri, but when I got there, Henri said you'd canceled—something about a broken violin. Then he mentioned your mother came by the club."

Jules knew he should say something, but he couldn't find the words. He felt like a complete fool. He'd let her use him again. He'd let her use Guy as a weapon. How many times had he said she didn't have any hold over him? And yet each time she'd come back, wanting something from him, he'd given in.

"I'm not stupid, Jules." Jason pressed his lips together and his brow knitted in a loving and sympathetic expression. "It didn't take much to figure out why you wanted the money. But selling your violin…." He sighed.

"She's using Guy. She knows she can manipulate me by threatening to take him out of the school. I don't want him to go back with her…. He *can't* go back to that place… but she's his guardian and I…." Jules turned his back to Jason, fighting tears once more.

"Hey." Jason touched Jules's shoulder. "It's okay to be upset."

Jules tensed at the touch. "I'm not a child." The words were for himself—a reminder of sorts—but he knew they wounded Jason.

"Being afraid for your brother doesn't make you a child, Jules."

"I don't want you to think I'm weak," Jules said. Pity was the last thing he wanted from anyone, especially Jason.

"Not gonna happen." Jason wrapped his arms around Jules again and hugged him tightly. "Knowing you—who you are even after all you went through as a kid—that's strength, Jules."

Jules leaned his head against Jason's arm.

"I know you love your brother," Jason continued. "I know you'd do anything to keep him safe."

"I left him with *her*. This is all my fault." Well, it was. If he hadn't left Guy with her….

"You were *sixteen*, Jules," Jason countered. "And it was your mother who kicked *you* out—it wasn't the other way around."

For a moment Jules was silent. Then, realizing what Jason had just said, he asked, "How do you know that?"

"I saw her today—your mother."

Jason's body tensed against his. "You… you *saw* her?"

"I spoke with her."

"You… *what*?" Jules's heart pounded hard against his ribs as the reality of what Jason was saying sank in.

"I had a little conversation with her this afternoon."

"But now she'll—" Jules began, rounding on Jason.

"No," Jason said firmly, "she *won't*."

"But how do you know she won't?" If his mother had her way, Guy would be right back where he'd been. Could she take him out of the school, drag him back home?

"This is my job, remember?" Jason smiled at Jules, clearly trying to reassure him. "I made a few phone calls before I spoke with her. The first was to Juliette."

"The attorney?"

Jason nodded. "Seems as though your uncle wasn't notified about Guy's situation."

"Uncle Louis?"

"Yeah. Damn social services employees," Jason grumbled. "They never called him like they should have. They should have contacted him years ago. When he found out that Guy was in trouble and what your mother was up to, he offered to take custody of Guy. Juliette got an order signed giving him temporary custody, at least until a full hearing can be held. They won't be contacting your mother. She can't use Guy to manipulate you anymore." Jason smiled at Jules once again, and this time Jules relaxed a bit. He wasn't sure he believed his mother was out of the picture, but getting Guy away from her, even temporarily, was progress.

Jules slipped out of Jason's embrace and walked to the table. He ran his fingers gently over the green violin case. "How did you find it?"

"That was the easy part." Jason laughed. "I figured you'd pawned it. I just asked Henri where he'd take his drum set if it were him."

"But they weren't supposed to sell the violin. I mean, I'd have paid back the loan and—"

"I asked Henri to speak to the shop owner. He explained that I was your friend and I'd be returning the instrument to you." Jason grinned and added, "Turns out the shop owner's heard you guys play a few times. He gave the violin back to me for the amount of the loan, with no interest."

Jules looked up at Jason. "What did I do to deserve you?" He meant it too.

"More than you know" was Jason's response.

"I'll repay you."

Jason shrugged.

"I mean it, Jaz."

"That's fine," said Jason, "but you don't need to."

"I *want* to."

"Works for me. In the meantime, a hug will do just fine."

Jules grinned. "You missed me again, didn't you?"

"Damn straight I did." Jason wasn't going to lie about it. Why should he?

Jules walked back to Jason and threw his arms around him. "Thank you. I don't know how I can ever—"

"Don't worry about it. I'm just glad you're back."

Jules kissed him, then brushed his fingers over Jason's chin and cheeks. "I love you, Jaz."

THEY LAY together in the bed later, spent and exhausted. Jules was naked and cradled in Jason's arms, his head on Jason's chest. "She was really young," he whispered into the darkness.

"Your mother?"

"Yes," Jules answered. He snuggled against Jason and into the warmth of that broad chest and found the strength to go on. He wanted Jason to understand. He *needed* him to understand, even if he wasn't sure why. "She was seventeen when I was born. She and I lived with Mémé back then—Mémé was a mother to both of us, I think.

"I don't remember the first few years, of course—I was too young. But I do remember later on, when Maman left. Mémé told me my maman loved me… that she was trying to become stronger so that she could make a life for us." He repressed a sigh and fought the heartache that always seemed to accompany the good memories. "Maman used to read me stories when she was home. Fairy tales, I guess you'd call them. She'd tell me we'd go see some of the places in those stories when she had enough money…."

Jason held Jules tighter and kissed the top of his head, a reassuring reminder that Jules was no longer alone and an encouragement to continue his story.

"I believed her," Jules whispered. "And when Guy came along, I thought she'd come back to stay. She didn't, though. We'd see her a few times a year. And then Mémé died, and we went to live with Maman.

"For the first few months, I thought maybe she'd changed—that she really had gotten her life together. But then she started to bring men home. I was old enough to realize why they were there—she stopped working, but she still had enough money for alcohol and drugs. I knew it, but I didn't do anything about it. And when…."

For several minutes, Jules said nothing. He didn't want to cry, and he wasn't sure he could say what he needed without crying. He also wasn't sure how much he should tell Jason. Some things he didn't want Jason to know.

Jason must have understood this, because he held Jules and didn't push him. Didn't ask him questions. Jules knew he was waiting, that he'd wait until Jules was ready, even though he also knew Jason wanted to help him. That knowledge made all the difference in the world.

"A few weeks before I turned sixteen," Jules continued at last, "she and I got into a huge fight. She kicked me out of the apartment. I had saved up a little money, but it didn't last long. I tried—I really did—but I just couldn't do it. I couldn't find a job that paid enough for an apartment. I didn't know how to do anything. I think I would have died if it hadn't been for Henri and his family…. They took me in. They never asked any questions. They even helped me apply to the conservatory."

Jason ran a gentle hand over Jules's hair and kissed him again. "You *are* strong," he said. "You just don't give yourself credit, Jules."

Jules sat up abruptly, pushing Jason away. "You don't know what I did. If you knew, you'd hate me."

"I don't need to know. We've all done things we're not proud of, things we wish we could take back. There's nothing you've done that would change how I feel about you." As he said this, he sat up and gathered Jules in his arms, then kissed him tenderly on the back of his neck.

Jules sighed audibly and leaned his head against Jason's. Of course Jason would say that. He knew Jason believed it too, but he wouldn't take that chance. He couldn't.

"You'll tell me when you're ready, Jules," Jason continued, brushing Jules's bangs off his forehead and kissing his cheek. "And if you're never ready," he added, "that's fine with me too."

"You really think I'm beautiful?" He spoke the words in an undertone, afraid to hear the answer to the question.

"I do," Jason answered without hesitation.

"I love you, Jaz," Jules murmured as he leaned in toward Jason's shoulder. And in that moment, Jules knew he *was* beautiful.

JASON SHOULD have known from the start that the trip to Italy wouldn't end up quite as they had planned. David arrived at the airport late, a half an hour before the flight, looking exhausted. Henri, who had gotten tired of watching Jules pace back and forth at the small gate, had shoved a pair of earbuds in and cranked up the music loud enough that half of the waiting passengers could hear it.

Mumbling something about his pregnant girlfriend trying to fatten him up before the baby came, David apologized halfheartedly to Jules and the others. Apparently Jules had been giving the woman cooking lessons. "At this rate," David moaned, "I'm going to get fat. That is, if she doesn't kill me first." He looked pale and sweaty.

Jules's anxiety evaporated, however, once the plane took off down the runway, and he gasped and held Jason's hand in excitement. "What d'you think?" Jason asked.

"It's incredible, Jaz," Jules gushed, pressing his nose against the window. He pointed at a group of high-rise buildings. "Do you think that's Nanterre?"

"Could be." Jason chuckled and leaned back in his seat. At times like this, he realized how fortunate he'd been to travel so much as a child. He guessed that he, too, had once been as excited to fly.

A few minutes later, the plane broke through the cloud ceiling, and Jules turned back to look at him. "I probably look like an idiot, don't I?"

"Why?" Jason asked. "Because you're enjoying yourself? How could that ever be stupid?"

Jules glanced around the cabin. Then, seeing that nobody was looking in their direction, he gave Jason a quick kiss on the lips. Jason, however, just pulled Jules against him, not caring if any of the other passengers noticed.

THEY ARRIVED in Milan around lunchtime and checked into the small hotel near Castello Sforzesco. After grabbing a quick lunch at a restaurant near the hotel, they headed over to the venue for the fashion show to meet Rosalie and rehearse in the space.

"Jules," Rosalie gushed, hugging Jules tightly and kissing him on both cheeks, "I'm so excited that you're going to play tomorrow!"

"For you, Rosie," laughed Jules, "I'd do anything."

"Flirt." Jason hugged his sister.

"Always," Jules replied with a wink as she proceeded to greet David and Henri.

"That's my partner, Stefano Fratelli," Rosalie said. She gestured to a tall, lanky man who stood on a stepladder on the large platform, hanging an enormous abstract poster in vibrant shades of fuchsia and blue. Stefano waved down at them, then said something to the woman who was helping him and climbed down.

"Nice to meet you all," Stefano said in heavily accented but passable French. "Rosie's told me all about you." He hopped down off the T-shaped runway, landing easily next to them and holding out his hand to Jason.

"Jason Greene," Jason said, shaking Stefano's hand. "And this is Jules Bardon, Henri Duvalier, and David Gilman."

"I've heard a great deal about you." Stefano shook hands with the men. "Rosie here can't stop raving about your music."

"Speaking of which," Rosalie interjected, "have you decided on a name for your trio? I'd like to introduce you tomorrow."

Jules grinned, catching Jason's eye. "We have. We're calling ourselves Blue Notes."

Jason smiled and slipped his arm comfortably about Jules's shoulders. "I like it."

"Perfect!" Rosalie beamed. "We've got you set up over here"—she gestured to one of the junctures of the stage—"if that's all right."

"That looks great," Henri said, walking over to the drum set and eyeing it with open wonder.

"I hope the instrument is acceptable." Stefano watched Henri appraise the drums.

"It's incredible." Henri sat down and pulled his drumsticks out of his backpack. "Much better than my set!"

David sat at the piano and played a few arpeggios. Jason noted with obvious pleasure that the piano, a Yamaha baby grand, sounded worlds better than the clunky old upright they'd been using at the Loup-Garou.

"You done good, sis," Jason said with a wide grin.

"I'm glad." Rosalie turned to Jules and asked, "Can we go over the plan for tomorrow? I've got a few ideas about the kind of pieces we need for each part of the collection."

"Of course." Jules allowed her to take him in hand and lead him over to a table covered with sketches and notes. "Jaz told me a little about what you wanted."

THE REST of the afternoon was spent rehearsing, with a short break for a fitting—Rosalie had designed suits for the musicians, along the lines of the slim suit she'd given Jules in Paris. It was nearly five o'clock when they finished practicing, and in the end, even Jules seemed pleased with the acoustics of the large space.

Stefano had brought along a good friend to handle the sound system. With Jason's help, they managed to amplify the music just enough to ensure that it could be heard throughout the hall without compromising the intimate feel of Jules's compositions or the warm tone of the violin.

Watching Jules wipe the rosin from under the bridge of his violin and release the tension in his bow, Jason walked over and put his hand on Jules's shoulder. "You guys sound great," he said proudly.

"You think?" Jules looked up at Jason. Jason wasn't sure he'd ever seen Jules so happy.

"Yeah, I think," laughed Jason. "So how about some dinner? I've got a little surprise for you tonight."

"A surprise?"

"Ouais. But if we don't get moving, we'll be late for it," Jason added as he directed Jules toward the exit and waved at the others.

TWO HOURS later, dressed in his suit and having eaten more than he ever remembered eating in his life, Jules walked down the via Filodrammatici, hand in hand with Jason. "You're not going to tell me where we're going?"

"Nah, but you'll see in a minute," Jason answered as he repressed a grin.

"You know I hate surprises," Jules warned.

"You should learn to like them, Jules." He stopped walking and squeezed Jules's hand.

For a moment Jules just looked at Jason. Jason watched as the realization of where they were slowly occurred to Jules, whose eyes grew wide and jaw dropped. "This is…," he began, unable to finish the sentence.

"The Teatro alla Scala," supplied Jason. "And"—he pulled an envelope out of his pocket—"I have two tickets for tonight's performance of *Tosca*."

"*Tosca*? Really?"

"Yes, really." Jason chuckled. "You like Puccini?"

"I *love* Puccini!" Jules took the tickets from Jason's hand and scrutinized them as though he didn't believe it. "But how did you get them? I heard that it's almost impossible to get tickets to La Scala at the last minute, especially for an opera."

"I've got a few friends in the business," Jason explained, guiding Jules under the brick entryway and through the doors. "Comes in handy sometimes."

"I've never seen an opera," Jules admitted later, as they were shown to their seats in the center of the orchestra section of the enormous hall. "I mean, I saw some of the opera singers at the conservatory perform scenes from them, but I've never seen an entire opera."

"My dad loves opera. He'd take us to Chicago from time to time. You know, toss the kids in the car and spend the weekend there. *Tosca* was one of his all-time favorites. Mine too."

And as the lights dimmed, Jules took Jason's hand and squeezed it tight. Jason couldn't remember ever having been happier in his life.

BACK AT the hotel hours later, Jules was still babbling on about the opera. "It was so sad." He sniffled as he recalled the execution scene at the end where Tosca mistakenly believes that her lover will be spared and they will escape Italy together. "That bastard Scarpia, he *lied* to her. He never intended to let Mario go."

"She *killed* Scarpia," Jason pointed out as he chuckled at Jules's enthusiasm.

"Yes, but not until the bastard tried to rape her!" Jules was indignant. "And when she climbed up to the top of the parapet and jumped," he continued, pacing back and forth by the window, "I thought she might still escape. But she killed herself."

"She couldn't live without her lover. She didn't care about fame or power—she just wanted to be with him. When he died, she didn't want to keep living."

Jules finished taking off his clothes and fell back onto the bed with a shake of his head. "The conductor was amazing too," he continued somewhat breathlessly. "*Everything* was so unbelievably amazing, Jaz!"

Jason lay on the bed next to Jules, naked and grinning from ear to ear. "I'm really glad you liked it. I was hoping you would." He sighed as he rolled over and planted a kiss on Jules's lips.

"Sometimes I wonder if all this is real." Jules settled into the crook of Jason's arm.

"I've got one other surprise for you," Jason said. He kissed Jules on the head and turned to look at him.

"Another surprise? I'm not sure I deserve that!"

"Oh, you deserve this one, believe me," Jason answered. "But it's up to you and David and Henri to make it pay off."

Jules sat up and frowned. "Pay off?"

Jason laughed. "Another American expression. It means it's up to you to make something happen with it."

"What do you mean?"

"I've arranged for an agent to be in the audience for the show tomorrow. He's a friend of a friend, and he does bookings for jazz artists in Europe."

"An agent?" Jules looked horrified.

"What are you worrying about? You guys are really good—you deserve to get some more work out of this gig. He's going to love your music. Trust me, Jules."

For a moment Jules said nothing. Then he looked down and turned away.

"Hey," Jason said, "what's the matter? Have I done something wrong?"

Jules's response came through tears. "No. You haven't done anything wrong, Jaz. It's just that…." His shoulders began to shake.

"Jules…." Jason sat up and put his arms around Jules from the back, holding him close. "I'm sorry. If you want me to tell him not to—"

"No." Jules's voice broke. "It's not that. Of course I want him to hear us."

"Then what? Have I done something to hurt you? God, Jules, that's the last thing I'd want to do."

Jules pulled away and bounded off the bed, heading for the window and peering out onto the street below. His body continued to shake as he sniffled.

"What is it, Jules?" Jason had seen Jules fight back tears, but he'd never seen him cry. Not like this. "Please. You know you can tell me anything. What's wrong?"

"It's nothing you've done," Jules answered. His voice was husky and nasal. "It's me."

Jason got off the bed and walked over to Jules, then rested his hands on his slumping shoulders.

Jules pulled away. "You don't *know* me. I don't deserve this—*any* of this. I don't deserve *you*. Maman was right. I'm nothing but merde."

"She's *wrong*, Jules," Jason said, startled at the intensity of Jules's words. "And you *know* it! And there's nothing you can tell me that will change that. *Nothing*."

"You don't know," Jules whispered between sobs. "You don't know what I've done." He spoke the words so softly Jason could barely understand him.

"I know that you're one of the most loving people I've ever met. You'd never do anything to hurt another person."

"You're wrong!" Jules shouted. His eyes were red and his face streaked in tears. "I've done terrible things! Things I can't forgive myself for!"

"I forgive you," Jason reassured him in a low voice. "Whatever you did, you had a good reason for it." Jules looked so desperate it frightened him. He had no idea what to do for Jules except to put his arms around him once again and reassure him physically.

"I don't deserve you. *You're* the good person, Jaz. You deserve better than me. I've been so selfish, telling myself that at least I could have you for a little while.... I kept telling myself that it was only for a few weeks, so it was okay. But now...."

"Stop this!" Jason shouted. "You can't let that bitch win. *She's* the one who's made you feel this way. *She's* the one who never gave you the love you deserved!"

"It's not all her." Jules's tears gave way to anger. "Yeah, she kicked me out when I told her that her fucking boyfriend forced me to give him a blow job and tried to screw me in the bathroom. But she didn't tell me to sell myself on the street! She didn't tell me to take their money after I sucked them off! If it hadn't been for Henri, I'd probably be dead by now. Maybe I *should* have died back then."

The words in French came so quickly that for a moment Jason struggled to understand what Jules had just confessed. Silence hung heavy as he realized that he *had* understood Jules's words. "Oh God, Jules," he moaned. He held Jules's slim body closer, not allowing himself to be pushed away this time. Jules didn't speak, but he didn't try to pull away either. "Jules," he murmured, kissing Jules's flushed cheek, "you were just sixteen years old. *They* abused *you.* You had nowhere to go. You were scared, hurt, and hungry."

Jules began to shake uncontrollably in Jason's arms. "I wanted to tell you," he sobbed. "I really wanted to tell you. But I was afraid. I thought you'd hate me, that you'd push me away."

"Never," Jason insisted, his own eyes now full of tears. "I told you. You're beautiful. I meant it." Jules's sobs subsided, and he clung to Jason. "It must have been terrible, keeping that from me—worrying that I'd hate you." Jules nodded. "But I don't hate you, Jules. You have to believe me. You don't know how much it means to me that you trusted me enough to tell me the truth."

"Really?"

Jason kissed Jules's head again. "Really, gosse. I mean it."

They stood there embracing for the longest time. Finally Jules stopped shaking. "Better?" Jason said. Jules nodded. "Then come to bed with me. It's going to be a long day tomorrow, and you need to get some sleep." He handed Jules a tissue.

"I'm sorry I didn't trust you before." Jules blew his nose.

"No more apologies, all right?"

"Yeah," Jules said with a forced laugh. "I won't apologize for being a sniveling kid."

"Nah. No need to. Come here." Jason reached out his hand, and Jules took it, allowing himself to be pulled back over to the bed.

"Okay," Jules responded. He still sounded tentative, but Jason did not hesitate to gather him into his arms and hold him against his chest.

"That's better." Jason kissed Jules's neck. Jules shivered and spooned closer. "You believe me when I tell you it doesn't matter to me, don't you?" Jules nodded. "Good. Then you also have to believe me when I tell you that I've never been happier. Got that?" Jules nodded again. "You really *are* beautiful, you know."

"Thanks, Jaz."

"No need to thank me," Jason answered. "Just believe me, that's all. D'accord?"

"D'accord," Jules whispered. "And Jaz?"

"Hmm?"

"Je t'aime. Vraiment."

Jason sighed and kissed Jules.

You know you love him, he thought as he clung to Jules. *Why can't you just say the words?*

CHAPTER 11

THE SOFT light of dawn filtered through the hastily drawn curtain of the hotel room. A sliver of brightness where the panels did not meet fell onto Jules's face as he lay nestled in Jason's arms. He was already long awake. For him, this day was like the greatest gift. Jason was still here, in spite of everything.

"Good morning." Jason's sleepy voice was the sexiest sound Jules could imagine hearing first thing in the morning. His cheek against Jason's chest, Jules smiled. *I've never been happier*, Jason had told him last night. Now, feeling those powerful arms wrapped around his naked body, Jules could honestly say the same.

"It *is* good," Jules answered with a grin. He shifted his body so that he rested his weight on his elbow and looked down at Jason. He brushed his lips against Jason's in silent gratitude for the acceptance he'd so feared would not come. Nothing—not even the opportunity to play his music in front of so many people—*nothing* meant as much to him as the knowledge that Jason knew the entire truth and still cared for him. Jason was still here, at his side.

If only you knew how much I love you, Jaz.

"Come here." Jason claimed Jules's lips. There was nothing tentative about his kiss, and Jules rolled on top of Jason and responded in kind. Jason's touch was far more languid, almost reverent this time. Jules felt the love that Jason could not yet express in words in that touch. He didn't mind, though, because when Jason traced his fingers up Jules's neck, their mouths still pressed together, Jules *felt* loved.

"Do you trust me?" Jason asked as his eyes met Jules's. Jules only nodded, too full of emotion to find words to express the depth of his trust. Everything—his mother's anger, the sting of her hand against his cheek, the abuse he'd suffered—all of it seemed a distant memory when Jason touched him.

"Good." Jason grinned. "Because I'm not sure I could handle it if you took off again without asking me to help."

"I know." Jules's breath caught as Jason nipped and sucked on the sensitive skin of his neck. *But sometimes I feel so afraid....*

"THE BASTARD'S name was Charles," Jules began as they lay on the bed later, limbs intertwined, sheets in a state of disarray. "I don't even think he was interested in my mother—I'm pretty sure it was me he wanted all along."

"You don't need to do this, Jules." Jason kissed Jules's neck tenderly.

"Yes," Jules replied with calm resolve, "I *do*. I've never told anyone before. I need to tell someone. I need to tell *you*."

"I'll be here when you've finished." Jason hoped he sounded encouraging, even if he wasn't sure he really wanted to hear this, but he knew it was something that Jules needed to purge and make peace with.

"I know," Jules answered. He caught the edge of Jason's lips and murmured, "Thanks." Gone was the haunted look of the night before; his expression reflected the grim determination in his voice.

"She took us with her to an open-air concert in the center of town," Jules continued after taking a deep breath. "Guy loved music too. Funny, how we both seemed to get that from her. Maman played clarinet when she was in grade school—at least that's what Mémé told me.

"She knew Charles and his friends—she saw them there and invited them to join us. He wanted Guy to sit on his lap." Jules clenched his jaw and shook his head. "Guy didn't mess around. He stuck out his tongue at the freak and came over to me. So Charles decided I looked more interesting. Tried to talk to me. Asked me if I liked girls. He must've guessed from my expression that I wasn't really into them. Next thing I knew, he'd come home with us. He'd had a lot to drink at the concert... said he had a headache and asked me if we had something for it. I went to the bathroom to look, and he followed me in there and locked the door behind him.

"I tried to ignore him. I pretended I didn't know what he was trying to do. I handed him the bottle, and he grabbed my hand. I saw his dick hanging out of his pants…. He told me to put it in my mouth—that if I didn't, he'd make sure my mother knew I was a môme. A fag. A queer. He said he'd tell her I'd come on to him…." Jules put his hand to his face and rubbed his eyes. "She'd have believed it. She'd kind of caught me with Henri a few times—just exploring, you know, nothing big. But still…."

"You okay?" Jason asked after the silence stretched on for more than a minute.

"Yeah. I am. Really." Jules got out of bed and crossed to the window, as he had the night before. He pulled the drapes shut, and the narrow strip of light was extinguished. There was still enough light in the room that Jason could see the outline of Jules's body.

"He told me he wouldn't tell her I was gay if I sucked him off. I knew she'd kick me out if he told her it was my idea, and I didn't want Guy there by himself. So I did it. Fucking asshole made me swallow it too. I thought I'd throw up. I thought that'd be the end of it. But later that night, he came into my room. Said I was a slut and that he'd decided what I really needed was a good ass-pounding…."

Jules rubbed his eyes, but Jason knew he wasn't crying, just catching his breath. "I just couldn't do it," he continued a moment or two later. "I hit him, told him to get the hell out of my room. He wasn't lying about going to my mother. He went to her and he told her what I'd done to him… said it was my idea. She believed him. Hell, she was drunk or high, or both—I'm not even sure. But she believed *him*. Who was I, anyhow? I was just a kid…. Just her son…."

"Shit, Jules," Jason groaned. He got off the bed and turned Jules around so he could hold him close. "No one should have to put up with that. Especially not a kid."

"Yeah," Jules whispered. "I know. I was so fucking scared for Guy—you know, living in that place. I tried to convince her to let me stay just so I could keep an eye on him. I didn't even care if that bastard came back. At least it'd be me he'd mess with and not my brother."

Jules sighed. "She told me to get the hell out and stay out. I knew the name of her caseworker. I told her if anything—*anything*—happened to Guy… if *anyone* even touched him like that, I'd go to social services. She knew they'd believe me over her."

"You kept your brother safe."

"Yeah," Jules said with a hint of fierce pride in his voice. "I kept him safe. From everyone but himself, I guess."

"He's going to be all right. Things are going to be better for him now."

"Thanks to you, Jaz."

"No," Jason told him. "Thanks to *you*, Jules. Because he knows *you* love him and *you* care what happens to him. I only helped a little. You'd have made it work, even if I hadn't been in the picture."

"In the picture?" Jules laughed.

"Another American expression," Jason answered with a roll of his eyes. "It means—"

Jules kissed Jason. "Just joking," he said, laughing harder this time. "I know what you meant."

"Gosse."

"Yeah, but a cute one, right?"

"Exactement," Jason replied, smacking Jules gently on his ass. Jules smirked and licked his lips. "And don't you get me started again," Jason added with a chuckle. "It's time for breakfast."

"I'm not hungry for food," Jules teased as he pushed Jason toward the bed.

Jason was just about to start nibbling at Jules's ear when the room phone rang.

"Shit," Jason growled as Jules rolled off of him. He grabbed the receiver from the nightstand.

"Jaz?" Jason recognized Henri's voice.

"Yeah, why are you calling so—"

"Jaz, David isn't doing well. He's… I'm not sure… but he's not himself. He's talking crazy. I think he has a fever. He was up all night and—"

Jason sat up and glanced at Jules, who watched him with a look of obvious concern. Jules frowned and mouthed, "What?" Jason shrugged.

"Wait a minute. Henri. Slow down. My brain's too fuzzy to follow you when you talk that fast.… What's the matter with David?"

"I think he's sick. He's throwing up and he's shaking." Henri didn't sound so good himself. Jason guessed he'd been up all night with David.

"Shit, Henri. The guy needs a doctor." Jason frowned and shook his head. "Look, I'll call Rosie and see if she can get someone over to the hotel to look at him. We'll come right down, okay?"

AN HOUR later, Jules, Jason, and Henri watched from the hallway as the doctor walked out of David's hotel room. Rosalie, who had been talking on her phone to David's girlfriend, Marie-Claire, in Paris, spoke briefly with the doctor as he left.

"He's going to be fine. I've asked a friend of mine to come and sit with him for a few hours until Marie-Claire's flight arrives," she said. "The doctor says it's the flu—it'll be at least a few days before he can go home."

"*Home*?" Henri shook his head. "But what about the show?"

Rosalie glanced at Jules, who nodded in silent assent. "The show must go on," she said, putting her arm around Jason's shoulder.

"No," Jason said firmly. "I know exactly what you're both thinking."

"Jaz…," Jules began. "You know this music almost as well as we do."

"Giving you pointers is one thing," Jason said. "*Playing* with you is something else entirely."

"Go get ready," Rosalie told Jules and Henri as she took Jason by the arm and began to lead him down the hallway. "We'll all meet downstairs in two hours, okay?"

"Rosie…," Jason warned.

"Come on, little brother," she said as she pulled him into the elevator. "We've got a little something we need to discuss."

JASON SCOWLED at his sister across a table in the hotel's small bar about an hour later. He'd eaten breakfast and spent the better part of the past ten minutes throwing it up in the men's room. "This is insane, Rosie."

"What's insane, Jason Matthew Greene"—she used his full name, and it immediately reminded him of when he was caught getting into trouble as a child—"is that you're willing to fuck this whole thing up for those boys just because you're scared."

"I'm not—"

"Don't lie to me, Jason. You're scared to death of playing. Look, your hands are practically shaking."

Jason glanced down at his hands and saw she was right. "I can't do this, Rosie," he mumbled, unwilling to look her in the eyes.

"You're *damn* well going to do this." He felt her looking daggers at him. "You'll do it because you're a grown man, and you'll do it for Jules."

He felt like a schmuck. *Jason Greene. Knows his way around a courtroom. The guy you go to when you want to settle the case, because you know he won't blink until he's gotten you the best deal. Jason Greene. Scared shitless.*

He closed his eyes and drew a deep breath, doing his best to slow down the heart that threatened to jump out of his chest. "Rosie…."

She brushed her soft hand against his cheek. "You'll do this, Jaz. You'll do it because you *need* to do it. And you'll do it for that boy you love. *Because* you love him."

Jason looked up at her with surprise.

"Yeah, of *course* I know you love him. What kind of an idiot do you think I am? I can see it in your eyes." She paused for a moment and frowned. "Have you told him yet?"

He should have known he couldn't get anything by his Rosie, and he sure as hell knew he couldn't lie to her. "No."

She sighed dramatically and narrowed her eyes at him. "You know, little bro, for such a smart guy, you're incredibly stupid sometimes. Just don't wait too long. You've got to give up control of your life sometime, or you're going to stay miserable." And with that, she stood up and kissed him on the top of his head.

"You coming?" she asked when he didn't follow.

"Yeah," he said, feeling as though he were ten years old again. "I'm coming."

JULES WATCHED Jason, seated on the bench, staring at the closed piano. Jason was pale, and in spite of the cool temperature of the hall, tiny beads of sweat were visible on his forehead. He turned to Henri. "You good?"

The drummer nodded, looking a little nervous himself and rooting around in his pocket for a cigarette. "I'll be back in five minutes." He popped the unfiltered Gitane into his mouth and headed for the side door.

"Okay." Jules waited for Henri to leave, then turned back to Jason. Jason was running his fingers over the cover on the keyboard as if he were playing. Jules smiled and sat down beside him until Jason's large hands stilled.

"Brahms?" Jules ventured with a coy smile.

Jason raised an eyebrow. "How did you know?"

"I play a little piano too. And that's not my music."

"No," Jason said. "I guess it's a bit of a habit with me, the Brahms."

"I've got a few pieces like that—you know, the ones I play when I'm upset… or afraid."

"I don't want to mess this chance up for you, Jules." Jason's warm baritone was a tad higher than usual.

"You won't," Jules answered with unbridled confidence. "You're really good."

Jason remained silent this time but lifted up the cover and rested his fingertips on the keys. Then, as if making up his mind about something, he stood abruptly and said, “I’ll be back in a few minutes.”

Jules realized he must have looked worried, because Jason said, “I’ll be back. I promise.”

Jules watched as Jason exited through the same door Henri had minutes before. Then, taking a deep breath, he set down his violin case and pulled out his instrument to warm up for the show.

JASON SAW Henri standing outside the hall, smoking. He nodded briefly, then turned the corner of the building to find a spot where he could be alone. A few hundred feet away, he saw people beginning to arrive at the front entrance.

Shit. He held his shaking hands up to his face and stared at them for a few moments. *If only I’d had some time to prepare....* But he knew it wouldn’t have mattered—he probably would have been more nervous if he’d had more time to think about things. He closed his eyes and forced himself to breathe.

“Monsieur Greene,” said the voice from the darkness at the back of the large concert hall. “Do you want to begin again?”

He was sixteen and seated at the enormous grand piano on the stage of the Conservatoire de Grenoble. It was his first juried exam—the moment he’d been silently dreading all year. The moment when all his hard work and all the hours of practicing would pay off and he would get the grade he deserved in his instrument. Except that he’d blown it—his mind had simply run away and left him sitting there in front of the three judges. He’d lost his place, forgotten where he was in the sonata. And so he stopped dead.

The silence—his silence—pained him. He was supposed to be playing! He knew this piece! And they were out there in the audience. Waiting for him to do something. Anything. And he was frozen there. He hoped the stage would swallow him up, devour him whole. Then there would be nothing left. What did it matter, anyhow? The way he’d just fallen flat on his face, he’d be perfectly happy never to see the inside of the conservatory again. The only thing that made the entire pathetic situation more tolerable was that there were only three of them—none of his friends and classmates were here to see him fall apart.

"I...," he croaked. "Y-yes. If you don't mind. I'd like to start again." But he knew from the moment he tried to recover from his lapse of memory that this attempt would be far, far worse. The walls of the great room were closing in on him. His fingers shook so badly he missed the simplest of chord progressions. Oh God, oh God, oh God….

"Monsieur Greene," the disembodied voice repeated as the silence descended once more. "Since you cannot complete your exam, you will repeat the same level next year."

He rubbed his hands over his face. More people arrived for the show, and the temperature outside had dropped a few degrees—or was that just him?

Get it together, Greene. He groaned inwardly. *You can do this. For Jules.* But then another memory stirred, and even though he tried to force it away, it hit him even harder than the first. He clenched his jaw and fought back a wave of dizziness.

He was seated at a Steinway grand in a large rehearsal hall at the Curtis Institute. Thirty feet away, three judges waited at a long table in the back of the room—faculty members all of them, including Martina Shiranova, the piano teacher he'd heard so much about and with whom he hoped to study. She was an imposing presence—tall, with broad shoulders and powerful arms. A pianist's pianist.

"What will you play, Mr. Greene?" she asked in thickly accented English.

"Liszt's Hungarian Rhapsody No. 2." Jason fought a wave of dizzying panic.

"Very well," Madame Shiranova said, nodding.

He stared at the keys, watching his hands shake, knowing how much was riding on this audition and how much he wanted this. Murmuring an improvised prayer, he began to move his hands over the keys—

"Please stop there, Mr. Greene."

Jason stopped playing. Oh God, I'm going to be sick.

"Mr. Greene?"

"Yes?" His voice cracked.

"Did you bring something else for us today?"

"I... I...," he stammered.

"Something you feel comfortable playing?"

Good Lord, he'd screwed it up. He knew it! In spite of all the hours he'd spent practicing until his fingers hurt, he'd let it get away from him. He knew it. It was worse than in high school—far worse than the ill-fated jury exam. Because this time, it wasn't just repeating a year of lessons. This time, it was his dream. *And he'd fucked it up big-time.*

"I have some Brahms I could play," he offered tentatively.

"That would be lovely," Madame Shiranova told him. She didn't smile, but Jason thought he caught a hint of something like humor in that owl-like face of hers.

He played—tentatively at first, but finally opening up and forgetting where he was and just letting the music lead his fingers. And when he was finished, he stared at the keys as his heart beat hard against his ribs once more.

"Thank you, Mr. Greene," Madame Shiranova said. "That's what I thought."

"Ma'am?" he nearly squeaked.

"I thought you had it in your soul." His eyes met hers. "The love of the music. The power there."

"Thank you."

"You have talent, Mr. Greene," she continued. A hint of a smile played on her lips as she spoke. "But you are afraid to share it with us. Come back again when you have let go of your fear—when you are willing to open your soul and play what is inside. Then, Mr. Greene, I will be happy to have you as my student."

He rubbed the bridge of his nose with a trembling hand as he willed the memory away. It had always been like that with his playing. In private or with people he felt comfortable with, he played well. In public, he was a disaster waiting to happen: unable to concentrate and racked with nerves. It was why he finally decided to go to law school. When he was in the courtroom, he didn't *have* to be himself; he could be Jason the lawyer, strong and unflappable. It was a mask he wore, one he could put on as easily as his suit jacket. There was nothing remotely emotional about his performance when he wore that suit, and as a lawyer, nothing more was required of him. But music….

Music was something more. It was deeply personal to him, an integral part of his heart. And he'd long since realized that expressing his music openly left him feeling vulnerable and weak. Out of control.

I have to do this for him. He clenched his teeth and turned back toward the entrance.

THE SHOW went off without a hitch. Rosalie and Stefano had planned it well, and the crowd seemed to enjoy both the collection and the music. For his part, Jason played passably well—but he didn't enjoy it. It was all he could do to stop his hands from shaking on the keyboard for the first few pieces. By the end, at least he'd relaxed enough that he wasn't as worried his playing would detract from Jules's music.

Afterward, the musicians greeted Jean-Claude Bernolin, the agent Jason's friend had invited to hear the group. In spite of his discomfort during the performance, Jason took charge, introducing Henri and Jules and explaining his last-minute substitution.

"Jim didn't tell me you doubled as a musician," Jean-Claude told him. "I'm impressed, Jason."

"Don't be," Jason replied with a self-deprecating laugh. "I'm just happy that you were able to get a feel for Jules's music."

"You're quite gifted, you know," Jean-Claude said to Jules with a warm smile. "Your music is modern, but it has a down-to-earth sensibility to it."

"Thank you." Jules blushed charmingly at the compliment.

"So do you think you might be able to do something for my boys?" Jason pressed, happy to be back in his element as a negotiator for a change rather than behind the piano.

"Most definitely," said Jean-Claude. "I handle large bookings, mostly—you know, Montreux and the other jazz festivals, that sort of thing. But I work with several other agents who handle smaller venues in the larger cities—Paris, Lyon, Marseille, and some in Switzerland and Belgium. Should I have them contact you, Jason?"

Jason looked at Jules and Henri, who both nodded enthusiastically. "Sure." Jason pulled a business card out of his suit jacket. "My cell number is at the bottom. I'll be in Europe for a few more weeks."

"Perfect," said Jean-Claude. He shook hands with Jason, Henri, and Jules. "Monsieur Bardon," he added as he turned to leave, "I look forward to hearing more from you in the future. I've no doubt you'll do well for yourself."

"Merci beaucoup," Jules answered, clearly doing his best to keep from shouting his excitement. "It's been a pleasure to meet you."

Rosalie, who'd been seeing the rest of the guests out of the hall, now ran over to the three men and threw her arms around Jules. "I can't believe how lucky I was to find you!" she cooed as she planted a kiss on Jules's cheek. She glanced at her brother with a knowing look.

Jason managed a slight smile and said, "It looks like Blue Notes will be playing again soon."

"That was the agent?" Rosalie asked as she released Jules from her embrace.

"He's going to put us in touch with some of his colleagues in the business," Jules answered.

"That's terrific!" Rosalie bit her cheek and looked at Jason again as if to say, *See, I* told *you you'd be fine.*

"Don't…," Jason warned.

"I'm not saying anything, Jaz. I'm just happy for the boys, that's all. And speaking of the boys," she added, changing the subject, "has anyone heard from David?"

"Marie-Claire texted me a few minutes ago," Henri told her. "She says David's feeling a little better. She even got him to eat some soup."

"Good. Then you three will join me and Stefano for a little snack at our apartment tonight?"

"We'd love to." Jules tugged on the collar of his shirt to loosen his tie.

"Jeans are fine," Rosalie said with a smirk. "Why don't you go back to the hotel and rest for a few hours. We'll be a little longer here, anyhow. Stefano's still speaking with a few of the buyers—he's much better at the business end of things than I am."

"Thanks, Rosie," Jason said as Jules and Henri went to pack up.

"No problem, Jaz." She took his hand in hers and squeezed it. "I knew you'd come through."

"Yeah."

"You didn't enjoy it, though, did you?"

"You know me too well, Rosie," Jason answered.

"I do, don't I?" came the glib response. "But I wish I were wrong. Really. I know how much you love to play. I loved hearing you play for me. You always seemed so happy when you used to play for me."

"I *was* happy playing for you. But this—" He hesitated and drew a long breath. "—playing in public, it's just different somehow. I'm not sure why. I guess it's always been that way for me."

Jules joined them again, his violin case now slung over his shoulder, and Jason found himself immensely relieved that he didn't have to continue the discussion. "Ready?" he asked Jules.

Jules nodded. "See you later, Rosie." He kissed her on both cheeks, and she beamed.

"You bet." She winked at Jason.

"I'm proud of you," Jules said as they walked out of the building, his arm around Jason's waist and under his jacket. "I know that was difficult for you. Anything I can do to thank you?" Jules's eyes glittered with the invitation.

"Maybe." Jason's empty stomach growled audibly. "But first I need to eat something, or I'm going to collapse. Food, maybe a stiff drink, and then dessert. Okay?"

"Bien sûr." Jules giggled and slid his lean fingers down the waistband of Jason's trousers.

"You're incorrigible, you know."

Jules winked and squeezed Jason's ass underneath his boxers. "Ouais. Je le sais."

CHAPTER 12

THE "LITTLE snack" Rosalie had invited them to turned out to be a full-blown launch party, and the spacious loft apartment was packed with friends and admirers eager to congratulate Rosalie and Stefano on the success of their new line. Rosalie had decorated the apartment in shimmering jewel tones with lavish silk saris hung from hooks in the ceiling. The food was exotic—an eclectic blend of Thai, Japanese, Filipino, Indian, and North African. The servers, male and female alike, wore eye makeup in surreal colors and sported Rosalie's own creations.

Jules and Jason spent a good hour greeting guests who wanted to compliment them on the performance. Each time the conversation veered toward Jason, he inevitably steered it back to Jules, playing down his own part in the show. And when he spotted an old friend by one of the large windows, he saw an opportunity to escape. He quickly took Jules's hand in his and led him over to the two men standing there.

David Somers's face lit up when he saw Jason. "It's been far too long, Jaz," he said as they embraced.

"Good to see you, old man."

"Six months older than you, if I recall?" David countered with a barely repressed grin. "Besides, I prefer to think of myself as 'distinguished.'"

Jason turned to Jules. "Jules, I'd like you to meet Maestro David Somers. David, this is Jules Bardon."

Jules glanced briefly at Jason, then shook David's hand. "M-Maestro," he stammered, "i-it's an honor to meet you."

"Please," David Somers replied, clearly used to such a reaction, "call me David."

"David and I are old friends from college. I heard he was conducting at La Scala while we were here, so I asked him if he could spare a few tickets."

"The *Tosca* was incredible," Jules gushed. "Amazing, really."

"I could say the same of *your* music," David countered gracefully. "Quite beautiful. Innovative, as well." Jason knew David wouldn't have offered the compliment it if he hadn't meant it. Not that he'd doubted David would enjoy hearing Jules play. "Your pianist is quite good as well," David added after a pause.

Jason swallowed hard, uncomfortable with the praise. "Thank you," he managed quickly.

"Y-you came to the show?" Jules was wide-eyed now, his face flushed with what Jason guessed was a mixture of embarrassment and pleasure.

"Jason has a good ear. When he suggested I come, I knew I wouldn't be disappointed." David smiled and turned to his companion, a tall man with auburn hair, and added, "This is Alex Bishop, my partner. Alex, Jules Bardon and Jason Greene."

"Nice to meet you both," Alex replied warmly, taking Jason's hand.

"So *you're* the reason David looks so happy," Jason said with a nod in David's direction. "It's a pleasure to finally meet you."

Jules's eyes widened as he shook Alex's hand. "Alex *Bishop*?" The thrill of recognition was plain on his face.

Alex laughed and leaned a tattooed arm on the windowsill. "That's me."

Jules continued to stare at Alex in openmouthed shock.

"You know his music?" Jason asked Jules, catching David's eye and winking.

"You're joking, right?" Jules asked.

Jason laughed. "Yeah, actually, I am." Of course Jules—and just about everyone else—had heard of Alex Bishop. He was one of the hottest commodities on the classical music scene. Not to mention he'd just won a Grammy for his crossover jazz/rock album, *The Lake*.

"Y-you were there today too?" Jules choked out.

"Yeah," Alex answered with a grin. "And David's right—you *are* very talented. Maybe we can play together some time."

Jules paled. "I… I… yes, I'd love that!" he managed at last.

Jason squeezed Jules's shoulder. "I'd love to hear that."

"Jaz!" Rosalie shouted, her voice carrying over the din of the crowd. "Come over here so I can introduce you to my friend Antonio!"

"I'll leave you two to talk shop," Jason offered. "David, thanks again for the tickets. Let's catch up when you're in Philly in June. There's a new Vietnamese place I think you'd enjoy."

David nodded and shook his hand once more.

"Nice to meet you, Alex."

"You too," Alex replied.

Jason grinned at Jules and, donning his best "lawyer" demeanor as if it were armor, proceeded to snake his way in and out of groups of conversing people toward his sister. He clutched a glass of red wine in his left hand—his third since they had arrived—and reached out with his right to shake the hand of the man standing beside Rosalie. "Nice to meet you," he said in Italian.

"My pleasure," Antonio replied in English. "Rosalie's told me all about you." He smiled, his perfectly straight, blindingly white teeth complementing his blond hair and the near-turquoise of his eyes. Jason swallowed hard as he realized that he was studying Antonio a bit like he might have studied a woman just months before. The man was gorgeous. This fact did little to assist Jason in maintaining his fragile composure; even with the wine, his hands still trembled slightly, an aftereffect of the afternoon performance.

"She told you everything and you're still here talking to me?" laughed Jason. Another guest grabbed Rosalie's arm, and he found himself alone with Antonio.

Antonio laughed. "Don't worry, it's all been good." He raised his glass to his lips and sipped his wine. "Besides, I like lawyers."

"*That's* where I've heard your name." Jason's alcohol-dulled mind finally put the pieces together. "You're Rosie's attorney, aren't you?"

"Guilty." Antonio grinned. "We have a friend in common, you and I—John McCarthy? I handle some work for him over here."

"Right. John mentioned it last time I was in DC." One of the other guests bumped into Jason and splashed his wine onto his shirt. Jason looked down at the burgundy stain on the crisp white fabric. He shook his head and sighed.

"Kitchen?" Antonio offered sympathetically.

"Good idea," replied Jason, "or Rosie'll try to send me home with one of her own creations."

"Not your style?"

"Actually," Jason admitted as they walked into the kitchen, "I love her stuff. But she loves to tease me about my boring wardrobe."

Antonio smiled, and Jason saw him take full (and appreciative) measure of him. He found himself both flattered and a little bit uncomfortable at the realization.

Once inside the kitchen, Antonio handed Jason a damp paper towel. The brief touch of his hand on Jason's was surprisingly sensual, and Jason forced himself to concentrate on his shirt. If Antonio noticed Jason's reaction, he didn't let it show. Instead he leaned back against one of the counters and took another drink.

"So where did you learn to play the piano like that?" Antonio asked. "Rosie said you were talented, but I didn't realize just *how* talented."

Heat rose in Jason's cheeks. Doing his best to hide his embarrassment, he answered, "I played some when I was a kid. I'm really not all that good."

At this, Antonio just smiled and changed the subject, perhaps sensing Jason's uneasiness. They chatted for a few more minutes, briefly touching on topics such as their work, the weather, and Jason's stay in Paris. It didn't take long for Jason to realize that Antonio was flirting with him.

Maybe it was the three glasses of wine, or maybe it was the fact that he had survived the performance without completely losing his mind—either way, Jason found himself enjoying Antonio's attention. It wasn't until nearly an hour later, when Stefano came into the kitchen to get some more white wine from the fridge, that Jason realized just how long he'd been enjoying Antonio's company. He felt a stab of guilt about having abandoned Jules in the other room.

"Listen, I'd better get back out there or I'll never hear the end of it," he said with a sheepish grin. "It's been great getting to know you."

"I've enjoyed our conversation." Antonio offered another charming smile. Then he added, "And Jason—" He paused for a moment, searching Jason's eyes. "—maybe you and I could get together for coffee before you fly back to France." From the expression on the man's face, Jason had no doubt that the offer was for more than just coffee between friends.

Jason returned the smile and sighed. In truth, if Jules were not in the picture, Jaz knew that he would have taken Antonio up on his offer without a second thought. "I'm here with my boyfriend," he heard himself say. Another surprise, that he'd come to think of Jules that way.

Antonio looked disappointed but pulled a card out of his pocket and handed it to Jason, saying, "If things don't work out, call me." He pressed the paper into Jason's hand and let his fingers linger a bit longer than necessary. Then he was gone, and Jason was left standing in the kitchen, feeling a bit overwhelmed. He tucked his damp shirt in, slipped Antonio's card in the back pocket of his jeans, and walked out of the room, intent on finding Jules.

JULES HAD noticed the stunning blond almost right away. He'd also noticed the way the man looked at Jason, and he didn't like it one iota. He wanted to walk over to the two men and stake his claim to Jason. Instead, he'd continued to converse with Alex and David for a half hour or so. After they had left—and he'd exchanged contact information with Alex—he made his way over to the drink table and poured himself a glass of cognac, deciding that he needed something stronger than the wine he'd been drinking. The warmth of the alcohol released some of the mounting tension in his shoulders.

"Jules," Rosalie said as she wrapped an arm around his waist and kissed him on the cheek, "Jaz told me the trio already has an offer of a gig in Paris."

Happy to get his mind off of Jason for a few minutes, Jules did his best to focus his full attention on Rosalie. "Jean-Claude called right after we left the hall—there was a cancellation. We're playing at the Sans Silence a week from Friday."

They spoke at length about the gig, about whether David would be well enough to play at it (Jules guessed that he would be), and about whether Rosalie could get back to Paris to hear them (she said she would fly in if she wasn't too busy). All the while he kept glancing around the room. Jason was nowhere to be seen.

Finally, unable to contain himself any longer, Jules managed to escape Rosalie's grasp to find Jason. That was when he saw the blond coquin—the rogue, as he had not-so-affectionately dubbed the man—walking out of the kitchen, followed a few moments later by Jason. Jules frowned, watching the well-dressed man wave casually to Rosalie, then grab a jacket from a hook by the door and head out of the apartment. He was smiling, and Jules fought back the urge to rush after him and find out exactly what he and Jason had been doing in the kitchen for so long and why he looked so happy about it.

"Miss me?" Jules nearly jumped out of his skin when he heard the familiar voice in his ear. He turned around to see Jason standing beside him, grinning.

"Should I have?" Jules countered. His voice was a bit higher, a bit edgier than he'd meant it to sound, his jealousy not quite held in check. He was tempted to ask Jason directly what he'd been up to in the kitchen, but he bit his tongue. What Jason did wasn't his business.

Jason raised an eyebrow. He looked a little taken aback by Jules's reaction, but he didn't push the issue. "Ready to head back to the hotel?" he asked.

"Ouais." Jules followed Jason over to Rosalie to say their good-byes. She looked exhausted but completely happy.

"You call me before you decide to head back Stateside," she admonished her brother, hugging both men with genuine warmth. "And *you*," she said, looking at Jules this time like a proud mama hen, "you e-mail me the schedule of Blue Notes' gigs. I want to come hear you play, okay? Promise?"

Jules smiled in spite of himself. "Promise," he told her, although he wondered whether seeing her after Jason had returned home would be a good idea, since he was already so possessive of Jason. The reminder that Jason would be leaving in less than two weeks was difficult enough for him to think about, and he knew seeing Rosalie would just make it worse.

JULES SPOKE very little in the cab on the way back to the hotel. Jason didn't mind; he was overwhelmed by thoughts of his halfhearted promise to Jules that he would go to Grenoble and confront his ghosts. Already he was trying to figure out a way to back out of the trip. They didn't make love that night, although Jason wrapped his arms around Jules under the sheets and pulled him against his chest. Several minutes later, Jason felt the subtle change in Jules's breaths as he succumbed to his exhaustion.

At 2:00 a.m., Jason glanced at the clock next to the bed. Jules slept beside him, his face peaceful, almost childlike. Jason had watched Jules sleep for almost an hour, but he was still wound tight, despite the large amount of alcohol he'd consumed at Rosalie's after-party. Deciding that it was better to get out of bed than risk waking Jules, he slipped out from under the sheets, dressed in a hurry, and shoved his wallet into his back pocket. Glancing back to reassure himself that he hadn't awakened Jules, he left the hotel room, grabbing his shoes as he went.

The hotel bar was, as Jason suspected, still open. There were several couples sitting pressed against each other in some of the booths, as well as a few businessmen at the bar. He smiled, realizing how rapidly he'd eschewed his routine of late nights spent in the office, poring over documents. Jules wasn't the only thing he was going to miss when he got home.

"What can I get you?" the bartender asked him in English. Jason recognized him as having been at the bar earlier in the day, when he and Rosalie had spoken before the show.

"Scotch and soda," Jason said.

The bartender smiled. For the second time that day, Jason became aware of another man's eyes assessing him with interest. It was a bit unnerving for a man who had, until just months before, considered himself straight. But Jason realized he didn't mind. In fact, he was beginning to enjoy the attention. But it did take a bit of getting used to.

He watched the bartender pour his drink. He thought briefly of Jules asleep in their hotel room and nearly grinned—whatever interest other men might take in him, his attentions were firmly focused on

Jules. It was *Jules's* body that Jason dreamed about: the feel of his soft skin under his fingers, the taste of his mouth, his warm brown eyes, the lean muscle of his thighs wrapped around Jason's waist, the childlike wonder Jules took in the world around him, and his loving heart. Jason shifted in his seat to accommodate his body's physical response, thinking that he'd been a fool not to wake Jules up and have his way with him.

It had taken him by surprise at first, the almost uncontrollable lust that accompanied thoughts of Jules. He couldn't stop wondering how he'd ever get used to being alone again. The idea of returning to the States in a few weeks weighed heavily on his mind.

You are so *going to have to figure this out. You owe it to him.*

It was all too much—the performance, the way he felt about Jules, the realization that his leave of absence would be over in less than two weeks. For the first time in a very long time, Jason felt as though the control he thought he'd had over his life was an ephemeral thing. That, or a lie he'd told himself often enough that he'd come to believe.

"Here you are, sir." The bartender sat the glass of amber liquid on the bar in front of him. This time, Jason took a moment to look back. The man was handsome, classically Italian, with wavy dark hair, olive skin, and green eyes.

Shit. You really are a piece of work, Greene.

He brought the cool glass to his lips. The alcohol burned his throat, warming it. It was going to be a long night.

JULES AWOKE, reached for Jason, and realized he was alone in the bed. He'd seen Jason's anxious anticipation of the show and the pale face that still echoed with fear, even after they had finished playing. He'd seen the way Jason had been drinking at Rosalie's impromptu celebration, the slight tremor in his hands. He'd seen it all, and he'd somehow convinced himself that Jason would be fine—that the strong, controlled presence he'd come to depend upon would reassert itself and all would be right with the world. But really, he knew better.

He'd acted like a child by allowing his jealousy to get the best of him. Jason was obviously upset, anxious. *He needs me.* It was almost a relief, knowing that *he* might be able to do something to help Jason for a change.

Time to act your age. Time to show him what you mean when you say that you love him.

JASON LOST count of how many drinks he'd downed after the fourth, but at least now the restlessness that had kept him from sleeping was replaced by a warm, comfortable numbness. He closed his eyes and listened to the music being piped into the bar, a soundtrack of cheesy Italian hits from the fifties. He was just drunk enough that the sappy music made him chuckle.

"Something funny?" The bartender gazed at him in amusement.

"No," Jason replied. "But I'm thinking another scotch might be nice."

The bartender leaned over the counter. "My shift's over at four. My friend owns a club not far from here. Good music too. Why don't you join me?"

Jason had no intention of taking the man up on his offer, but he didn't want to be rude. "That's really nice of you—" he began.

"But his boyfriend might not think it's such a good idea," a voice from behind him finished. That word again, this time from Jules's lips.

Boyfriend.

Jason liked the sound of that word. He turned to see an irritated-looking Jules frowning back at him as he leaned against the bar. He smiled up at Jules. "How did you find me?" He was happy to see Jules, although Jules did not look as pleased.

"The way you were drinking tonight at Rosie's," Jules said, "it was a pretty good guess. Although I worried you might be on your way back to the United States."

"Nope. Just getting intimately acquainted with a bottle of Scotch whiskey." Jason laughed as he leaned his cheek against Jules's shoulder. "Sorry if I woke you."

"You didn't. When I realized you weren't lying next to me, I got worried about you."

"No worries." Jason slurred his words, and his cheeks warmed.

"Let's get a table." Jules held out his hand to steady Jason. "Talk a little."

Jason wobbled off the barstool and waved to the bartender. They settled into a small booth, and Jules ordered a beer when the bartender delivered another scotch for Jason. Jason was a little embarrassed. For a moment, at least, until that thought fled his mind with the onslaught of alcohol, like the rest of his thoughts had.

"Tu es ivre." Jules shook his head.

"The proper term is 'shit-faced.'" Jason laughed, reverting to English.

"Never heard that one," Jules replied with a frown.

"I'm happy to have enlightened you, then." French again, but the words came out with an American twang. "You look pissed." Jules also looked edible, but Jason tried to put that thought out of his mind for the time being.

"Surprised would be a better word."

Jason frowned. "Why?" His brain was simply too tired and too fuzzy to manage anything more.

"You were flirting." Jules pursed his lips and furrowed his brow.

Jason remembered something from earlier in the evening, at Rosalie's party—Jules had the same look on his face then as now. "Flirting?" Through the dull haze of the alcohol, Jules's words began to sink in. "Are you… jealous?" It seemed preposterous that Jules would be jealous. How could he not know how Jason felt?

"Of course not. You have every right to do whatever you like. You don't owe me anything."

Jason rubbed the bridge of his nose, trying to focus his wandering thoughts.

Jules continued, "I'm sure Rosie's friend… I'm sure he's a nice guy…."

"Shit, Jules." Jason shook his head slowly to keep the room from spinning too fast. "It wasn't like that. I was just talking to him, just…."

He stopped and looked into Jules's eyes. He saw the pain there, glittering. "Jules." He reached across the table and took Jules's hand in his own. "I'm so sorry. I had no idea."

Jules looked mortified. "You don't owe me anything," he repeated.

"The *hell* I don't," Jason said, his voice louder than he'd intended. He squeezed Jules's hand. "Dammit. I didn't mean for it to be like this. Shit, Jules, I'm not interested in Antonio. How can I be when I'm in love with *you*?" The words were out of his mouth before he'd even realized he'd said them.

Jules's eyes widened. "You…," he whispered, "you're drunk."

"Yeah, we established that a few minutes ago," Jason chortled. Then, realizing why Jules might be concerned, he added, "But not so drunk that I don't know what I just said."

"You love…. Then you're not down here because of me?"

"What? You thought I was trying to get away from *you*?" Jules's expression told Jason that was exactly what Jules had thought. "Jules—shit—I'm so sorry. I should have told you weeks ago how I felt about you. It's just that… I've never been very good at expressing my feelings. And after Diane, I don't know… I just… I was just *afraid*, I guess."

You're babbling, Greene. Any more verbal diarrhea and he'd propose. He always ran on at the mouth when he'd had too much to drink. He scooted around the booth so he was sitting right next to Jules.

"I know all of this—us, being with a man for the first time and everything—it was just so fast. I didn't want you to feel—"

Jason cut Jules's word short with a kiss. "I love you, gosse," he said as their lips parted.

"So if you're not here because of me," Jules said, his tone tentative, "then why?"

Jason looked away.

"Jaz, please. Tell me what's wrong."

Jason stared down at his half-empty scotch, absentmindedly swirling it about. "You were incredible today, Jules."

"Really, I wasn't—"

"You were *amazing*, Jules. You played better than I've ever heard you play before. It was like being there in front of all those people… it was like you came alive." Jason paused and wished he hadn't had quite so much to drink. Maybe he'd make more sense if he weren't so trashed. Maybe he could make Jules understand what he'd heard in his playing. "You really *were* incredible."

"You're too kind," Jules murmured, obviously embarrassed at Jason's praise.

"No," Jason said. "I'm really not. Anyone who was there felt it. There was such joy in your face—in your music."

"But even if that's true, I don't understand."

The bartender brought Jules his beer. "Another one?" he asked Jason. Jason shook his head, and the man disappeared again behind the bar.

"Jaz," Jules tried again, "tell me why you stopped playing. The truth, I mean. What happened?"

"Why would you think something happened?" He couldn't look into Jules's eyes, couldn't quite bring himself to come clean.

"It's just a guess. I've never seen you so frightened before. You… you're usually so sure of yourself. But at the show today… Jaz, you were shaking. You *still* are."

Jason looked down at his hands and scowled. As usual, Jules had seen what he himself had tried to ignore.

"Please, Jaz. You've done so much for me. Let me help *you* now."

Jason wrapped his hands around his almost empty glass.

Jules leaned over and, in an uncharacteristic move, pulled Jason's face toward him so that their eyes met at last, forcing the contact Jason had avoided. "Please," Jules repeated as his lips brushed Jason's.

Jason nodded. It took him some time to form the words, and even then, they were just barely audible. "I'm afraid," he whispered, still unwilling to face Jules. The bar suddenly felt stuffy, the air thick.

"Afraid of what?"

"Of performing. Afraid I'm not good enough. Afraid I'll fall flat on my face. Afraid I'll embarrass myself, that I'll embarrass other people. Afraid I'll let you down… that I'll let *me* down." He paused again, emptying his glass this time but still not looking up. His hands were shaking, and he scowled at the realization that his fear could affect him even when he wasn't playing. "I love the music. I love playing it. Shit, I *wanted* to play with you, Jules. But it was torture today…."

Jules wrapped his arms around Jason. "But you were great."

"Was I? Because I don't even remember it. I didn't enjoy it. I just thought I was going to die. Either that or get sick all over the piano."

Jules said nothing, he just held Jason. Jason tried to calm his breathing and relax a bit. They remained in the embrace for a few minutes, and when Jules spoke again, Jason heard nothing but determination in his voice. "When do we leave?"

"For Paris?" Jason asked stupidly.

"No. Not Paris. When do we leave for Grenoble?"

"I never said I'd—"

"Yes, you did," Jules insisted. "You can't go on like this, Jaz. You *need* to go there and make your peace with it. Even if you never play again, you need to do this."

"I can always do it later."

"You go home in less than two weeks," Jules said, clearly unwilling to back down. "It's time, Jason."

Jason's shoulders fell. He knew Jules was right, and he was too tired to argue. "Okay." He knew when he'd lost.

"We'll go?" Jules's face was eager.

"We?"

"I told you, Jaz," Jules replied, "I've got your back. We do this together." He grinned and added, "You can hold my hand if you want."

Jason looked up at Jules and narrowed his eyes. "I was thinking about something a little more interesting than hand-holding." It was bluster, but he didn't care; he was tired of being weak. At least with his words, he could assert some semblance of control. "Unless, that is, you would prefer just holding hands."

Jules took a pull on his beer and licked his lips. "Nah," he answered with a wicked grin. "I like your idea better."

IT WAS 5:00 a.m. Jules lay naked, spooned in Jason's arms, satisfied. The sex hadn't lasted long, but he'd needed it and so had Jason. And now, as the first light of morning peered in through the drapes, Jules listened to Jason's soft snoring and felt truly safe.

He loves me. It was enough—*more* than enough for now. More than he'd ever had, really. And at that moment, even the thought of Jason leaving didn't bother him. *He loves me. He said he loves me.*

CHAPTER 13

BY THE time they made it back to Paris the next morning, Jason's head was pounding like something out of a heavy-metal nightmare. He'd spent the better part of the trip puking his guts out in the airport and airplane bathrooms. He felt weak and his body ached. As he walked across the courtyard to the apartment, he stopped and leaned on one of the wooden folding chairs as his head spun for the umpteenth time. His brow was covered in sweat, and he wondered vaguely if he was going to make it to the bathroom before vomiting again. He'd only managed to make it from the airport in the cab with an enormous effort of concentration.

"Jaz," Jules asked with concern, "are you all right?"

"It's just a hangover," Jason muttered as he fumbled for his key.

"I've got it." Jules pulled his own key from his jeans pocket and put his free arm around Jason's waist. Leaving their suitcases outside, he helped Jason down the hallway to the apartment. "You need to get into bed."

Jason scowled but leaned on Jules until they reached the bedroom, where he promptly collapsed on the mattress. Jules leaned over and started to unbutton Jason's shirt. "Shit," he said as he touched Jason's bare skin, "you're burning up."

"I'm fine," Jason lied as Jules pulled his pants off and managed to put the blankets over him.

"Like hell you are. This isn't a hangover, Jaz. You're sick."

"Oh shit." Jason struggled to sit up. "I'm gonna…." But Jules had already grabbed the wastebasket from the corner and held it out to him. "Geez," Jason gasped a few minutes later, "I'm sorry."

"Don't worry," Jules replied with an endearing smile, "I'm used to it. I held a few trash cans for my mother over the years. But this isn't a hangover. You've got a fever."

"Remind me to thank David." Jason tried to laugh. The irony that he would get the flu in Paris, when he hadn't been sick a day since he was a kid, wasn't lost on him.

"Let me get you some water and something to bring down your fever," Jules told him. "Should I call a doctor?"

Jason shook his head. "Nah. The doctor'd just tell me to drink lots of liquids and stay in bed."

Jules narrowed his eyes, but he didn't argue. "I'll get the suitcases," he said after he'd brought Jason some water and a cold compress. "Then I'll make you some soup."

Jason closed his eyes, thinking wistfully of his grandmother's matzoh ball soup.

WHEN JASON awoke, the sun was beginning to set. The cloth on his forehead was cool, and he guessed Jules had been in recently to replace it. He smiled, too weak to do anything but pull the covers up over his shoulders. The sound of Jules playing his violin drifted in through the bedroom door. Jason breathed in and closed his eyes, allowing his mind to drift along with the music.

Jules had chosen the music with care. His playing, ever soulful, was soothing and sweet—Bach, Mozart, and a few of his own compositions. With each note, Jason was reminded of the first time Jules had played for him in the apartment and of the deep and immediate connection he'd felt to Jules.

He had no idea how long he'd listened to Jules's playing, but at some point he must have fallen asleep, because he awoke to a darkened room and Jules sitting on the side of the bed, stroking his hair.

"Bonsoir," Jules said. His brown eyes reflected a mixture of love, concern, and something else. Happiness?

"Hey."

"I made soup for you," Jules said, nodding at the bedside table where he'd set a small tray with a bowl of steaming vegetable soup and a few pieces of baguette.

For the first time that day, Jason's stomach didn't turn over. It actually rumbled a little. "It smells great," he said. "Did you make it yourself?"

Jules beamed.

"Thanks." Jason tried to push himself up to a sitting position. It was not a simple task; he was far more exhausted than he'd realized.

"Let me help," Jules offered, his hand on Jason's shoulder, steadying him.

"Damn." Jason tried to catch his breath as the pain in his limbs reasserted itself with a vengeance.

"Hurts?"

Jason nodded, transported back to when he was a kid and his mother would dote on him when he was home sick from school. It was an odd feeling, being dependent on someone else again after so many years. Even when he'd broken his wrist on a ski trip with Diane two years ago, he hadn't asked her for any help. He guessed that she might have given it, although he doubted she would have done it as graciously or with as much tenderness as Jules.

"Here." Jules handed Jason a few pills and put his hand on his forehead. "That should help the pain. You don't feel hot anymore, though."

"Thanks." He took the medicine and picked up the glass of water by the bed. Setting the glass back down, he looked at Jules and smiled. "The music was beautiful."

"Did you like it?" Jules asked after he'd settled the tray of soup on Jason's lap.

"I love to hear you play." He noted Jules's slight blush as he dipped his spoon into the soup; the smell was heavenly. But when he lifted the spoon to his lips, his hand shook, spilling some of the liquid onto the tray. "Damn."

"Let me." Jules moved closer and picked up the spoon.

Jules ignored Jason's weak protests and grinned. He waited until Jason had finished scowling and opened his lips, then put the spoon into Jason's mouth.

When he thought about it, Jason wasn't sure if he loved or hated being fed by Jules. Either way, it was disconcerting. "Nobody's fed me since I was a baby," he grumbled.

Jules laughed. "I'd never have guessed." Then, meeting Jason's eyes, he added, "You really don't like to rely on anyone, do you?"

"I do fine by myself."

"Probably" was Jules's response. "But you're enjoying this a little, aren't you?"

Before Jason could reply, Jules had brought another spoonful of the warm soup to his lips. And what could he really say to that, anyhow? "Damn gosse," he replied with affection after he'd swallowed the soup. It was hard to stay irritated with Jules when he was so *sincere*.

Fifteen minutes later, having finished the bowl of soup and being pretty much convinced that he wouldn't vomit it back up again, Jason was once again exhausted.

"Time to sleep." Jules rearranged the pillows on the bed. He tucked the covers around Jason and kissed him on the forehead. "No fever right now," he confirmed. "I'll come back in a few hours and check on you, d'accord?"

"Thanks," mumbled Jason. Jules smiled and closed the door to the bedroom. As he fell asleep once more, Jason thought how lucky he was to have met Jules; it wasn't only the soup that had warmed his body.

JULES SAT in the living room, legs tucked underneath him on the couch, his eyes focused on the window that looked out onto the courtyard. Overhead, he saw stars and heard the vague drone of traffic from the boulevard. It was Wednesday, and Jason would be leaving a week from Monday. And no matter how many times he told himself he'd be fine once Jason left, he knew he was lying to himself. This would be worse, *far* worse, than when he'd left Guy with his mother.

The phone rang, interrupting his train of thought. He looked over at the answering machine; he was still unwilling to answer it. He knew Jason thought him silly to worry about who might be on the other end. The telephone was the one connection to Jason's life in the US that Jules did not dare encroach upon—the boundary between the surreal, dreamlike world they both currently inhabited and the harsher reality of their future. The machine clicked on….

"Jason?" It was a woman's voice, but not Rosalie's. This voice was slightly deeper, like the sound of cream poured into dark coffee. Sexy. "Jason… this is Diane."

Diane. Jules swallowed hard, glancing at the bedroom and debating whether he should wake Jason up.

"Jason. I know I should have called sooner," Diane said. Jules couldn't miss the tentative quality in her voice. That, more than anything else, made his body tense. "I guess I was hoping you'd call me." She laughed, then added, "I need to stop acting like a child." Jules heard her inhale a long breath.

"I was wrong, Jason," she continued. "I knew I wanted more from our relationship, but I didn't tell you. I know I should have—you deserved at least that much from me. But you know, I guess I wanted… I'd hoped you'd realize what I needed… that you'd be able to read my mind. That was pretty stupid of me."

Jules heard the remorse in her voice and fought the urge to turn the answering machine off. That, or throw it against the wall.

How dare she? How could she, after she hurt him so badly?

"Jason," Diane was saying, "we really need to talk. I know it won't be easy, but I… I'm sorry, and I want to make it up to you. Please, Jason, give me a call, and we can talk about what happened." There was an extended pause, then finally: "I hope you'll be able to forgive me, Jason. I… I love you. I really do." The speaker clicked off, and the answering machine beeped softly.

Jules stared at the flashing light on the display. Much as he wanted to delete that message, much as he hated what would happen when Jason heard it, he knew he couldn't—he *wouldn't*—do anything. There might not be a lot of time left for him in Jason's life, but he knew that there was one thing he wanted more than any other: for Jason to be happy, even if it meant that Jules would not be a part of that happiness.

I'm already lucky. Far luckier than I deserve.

THEY LEFT for Grenoble five days later than planned, as soon as Jason felt well enough to make the trip. The new schedule meant that Jules would have to return to Paris a day early so he'd be back in time for Blue Notes' gig at the Sans Silence on Friday. Jason offered to travel back to Paris with Jules, but Jules insisted Jason stay the full four days. They'd have Saturday and Sunday together before Jason's flight back to the States on Monday morning. Plenty of time to say their good-byes. Jason hadn't argued about staying the last day by himself. He hated to miss Jules's gig, but he was at least honest enough with himself to admit that he needed some time on his own without Jules, just to think through some things.

Jason had heard the message on the answering machine from Diane, and it had been a bit of a wake-up call. He knew full well that he needed to make a decision about his future and that he and Jules needed to talk about their future together before he left Paris.

"So what do you think of the TGV?" Jason asked. He needed to think about something other than leaving, his work, or Diane.

Jules, gazing out the window of the high-speed Train à Grande Vitesse, looked exactly as Jason imagined he himself might have looked on his first ride aboard the sleek train. "It's so cool," Jules said with a broad grin. "I love the feeling when the train picks up speed and you're pressed back against your seat. It's like I'd imagine you'd feel blasting off in a rocket."

Jason put his arm around Jules's shoulder. He'd sprung for first-class seats, and the cabin was nearly empty. The only other occupant was asleep, so Jason grinned and pulled Jules's face away from the window and locked him into a kiss.

THEY ARRIVED in Grenoble in midafternoon. Walking out of the train station, Jason caught his breath as he looked up to see the three mountain ranges that surrounded the city: the flatter, more staid Vercors, and the taller Chartreuses and Belledonnes with their peaks covered in snow.

"Bring back memories?" Jules asked, eyes fixed on Jason.

"Yeah. I always loved the mountains. I could see the Vercors from the window of my room." Jason pointed to his left. "We used to hike a lot, bring the dog along, eat lunch. And that"—he pointed to the Belledonnes—"is where we used to ski. Chamrousse, where the 1968 Winter Olympics were held."

"Mémé told us about the schools in the Alps." Jules eyed the mountains wistfully. "Did you really go skiing with your friends in the afternoons?"

"Yes, but not every day," Jason answered with a grin. "We'd hop the bus to Chamrousse from the school parking lot on Wednesday afternoons and ski until it got dark. On the weekends, my parents would take Rosie and me when the weather was good. In the spring, we would ski in T-shirts and jeans, it was so warm."

"I'm jealous," Jules laughed.

"I had no idea how lucky I was," Jason admitted. "When I got back to the States, I missed the mountains. Ohio is pretty flat." There was more to it than that, of course, more things Jason had missed when he'd returned home, but he wasn't sure he really wanted to talk about those things. Not yet, at least.

The hotel wasn't far from the train station, and they dropped their bags off before heading out to explore the city. The weather was rather mild for February; the sky was clear, and the city's inhabitants walked around in spring clothing, jackets open.

"I thought there'd be snow," Jules remarked as they walked over to the river on cours Jean-Jaurès. The Isère River looked gray and cold in the fading afternoon sunlight.

"Almost never in the city," Jason explained. "But the mountains are always snow-covered this time of year. The best of both worlds, I guess."

Jules looked with interest at the four bubble-like cable cars rising from a building ahead of them, hanging over the river and up the side of the mountain.

"Les bulles," Jason said, using the French term for the bubble cars. "Would you like to ride them up? I always loved doing that when I lived here."

Jules nodded enthusiastically, and Jason took his hand and led him to the station. "At the top is the fort, the Bastille de Grenoble. The view of the city from up there is incredible."

When they climbed aboard the small cable car a few minutes later, Jules's grin was as wide as his face. Watching Jules, Jason remembered the view of the city the first time *he* had experienced it. He'd been fifteen and sullen, angry that his parents had dragged him away from an impromptu soccer game he and his friends had been playing in the open field near the elementary school. But when they had begun to climb over the river and up the side of the mountain, he'd forgotten his anger. Even the view of the valley from Chamrousse wasn't as spectacular as seeing the city from a vantage point suspended from the narrow cables.

"It's like seeing Paris from the Eiffel Tower, isn't it?" he remarked, leaning over Jules and resting his chin against Jules's shoulder.

"Better, I think," Jules replied. "I mean, with the mountains in the background, it's so amazing!"

Thankful that they were alone in the cabin, Jason kissed Jules's cheek and sighed deeply. The tension in his upper body began to dissipate. "I'm glad we could do this. It means a lot to me," he said.

LATER, THEY stood atop the Bastille. "I lived over there," Jason said, pointing off in the distance to the south of the city. "The conservatory's a little bit closer in, over there."

"Are we going to visit the conservatory tomorrow?" Jules asked.

"I was thinking we could take a trip up to Chamrousse."

"Oh." Jules bit his lower lip and glanced down. Then he turned away from Jason and added quickly, "Sure. I'd love to see the mountains." Jason couldn't see Jules's expression since he was leaning over the railing, but he was pretty sure Jules was frowning.

"Something the matter?"

"Nothing," Jules said.

BACK AT the hotel after dinner, Jason gazed out the window at the busy street below. Jules walked up behind him and snaked his arms around his waist. "It's hard, coming here, isn't it?"

"Yes." Jason sighed. "But it's good too." He turned around and touched Jules's face. "I'm glad you came."

Jules's face warmed. He'd hoped he'd done the right thing by pushing Jason to come. Now he was pretty sure he had.

Jason kissed him, rubbing his cheeks with his thumbs. Jules pressed his tongue into Jason's mouth. He tasted so good, familiar and warm.

Jules moaned softly and snaked his fingers through Jason's hair. Then, after a moment's hesitation, he skated his hands down Jason's neck and chest and started to unbutton Jason's shirt. It had been a few days since they'd had sex, mostly because Jason had been so sick. Jules had cared for Jason when he'd been too weak to do anything for himself, even helping Jason bathe and use the bathroom. Surprisingly, Jules found some of those moments nearly as intimate as when they'd made love, although the expression on Jason's face when Jules refused to leave the WC for fear that Jason would pass out still made him laugh. "You're a sick man, Jules, that you'd want to watch me pee," Jason had said.

The night before the trip, they'd sucked each other off in the shower, but it had been frenzied and over too soon. Tonight, Jules was determined the seduction would be more gradual. He wanted to commit Jason's body to memory: the feel of his skin, the way he smelled, the sounds he made when they were intimate. Everything.

"Join me for a shower?" Jules suggested with a wicked lick of his lips.

Jason shook his head in mock defeat, then took Jules's hand and let Jules lead him to the bathroom.

"WHAT'S IT like?" Jules wondered aloud. "Being with a woman, I mean?" They were lying naked on the bed, their hair still wet, Jason on his side with an arm draped casually over Jules's chest.

"You mean having sex with a woman?" Jason asked.

"Yes."

Jason considered the question. "It's different than with a man. Softer, I guess." He wasn't sure what else to say. He had the definite sense that there was more than curiosity behind the question.

"Is it better with a woman?"

Jason looked down at Jules. "No." He studied Jules's expression, hoping to understand. "Not better… just different."

"Oh."

"Sex with you is the best I've ever had, Jules." He bent down and kissed Jules—a reassuring and tender kiss. Jules said nothing but looked up at him with wide, loving eyes. "But I don't think that's really because you're a man—it's how I *feel* about you that makes it so good." He realized his words hadn't adequately conveyed what was in his heart and added, "Although I love your body and how it feels—the way your skin is so soft, but I can feel the hard muscle underneath… how tight you are around me when I'm inside of you. God, Jules, I love that so much."

Jules smiled, but there was sadness in his eyes. "Do you miss her?" he asked. "The truth. I need to know."

Jason's jaw tensed with the realization that this wasn't about women in general but one woman in particular: Diane. "Sometimes," he admitted. "We were together a long time."

"I see," Jules said. Jason could read the disappointment on his face.

"It's not like that, Jules." Jason took Jules into his arms and kissed him gently on the top of his head. "In the end, we were much more like friends than anything else."

"But you loved her, didn't you?"

"Yes. Or at least I thought I did, once," Jason answered. Jules was silent again. "I love you, Jules." Jason tilted Jules's chin up so that their eyes met.

"I love you too," Jules replied as Jason drew him tighter against his body.

SLEEP CAME slowly to Jules that night. Even in Jason's embrace, he couldn't forget the sound of Diane's voice on the answering machine. *You knew this would happen*, he thought as he listened to the sound of Jason's gentle breaths. *He deserves to be happy, and if she wants to give their relationship another try, who are you to interfere?*

CHAPTER 14

THE NEXT day dawned perfectly clear. They arose early and, after a quick breakfast, walked over to a car rental agency to pick up a Renault Clio for the drive to the mountains. Jules laughed to see Jason squeeze his broad frame into the tiny car, and Jason laughed in spite of himself too. Hearing Jules's sweet laughter calmed his anxious thoughts; it always did. That, and Jules's close proximity inside the small vehicle, and the fragrance of his freshly washed hair and skin.

The ride to the mountaintop ski resort was uneventful. The tight switchbacks of the mountain road had Jules in openmouthed wonder—especially when the large tour bus in front of them navigated the sharp turns with relative ease.

"I expected more people on the road," Jules said, looking much like he had on the train, eyeing the valley far below with his forehead pressed against the window.

"It's late," Jason explained. "The hard-core skiers are on the slopes by eight in the morning."

They parked near the téléphérique—the imposing cable car was centered on the face of the main slope that had been created for the men's Olympic downhill race years before. Jason remembered the hushed, reverent tones in which his French friends had spoken of Jean-Claude Killy, the French skier who had won gold medals in all three 1968 Olympic downhill skiing events, more than twenty years after the fact.

A half-dozen smaller chairlifts surrounded the main cable lines. For nearly ten minutes, they just stood and watched the skiers descend. The more experienced skiers came almost straight down the mountain, barely touching their poles in the snow as they barreled toward the base, snow flying about them.

The air was cold and fresh; the smell of the snow reminded Jason of the many times he'd skied here. "Want to try skiing?" he asked, seeing Jules's excited interest. He longed to be back on the slopes—it had been three years since he and Diane had last gone skiing in Vail.

"Maybe another time," Jules replied. "I can't risk breaking an arm, especially with our next gig so soon."

Jason nodded in understanding. "I broke my ankle one of the first times I was out on the slopes." Jason chuckled and shook his head. "Thought I'd be a hotshot and take that trail there"—he pointed to the steep trail in the shadow of the cable car—"figuring if the Olympic skiers could do it…." He shook his head. "I was a fucking idiot."

"Sounds like you were just being a kid. Besides, I kind of like thinking about you as young and reckless."

"Ouais. I did some pretty stupid shit."

"Why did you stop doing stupid shit?" Jules asked.

Jason shrugged. "I was hanging around with some neighborhood kids one summer, and we got into trouble. They dared me to steal something from the store we hung out at. I ended up at the police station, and my parents had to come get me. I was terrified—thought they'd kick us out of the country for it. I know now they wouldn't have, of course, but still…. My folks grounded me for three months. After that, I decided to behave."

Jules laughed.

"What's so funny?"

"Nothing. It's just hard to imagine you as a bad boy," Jules said. "I'd have liked to have known you then."

Jason just looked at Jules with an unspoken question on his lips, then shrugged a second time, deciding not to ask. "So," he said, changing the subject, "do you want to take the gondola to the Croix de Chamrousse, the summit? There's a nice café up there. I could use something to eat."

THEY ENDED up eating lunch at the restaurant at the top of the cables, at a table complete with a panoramic view of the valley below and of the slopes. “I always loved the way the French put restaurants in the middle of nowhere,” Jason said as they sipped their coffee. “Much more civilized than in the States.”

“What’s it like,” Jules asked, “Philadelphia?”

“Big.” Jason’s gaze wandered to the snow-capped mountains in the distance. “Like Paris, I guess. Not as pretty, though. Don’t get me wrong, there are some beautiful areas downtown, but it’s just not the same. Every time I come back to France, I wish I still lived here.”

“Why haven’t you moved back?” Jules asked before blushing scarlet, clearly realizing he was treading on thin ice.

Jason knew the question of their future had been hanging between them like a particularly stubborn ghost the past few days, and he struggled not to show his unease. “I thought about it after I finished college—before I went to law school. But it was so damn expensive to live in Europe, and I didn’t have a job or anything. That was before Rosie bought the apartment too.”

It would be different now. I’ve got enough money to live on for years, even in Paris. The thought was tempting. He could live here in France with Jules and….

“You all right?” Jules asked.

Jason realized he’d crumpled his napkin in his hand, his fingers so tight around it that his knuckles were white. *You’re scared.* “Yeah, I’m fine,” he said aloud. Then, changing the subject for the second time that day, he added, “So what would you like to see next? We can drive to Annecy—it’s a beautiful city on a lake about an hour or so from Grenoble. Or we can—”

“Jaz,” Jules interrupted gently, his expression serious. “It’s beautiful here—don’t misunderstand me—but I….” He hesitated and fidgeted a little in his chair. “I get the feeling that you’re avoiding the very reason why we came here.”

Jason rubbed his forehead, then took a sip of his coffee. Jules was right, of course, Jason just wasn’t sure what to do about it. Thinking of making some sort of peace with his past made him really nervous.

“I’m sorry, Jaz. I didn’t mean—”

“It’s okay. You’re right.” He sighed. “I *am* avoiding things.”

Jules reached across the table and took Jason's hand in his. "I'm here, remember? What do they say in English? 'I've got your back'? Je te couvre."

"I know." Jason looked out the window again. "Come on," he said at last with resignation. He knew he couldn't put it off any longer. He was as ready as he'd ever be. "Let's go explore a bit of my past." He paid the waiter, and they took the cable car back down to the parking area, hand in hand. That simple contact—feeling Jules's hand pressed against his—was the most reassuring thing that Jason could imagine.

I can do this, he thought, willing his heart to calm its galloping beat. *I can do this. As long as I'm with him.*

IT WAS dinnertime when they arrived back in Grenoble, and the sun had already set beyond the mountains. Given the late hour, Jules had expected Jason to postpone their trip to his old neighborhood and the conservatory. But Jason did not immediately return the rental car; instead, he headed out of the heart of the city toward the Olympic Village. After Jason parked the car on a small side street, he and Jules walked into the large development, a sea of concrete and dark-brown wood connected by large, open pedestrian zones.

"We lived in this building." Jason pointed to a three-story apartment building that bordered the street. "The first month or so we lived here, I went to the local high school, but I transferred to the school connected to the Conservatoire after I was accepted there. Met a bunch of neighborhood kids, though. My best friend, Thierry, lived in that high-rise down the street." He pointed to a tall building a block away. "We actually kept in touch for a while after I went back to the States. Then he got married and moved. We lost track of each other after that."

"Did you play sports?"

"Other than competitive skiing, just soccer. I tried to teach some of my classmates to play baseball. Almost got myself hit over the head." Jason grinned at the memory.

"Was it hard, fitting in?"

"Not really. They knew I was American, and I was a bit of a celebrity because of it, I guess. I didn't speak a word of French, and they would all try out their English on me." Jason laughed. "I barely remember the first few months. After that, though, I caught on. By the time we had been here four months, I was fluent enough to talk to friends, hang out, that sort of thing. Classes were harder, but after a year, I was pretty much doing about the same level of work as the French kids. My second year, I got a B in French class. My teacher told me he'd graded me like any other French speaker in the class. I was pretty proud of myself."

"That's better than I did," Jules pointed out. "French was always my worst subject. All that dictation and memorization of poetry and shit. I hated it. I was just happy to finish. I knew I was going to be a musician. The rest didn't really matter much to me."

"How did you manage to pay for your lessons and your violin?"

Jules grinned proudly. "At first, my mémé paid for them. She bought me my violin. After she died, my teacher let me pay for my lessons by doing work at her house. Gardening, cleaning. That sort of thing." Jason guessed Jules's teacher had heard his natural talent and had understood how difficult his life must have been. "At the conservatory," Jules continued, "everything was paid for."

"What happened? Why didn't you stay at the conservatory?"

Jules chewed on his lower lip for a moment, then answered carefully, "I needed to get a job. My mother… she didn't take care of Guy sometimes. She'd spend the money she got from the government on drugs. So I gave her money. I tried to work and go to school, but it was too difficult." He sighed and shook his head. "Not that it mattered, in the end. They ended up taking him into custody and put him in foster care anyhow. But by then, I couldn't go back. So he bounced back and forth between my mother and foster care. She'd get better and they'd give him back to her. Then she'd start using again and they'd take him away again."

"I'm sorry, Jules," Jason said.

"It worked out anyhow. I don't think I'd have started writing my own music if I'd stayed. Maybe I'd have ended up playing in an orchestra, but I never wanted to be a soloist. Now, I wouldn't go back even if I could." Jules offered Jason a reassuring smile, and Jason could see he was telling the truth.

"You really are strong." Jason took Jules's hand. Jules blushed, and Jason decided he should change the subject. "So would you like to see the conservatory?" he asked. Jules nodded, and they got back into the car. A few minutes later, Jason pointed through the windshield to an imposing modern building of concrete and glass.

"That's it?" Jules wasn't looking at the building; he was watching Jason.

Jason, for his part, just took a deep breath and nodded. "It'll be closed now." He stopped the car in the parking lot and leaned back against the seat. The moon was now covered by clouds, and tiny drops of rain began to fall.

"You okay?" Jules took Jason's hand and squeezed it.

"Yeah. I'm not sure *what* I expected. I thought that just coming here would be like facing my demons—like an epiphany."

"Does it ever work that way?"

"No, I guess not. It's just that for so many years, I've tried to pretend it didn't matter, that I didn't miss playing. But after Milan…."

"What did you feel when you played in Milan?" Jules asked. Jason was sure Jules had wanted to ask the question before but was afraid to.

"Like I had to keep things together so I wouldn't just lose it. I didn't want to let you guys down." Jason closed his eyes.

"What would happen if you 'lost it'?"

An interesting question. Jules, he knew, never worried much about losing control; he'd always pretty much done what he felt was the right thing and dealt with the consequences afterward. It was something that had attracted him to Jules. Something he wished he could emulate.

"You know," Jason admitted, opening his eyes and focusing on Jules, "I'm not sure. When I used to play, the minute I'd try to handle something more technically difficult, it was as though this wall came down…. Like, if I let go, I'd make mistakes and embarrass myself."

"You're a perfectionist." It was a simple statement, but Jason couldn't argue with it.

"Yeah. So everyone tells me." Once again, Jules had gotten to the heart of things with uncanny precision. Jason appreciated the way Jules made him confront the truth; it reminded him a great deal of the way Rosalie always had.

"You don't agree?"

"I *am* a perfectionist."

Jules said nothing but leaned over to kiss Jason, who yielded without complaint.

"I was back then too. Had me all tied up in knots."

"What about when you're in court?"

"Pretty much the same, except that I don't need to wear my heart on my sleeve to be a good lawyer. With music, though, it's different. When I keep things under wraps as I'm playing piano, my music suffers. You don't have to be emotional to be a good lawyer."

Jules nodded his understanding.

"Will you come back here with me tomorrow?" Jason asked after a few minutes of silence. It was getting late; time for dinner.

"Of course, Jaz."

THEY SPENT a leisurely dinner drinking nearly two bottles of wine between them. They talked about easy subjects: music, the mountains, the differences between the schools in the US and France. By the time they returned to the hotel, Jules was tipsy from the alcohol, and Jason, who had drunk nearly a bottle and a half on his own, had one hand beneath the waist of Jules's pants. Not that Jules would complain—he'd been thinking about sex with Jason pretty consistently all day. Jules had barely closed the door behind him when Jason pressed Jules up against the wall, kissed his neck, and began to suck on his earlobe. Between the feel of Jason's mouth on him and the sound of Jason's stuttered breaths, Jules was hard in no time. He was just imagining Jason's hard cock inside him when Jason said something that took him completely by surprise: "I want you to fuck me, Jules."

Jason pulled Jules's shirt over his head and buried his lips once more in the bend of Jules's neck, nipping and licking there.

It took a moment before Jason's words sank in, but when they did, they were like an electric shock. "You… what?" Jules stammered. He pushed Jason away so he could see Jason's face and see if he was serious.

"I want you to fuck me," Jason repeated, clearly unfazed. His eyes were dark with lust, his breath shallow.

"What? Jaz?" The room suddenly felt very hot, his jeans far tighter than they had been only a moment before.

"You don't want to?" Jason's expression became unfathomable, but his voice hinted at disappointment.

"I…." Jules tried to speak, but the words seemed to get caught in his throat. Of course he wanted this! But it was so sudden, so unlike anything he'd ever expected from cool-headed Jason. It was as if the earth beneath his feet had shifted.

Jason looked crestfallen now, even a bit embarrassed. "I'm so sorry," he mumbled. "I never… I mean, I don't know anything about relationships between men except ours… I just figured that you'd… but I understand if you're not into that."

"Stop," Jules nearly shouted as he regained his grip on reality at last. Jason looked so… *insecure*? He'd already moved away from Jules, worried that he'd somehow offended him.

Jules put his hands on Jason's upper arms and waited until he saw Jason's eyes focus on his own. "It's not that," he said, making sure Jason could see the honesty in his face. "God, Jaz, how could you even *think* I wouldn't want you like that? It's just that it's so sudden. You took me by surprise. I didn't expect it."

Jason looked mortified.

"Really," Jules said. "I… I can't tell you how much it means to me that you'd want, that you'd trust me to…." He lifted his fingers to Jason's face and brushed the skin above Jason's lip to reassure him. Jason was so fucking sexy when he wasn't in control! Jules thought he might lose his mind just imagining Jason opening to him, allowing him to…. He fought to stay focused. "But," he continued, ignoring his pounding heart, "why now?"

"I don't know." Jason appeared as bewildered as Jules. "I was telling you about some of the stupid shit I would do as a kid. It made me think… my life is so damn… *predictable*. And I started to wonder what I could do differently—how I could live my life differently….”

Jules laughed. “I’d say not kicking me out of your bed that first night—that’s a little different from what you’d been doing before.”

Jason smiled. “Yeah,” he said. “But that’s the *point*, Jules. I’d thought about sex with a man before—a bunch of times—but I never did anything about it. But with you… I don’t know… it just felt right. And I can’t tell you how happy it’s made me, being with you. I want to be with you this way, before….”

Before he leaves, Jules finished silently.

The pain of this thought lingered, even as his lips met Jason’s. He pulled Jason’s face to his and brushed it with kisses, tasting the wine and the familiar muskiness there. “Are you sure you want this?”

“I’m sure,” Jason said, breathless. “But,” he added, “I *am* a little nervous.”

Jules smiled. “It feels strange,” he murmured as he took Jason’s hand and led him to the bed, “being the one to show *you* something.”

“You’ve shown me things before,” Jason reminded him for the second time that night.

“Yeah, but I didn’t really know you then.”

“Then it’s even better.” Jason sat down on the bed and pulled Jules on top of him.

Jules couldn’t find anything to say to that. Instead, he unbuttoned Jason’s shirt, pushed the soft cotton fabric from Jason’s chest, and bent over to lick his nipples. Jason arched his back, raising his body to meet the featherlight touch.

Jules flicked his tongue over the hardening skin, unbuttoned Jason’s jeans and pushed them down his hips. Stepping back for a second, he admired Jason’s body, memorizing every inch. “Lie back,” he directed, and Jason complied. It was a strange feeling—a heady feeling—being in control of Jason’s actions, but he found himself enjoying it immensely. He pulled off his own pants and boxers but did not move to touch Jason.

“Shit, Jules,” Jason moaned, “you’re making me crazy standing there.”

"I'm glad." Jules ran his tongue over his bottom lip, savoring the moment, wanting to tease Jason and knowing that he needed a bit of distance so he could do this right. Make it right and take it slow. He retrieved the bottle of lube and a condom from the bedside table, then rolled the rubber over himself and poured a generous amount of the liquid into his palm. Jason inhaled in anticipation and licked his lips as Jules slicked up his own cock, never taking his eyes off Jason.

"Oh… fuck. So fucking sexy when you do that."

Jules began to stroke himself. "You like it?" he asked, although he knew the answer.

"God, yes."

Jules knelt on the bed and took Jason in his mouth, swallowing him down to the hilt, then sucking so hard that Jason gasped. He ran a finger back under his balls, tracing a line until he felt the tight ring between Jason's cheeks, and slid a slippery finger over the opening.

"Please," Jason begged. "Please…."

Jules pressed his forefinger so that it only just breached the muscles of Jason's rim. "Relax," he said when he felt the tension there. "I won't hurt you. I promise."

"I know. I trust you." Jason relaxed a little as Jules pressed his finger in, working the muscles and urging them to release their taut grip. Jules took Jason's cock in his mouth once more, delighting in the moans and hitches that stuttered Jason's breathing.

"Jules… oh Jules…."

"Turn onto your stomach." Jules didn't want Jason's climax to come too soon.

Jason acquiesced and stretched out on the bed, legs splayed, the muscles of his buttocks straining against skin. Jules's cock ached. He wanted nothing more than to push his way into Jason and feel the warmth of Jason's body tight around him, but he restrained himself. This was for Jason, and he was determined that the experience would be one that Jason would remember—that he would cherish.

He leaned over and licked a line down Jason's spine, feeling Jason writhe beneath him, tasting the saltiness of his skin and the scent that was Jason's alone. He followed that line further, pausing for an instant at the tight ring that he longed to enter, then further until he reached the back of Jason's balls and felt them tense up under his tongue.

"You're killing me, Jules," Jason whimpered. By the time Jules withdrew his tongue and inserted two fingers, Jason was panting hard. "I want you inside of me," he moaned. "Please… need you… now…."

"It'll be more comfortable on your knees." Jules watched Jason move his legs under his body so that his entrance was neatly displayed. Jules was unable to hold himself back any longer, the sight of Jason in such a vulnerable position the most beautiful thing he'd ever seen. "Jason," he asked, "are you sure?"

"If you don't hurry up and fuck me," Jason growled, "I'm going to lose my mind."

Ever so gently, Jules pressed his slippery cock into the ring of pink flesh, feeling it give way against his tip. Jason mewled and pushed back against him, and their bodies meshed until Jules's pelvis met the hard muscles of Jason's ass.

"You all right?"

"Burns…," Jason whispered. But when Jules began to withdraw for fear of hurting him, Jason pushed back hard against his body, seating Jules completely inside. "No. I want to feel you move," he told Jules.

Jules didn't hesitate but began to thrust—gently at first, then increasing his tempo when he heard Jason's rumbling approval. "Harder," Jason begged. "Please… harder, Jules!"

"Merde alors!" Jules cried out. He hadn't fucked someone else this hard since he was in school, and he'd forgotten how incredible it felt—even better now that the body into which he thrust was Jason's. "I can't do this very long," he choked out, leaning forward so his chest was pressed against Jason's back. He reached around Jason and took his erection in his hand, fisting it hard. "Come with me, Jaz," he said as his balls drew up and the tingling at the base of his spine announced his orgasm.

"Yes!" Jason cried as he spilled himself all over Jules's hand and the rumpled sheets. "Oh hell yes!"

Jules closed his eyes, holding on to Jason for dear life, their bodies pressed so snug against each other that there was almost no separation between the two. He felt Jason shudder beneath him, trying to catch his breath. Jules kissed Jason's neck, then licked away the sweat there, releasing Jason's cock but unwilling to withdraw from his body. It felt so good like this, and he wanted to remember it.

He fought to hold back tears, scolding himself for behaving like a lovesick schoolboy but unable to control the conflicting emotions that roiled in his heart. In the end, he was just happy Jason could not see his face—neither the pain nor the joy there. He wanted nothing to spoil the moment.

"ET ALORS?" A grin spread over Jules's face.

Jason raised an eyebrow and smirked, then kissed Jules on his cheek. They'd dozed, then washed up before getting back into bed.

"Well, what?" From this angle, Jason could see Jules's face; he looked a bit apprehensive.

"Are you glad you tried something new?"

Jason contemplated the question as he gathered Jules in his arms. "Are you ki—?" he began, then decided that this was not the time to be glib. "Yes. That was incredible. I never guessed it would feel so damn good."

Jules looked relieved. Jason knew Jules wanted to be sure he didn't regret the reversed roles of their lovemaking, and even more, to reassure himself that he hadn't hurt Jason.

"Jules," Jason said, choosing his words carefully, "do you believe that I love you?"

"I…," Jules began haltingly, then answered, "yes, of course."

"You don't sound convinced." He hugged Jules, stroking his silky hair with a large hand. Jules remained silent, as if reconsidering his original answer. When he did not reply, Jason continued, "I know what you must think. That this relationship was all very sudden; that I haven't had a chance to think it through. But I *do* love you."

"I'm just happy you're here," Jules responded.

Jason frowned. He wasn't sure what he could say to alleviate Jules's fears. *He* knew how he felt about Jules.

Yeah, but you haven't exactly been the easiest person to pin down about your feelings. You need something more concrete to show him how you really feel.

He'd figure things out here, and he would be ready to sit Jules down when he returned to Paris. Then they'd talk about their future—their future *together*.

CHAPTER 15

"BONJOUR, MESSIEURS!" The blonde office assistant smiled pleasantly at Jules and Jason. "How can I help you?"

Jason returned the smile and offered his hand. "Jason Greene. And this is my good friend, Jules Bardon."

"Monsieur Greene, Monsieur Bardon," she said as she took the offered hand, "I'm Annette Duchamps. It's a pleasure to meet you both. What brings you to the conservatory?"

"I was a student here back in the 1990s," Jason explained, shifting on his feet. "I was hoping to look around, maybe show my friend the school."

"Of course. What instrument did you play?" Annette asked.

"Piano," Jason replied. "I studied with Jacques Vanier. Is he still around?"

"I'm afraid not," she answered. "Monsieur Vanier retired about four years ago. But if you'd like to look around, you're welcome to. The students are on vacation this week, so you can go just about anywhere you'd like." She handed them two visitor badges. "The individual studios are locked, but all of the public areas are open. Feel free to take your time. You're welcome to play any of the pianos, if you wish."

"Merci, mademoiselle," Jules said with a mischievous glint in his brown eyes. He ignored Jason's slight frown and turned instead to Annette as she followed them out to the main entryway.

"I assume you know your way around, Monsieur Greene," she said. "If you have any questions, though, please let me know. I'll be in my office all day."

"You've been very kind," Jason replied with his usual charm.

"De rien," Annette responded. "À tout à l'heure."

"À tout à l'heure," Jules said. Then, after waiting a moment until Annette had disappeared back into the office, he put his hand on Jason's arm and grinned. "So," he said, "are you going to give me the tour, then?"

Jason chuckled and shook his head softly. "You're so transparent."

"You mean 'cute,'" Jules parried with a bright grin, an obvious attempt to put Jason at ease.

Other than when he'd been charming the receptionist, Jason had felt like a lost child—anxious and awkward—ever since they had arrived at the school. "Right," he said in mock exasperation. "Cute."

In one of the classrooms on the second floor, Jason stopped and gazed out the window to the gray sky and mountains beyond. He was struck by a vivid memory of a similar gray day, years before in this very room, during his advanced music theory class. He recalled the complicated four-part dictation their teacher had subjected them to, which had been far beyond anything he'd learned in his studies with his mother or in his weekly theory classes at the local music school. When he managed to pass the advanced theory class by the skin of his teeth, he'd considered it a victory of sorts.

"Thinking about something?" Jules asked, bringing Jason back to himself.

"Just that you don't have to be the best at everything, I guess," Jason said. Jules gave him a questioning look, but Jason didn't elaborate.

Two hours later, having reminisced to Jules about what his life had been like as a student and what he thought of his teachers and classmates, Jason led Jules into the largest of the halls set aside for performances. It was here that Jason had sat for his juried exams—much like the audition at Curtis. Each student had been assigned several pieces of music over the semester, and along with final exams in subjects like theory, composition, biology, French, and math, they would perform for a group of faculty at the conservatory for their end-of-semester grade.

"I hated this place," Jason stated flatly as he studied the empty hall.

"Juries?" Jason knew Jules was intimately familiar with the process, having spent two years at a conservatory himself.

Jason nodded. "Yeah. Being judged on my ability to play piano—graded on it—that was the most intimidating thing about this place."

More than intimidating. Crushing.

They walked down the aisle toward the stage, and Jason felt a sense of déjà vu. A Steinway grand sat at the edge, and Jason wondered vaguely if it were the same piano he'd played more than fifteen years before. "I hated the juried exam system," he said with a sigh, doing his best to repress the memories that threatened to surface. "It's different in the States. At the universities there, your teacher grades you on the work you do in the studio."

"There aren't any exams?" Jules appeared surprised by this bit of information.

"You're required to do a junior and senior recital," Jason explained. "But it's not like an exam."

Jules looked at Jason, as if putting together the pieces of a puzzle. "That bad experience you told me about," he ventured. "It was a jury exam, wasn't it?"

Jason nodded. "I fucked it up. Spectacularly. Had to repeat a year with the younger kids." It had been humiliating.

Jules said nothing but touched Jason's arm in sympathy. The silence lingered until Jason climbed the steps to the stage and walked over to the piano. He appraised the instrument wistfully and ran his fingers over the closed keyboard. Jules looked up at him, observing but saying nothing.

Jason took a deep breath and sat down at the instrument. His hands shook as he lifted the cover from the keys. For a few minutes, he did nothing but contemplate the keyboard. Then, with deliberation, he touched the keys and he began to play scales—softly at first, then with more purpose. Jules settled into one of the front seats.

Five minutes passed, then ten. Jason progressed from scales to arpeggios, the familiar warm-ups coming back to him with little effort. How many hours had he spent just like this, warming up his fingers, working to increase his dexterity? He remembered his inner struggle to focus on the exercises, fighting the urge to plunge into the music without the proper preparation. Looking back on his childhood now, he understood that it hadn't only been the delay in his serious study of the instrument that had held him back; it had also been his lack of interest in practicing. He'd detested the hours spent indoors while all his friends were playing, unfettered, outside the apartment.

It's easy to forget, he thought with a twinge of regret. *It's too easy to lay the blame on things beyond your control.*

He sensed Jules's anticipation as he finished his warm-ups. It was a lovely instrument, with the rich tones of a full-size grand piano and the unique resonance of a Steinway. His mother had owned a Steinway baby grand, and he'd adored that instrument, but nothing in his experience was quite as powerful as playing its larger sibling. Even in a great hall such as this, the reverberations of the instrument reached into every corner, as if the room itself could not contain the sound.

Gingerly, he settled his fingers once more on the keys. He closed his eyes and recalled the joy he'd felt the day before on the mountain, with Jules at his side. He knew without hesitation what piece he wanted to play—the Brahms he'd so adored as a child clamored to fly from his heart directly to the keys—and the slow, passionate music burst from his soul and filled the hall.

JULES HAD heard Jason play this piece before, but it had been early on in their relationship. Now, after they'd shared so much, he became aware of how much of Jason's essence resided in this particular interpretation: the dark and brooding quality of the man, the focused determination, and the gentle heart that underscored incredible strength. He heard Jason's soul in each note, the beautiful and profound soul he loved and longed never to leave.

"That was beautiful, Jaz," he said after Jason had finished. "I don't think I'll ever hear that piece again without thinking of you."

Jason's face was a mixture of pain and great joy, and although Jules did not know for sure what had triggered those emotions in Jason, he could guess. It had taken great courage for Jason to come here and even more to play in this place.

JASON TURNED back to contemplate the keys once more. The Brahms relaxed him; it was a piece he could play under any circumstances, and play well. More challenging were the pieces that danced like demons in his heart—the beautiful, tantalizing music that had nearly paralyzed him but that held great promise, the promise of the same deep connection the Brahms had always held for him, but seemed so unattainable.

He drew a silent breath as the final chord of the Brahms still resonated in his mind. The hall seemed darker than it had before, and he imagined the table set up in the back, underneath the balcony. He felt suddenly small next to the huge Steinway, and he shivered.

"Monsieur Greene," a voice echoed from his past. *"Do you want to begin again?"*

His shoulders tightened, and he grew dizzy. *Breathe. You aren't that kid anymore.*

The hall was as silent now as it was then, in that moment suspended in time, that single moment that had never really ended for him.

I'd like to start again, he thought. Another echo. Start again? But how do you start again when something is gone forever?

This was the moment, he knew, the time for taking a chance and releasing the pain that clutched at his heartstrings. *There is no pressure in this place. No one to judge. Only love. Only Jules. Sitting there. Waiting for you.*

The sounds of music now replaced the ancient voices: Liszt's Hungarian Rhapsody No. 2. It was one of the most challenging pieces he'd ever studied, and the piece he'd attempted in his Curtis audition years before. It still terrified and fascinated him to no end. Passionate. Dark and brooding, certainly, but with a fire that connected with something deep inside of him. He looked out at the seats and saw Jules waiting patiently for him, and something within himself relinquished its hold. Another deep breath, and then….

JULES KNEW the piece well, and although he was no pianist, he understood it to be one of the most technically difficult written for the instrument. The opening was much like Jason, with his tough exterior that hid the grief and vulnerability in his soul.

This first section of music suited Jason technically as well. It did not require the flashy, note-pounding, hand-crossing technique that would follow. It was staid and resolute, and the entire hall resounded with the powerful beauty of the instrument and the man who commanded it. Much like he had the Brahms before, Jason attacked the piece with obvious relish, imbuing the notes with the very core of his being. He withheld nothing. Jules waited, almost nervous to hear how the rest of this piece would fare under Jason's stalwart fingers.

The grim opening gave way to the ebullient scales and arpeggios that populated the dance-like, playful second section of the piece. Immediately, Jules noticed a visible change in the way Jason held himself at the piano. Unlike in Milan, this time Jules saw none of the tension that had strained his neck and shoulders. He shifted forward in his seat, drawn in by the music.

The rendition was far from technically perfect. Jules guessed it had been years—more than a decade, perhaps—since Jason had practiced the piece. But the imperfections did not detract, because this time, unlike in Milan, Jules could finally hear Jason's beautiful soul coming through the music.

Jason's expression was one of intense concentration as he reached the frenzied, challenging finale. His fingers flew over the keys with abandon, and despite the flaws, Jules gasped for air, so taken was he by the emotional power of the music. And then there was silence, the piece finished. His eyes filled with tears, and he knew that Jason, too, must have felt the incredible power of the performance.

"I THOUGHT you had it in your soul," Jason heard Madame Shiranova say. *"The love of the music. The power there."*

He just stared at the keys as if he'd seen something there or perhaps understood something that had, until now, escaped him. He lost track of time until he felt hands on his shoulders and a gentle squeeze.

"Did you hear what I did?" Jules sounded tentative, almost as if he was afraid to ask.

"I… I…," Jason stammered. "I don't know." It was the truth; he was too overwhelmed to comprehend what had just transpired. "I made a lot of mistakes."

"I don't care," Jules said with a frown. "When's the last time you studied the piece?"

"I'm not sure. More than thirteen years ago, at least."

Jules laughed.

"How's that funny?"

"It's funny," Jules replied, shaking his head, "because you played it better than most people I've heard play it. And you hadn't practiced it at all for so many years." He kissed Jason on the cheek, then added, "I think I understand now."

"Please, O wise man," Jason quipped as he tried to rein in his fragile emotions, "enlighten me."

"I don't think it was ever really about technique."

"How so?" Jason knew he sounded defensive, but he really was curious.

"I think that you were so worried you'd make mistakes, it was like tying one hand behind your back. If you can play the piece that well after years of not practicing it, I can imagine how it would sound if you *did* work on it," Jules explained.

"I don't know," Jason repeated with a sigh. "I understand what you're saying, but…." He let out a long, slow breath. "But we'd better get going. It's getting late, and you have a train to catch—I was hoping we could grab lunch before I took you to the station." He realized that he'd often resorted to changing the subject lately and knew how it came across.

"Bien sûr." Jules squeezed Jason's shoulder.

Jason knew what Jules was thinking, and he was thinking about it too. For the first time in a very long time, Jason had lost himself in the music.

CHAPTER 16

THEY ATE in a restaurant near the river, the interior warm and comfortable despite the drop in temperature outside. Rain had begun to fall in large droplets, and Jason thought he smelled snow in the air. Sitting at the small table near the window, a candle flickering between them, Jason recalled the few snows he'd experienced in this town and the way the white powder looked on the walkways of the Olympic Village.

"You seem so far away." Jules sipped his red wine.

"Hmm. I guess. I think I'm a little overwhelmed."

Jules reached across the table and took Jason's hand, his smile sympathetic. "I like you this way," he said.

"You do?"

"Ouais."

"Thanks for making me come here," Jason said. "You were right—I needed to do it."

"But you're still not sure what it all means." It wasn't a question.

"No, I'm not," Jason answered. "But that's okay. I don't need all the answers right now."

THE TRAIN station was not very crowded at four in the afternoon; it was still too early for the evening rush. Jason's guess had been correct, and the snow had begun to fall in heavy, wet flakes. "Merde, for tomorrow," he told Jules with a heartfelt grin. "I know you'll play well. They'll eat you up."

Even on the covered tracks, the air was damp and cold. Jason shivered, although he wasn't sure if he could blame it on just the chill in the air. "I'll be on the first train out Saturday morning," he reminded Jules before taking his hand and walking him over to the first-class car. "We can eat breakfast together."

"I'll make your favorite, then," Jules told him.

Jason pulled Jules close. He didn't care that they drew a few surprised stares—he wanted Jules to understand how much this trip had meant to him. "I love you," he whispered in Jules's ear. "Don't forget that."

"I love you too." It was Jules's turn to shiver. He grinned, reached into his pocket, and waved the phone they'd picked up for him before leaving Paris. "Call me if you need me," he said.

"I will." Jason watched as Jules boarded the train, then waited until it pulled slowly out of the station. For a moment he just stood on the empty quay. It was the first time in nearly two months that he'd been without Jules for more than a few hours, and it felt strange to be alone. His phone rang, and he pulled it out of his pocket.

"Hello?"

"Jaz?"

"Hey, Rosie."

"Where are you?" Rosalie asked. "I've tried the apartment the past few days, and there was no answer."

"I'm in Grenoble."

"Really?" She could not hide her surprise. "Jules said he wanted to get you to go back. You gotta give that kid credit. I've been telling you to do it for years."

"Thanks, Rosie," Jason laughed. "So what can't wait?"

"Did you call Diane?"

Jason took a deep breath. "No."

"Did she call you?"

"Yes," he replied in a measured tone.

"Jaz…."

"Rosie," he warned, "this isn't your concern."

"But Jaz…."

"I love you, Rosie," he said, "but being a nudge doesn't suit you. I'll call her when I know what I want to say to her."

"Sorry." She sounded a bit sheepish. "You're right. It's just that she called me again a few days ago wondering where you were. I thought it was strange that she left a message but you hadn't called her back."

"I've got a few things that I need to work out," Jason told her as he walked back to the hotel. "I'll call her. Promise."

"How's Jules?" she asked.

"He's fine," Jason answered, pleased that the conversation had headed in another direction. "I just put him on a train. He'll be back in time for his gig with the trio tomorrow night."

"Did you tell him how you feel about him?"

Jason took a deep breath. He knew she was only asking because she cared deeply about him, but he didn't appreciate the pressure. "Yes," he said at last.

"Good," she responded happily. "So…?"

"Rosie," he warned, "let it go."

She sighed. "I know, you're right. Sorry. It's just that…."

"You want me to be happy," he finished. "I know. But you've gotta give me a little space on this. My flight back to Philly is on Monday, and I need to make some decisions."

"I'll stay out of it," she told him. "But if you need to talk, you know where to find me."

"Thanks, Rosie."

"You're welcome, little brother."

"Oh, and Rosie?"

"Yes?"

"I love you."

"I love you too. You take care of yourself and that delectable Frenchman of yours."

"Thanks, Rosie. I will."

BY THE time he hung up the phone, Jason had arrived back at the hotel. It was still too early for dinner, but the hotel had a small bar, and he decided he needed a drink.

"What can I get for you?" the bartender asked as Jason sat at the counter.

Deciding that scotch probably wasn't a good idea—he had no intention of getting drunk like the last time—he ordered a half bottle of red Bordeaux.

"Thanks," he said as the bartender poured him a glass. The bartender smiled politely and went back to drying glasses and putting them away behind the counter. For the second time that afternoon, Jason's phone rang.

"Hello?"

"Jason?"

"Scott?" It took him a moment to place the familiar voice. "Hey, Scott—good to hear from you! How are you?"

"The same." Scott snorted. "Just checking in with you, making sure you're coming back next week. The partners are chomping at the bit to see those billables."

"Warms my heart, Scotty," chuckled Jason. "Nice to know I've been missed."

"So how are *you* doing, Jaz Man? Enjoying the French wine and women?"

Jason coughed. "You're interrupting a damn good 2005 Château La Vieille Cure Fronsac."

"Right." Scott had never been much of a wine connoisseur. "I'll stick with my Heineken. So how about the women?"

"Not too much happening on that front," Jason answered. *Well*, he reasoned silently, *it's true.*

"Damn," Scott moaned. "I can't even live vicariously. You're killing me, Greene."

"Allison *will* kill you one of these days if you're not careful," Jason pointed out.

Scott laughed. "Good point."

"My flight gets in Monday night. I'll be back in the office Tuesday."

"You're not going to tell me any more?" Scott pressed.

"Nah, you'll have to wait. It'll be a good exercise in self-discipline," Jason deadpanned. "And God knows that's something you could work on."

"Yeah, yeah."

"Later, Scotty."

"Safe travels, Jaz Man."

Jason tapped the phone and slipped it back into his pocket.

"Jaz? C'est toi?"

Jason turned around when he heard his name. An attractive brunette stood by the bar, staring at him with wide-eyed surprise.

"Isa?" Jason grinned, and he stepped off the barstool to greet the woman—Isabelle Duhamel, a cellist who'd attended the conservatory and with whom he'd shared most of his classes. They'd been quite close; he'd thought of her as a little sister.

"I wondered if it was you," Isabelle said after they had exchanged the bises. "Not too many redheaded Americans in Grenoble, you know. What are you doing here? I thought you'd gone back to the United States years ago."

"I did," Jason answered. "I'm just in town until Saturday morning."

"Business?"

"No, this trip was purely for nostalgia's sake. Thought I'd visit—see how things had changed."

"Nothing's changed," Isabelle laughed. "Are you still playing?"

"Not anymore. I'm a lawyer. I live in Philadelphia."

"Really?" Isabelle seemed disappointed, but she didn't push the issue. "My husband's a lawyer too." She looked pleased to have found some common ground.

"Do you have children?" Jason asked.

"Three!" she said, throwing up her hands in mock exasperation. "They keep me busy. And you?"

"Still single." Jason had always wanted children, but Diane had been less than excited at the prospect, so he'd let the subject drop. "You still play the cello?"

"Only once in a while," Isabelle responded with a wistful look. "You miss it too, don't you? Music?"

"Yes," he admitted. "More than I realized. Coming back here's opened my eyes."

"I just finished drinks with a friend—I have about an hour before I need to get home," she said, gesturing to a table. "Care to join me?"

"I'd love to."

Having exhausted all possible topics of conversation, they parted company an hour later with a warm hug, an exchange of e-mail addresses, and a promise to keep in touch. Tired, Jason headed up to the empty hotel room. It was a letdown to find himself alone not only after meeting up with Isabelle, but knowing Jules would not join him in bed that night.

But this is what you need. Time to work things out. And what a lot there was to think about, not the least of which was what he might tell Scotty and his family. He tried to imagine telling his friend about Jules, but he had no idea how to describe himself. Bi? Gay? Confused?

Yep. That'd sum it up nice and neat. Not.

He looked out of the window; snow was falling harder now, illuminated by the soft glow of a streetlamp. He sighed and smiled to himself. It had been a good trip. He stripped off his clothes and slipped between the sheets in his boxers, hands behind his neck, still deep in thought. He had no idea what he'd tell Diane, how he would broach the subject of Jules following him to the States, or how he'd explain his French roommate to Scott and his other friends at the law firm, even if Jules agreed. He didn't suppose he would find the answers, but the questions wouldn't let him rest, and it was early morning before he slept.

AT TEN o'clock, he awoke to sunshine peeking in through the drapes. He chuckled to himself, wondering if he ever would be able to get back to his early schedule again. He'd gotten so used to late evenings with Jules and late mornings spent in bed or relaxing over good coffee and excellent food.

Better get your ass out of bed, Greene. The snow was too deep for his daily run, so he threw on sweats and went down to the tiny gym on the main floor—one of the advantages of an American-style hotel (another being the generous bathrooms in each room).

An hour later, having shaved and showered, he headed out into the city. The snow that blanketed the streets was reflected in the surrounding mountains—they were evenly dusted with white. It was cold, but the wind was forgiving, and he walked around a bit before deciding to take a bus to the Olympic Village.

He sat on one of the benches in the commons, watching the steady movement of people winding their way by the buildings. With the end of the holiday week approaching, children were out with their parents. Some clutched baguettes in their hands, nibbling at them when they thought their parents weren't watching. Others just chased one another around as they threw snowballs and kicked the fine powder about. Playing. He watched for a while, then ambled to the local bakery.

"Une millefeuille, s'il vous plaît," he asked the woman behind the counter. He handed her a few coins, and she offered to wrap the pastry up for him. "No, thank you," he replied, shoving his gloves in his pockets, "I'll eat it as I walk."

He wandered through the large development, remembering with fondness the many times he and his friends had run to the bakery after school to buy sweets. It had been a good life here, and it had left an indelible mark on him. The night before, he'd envied Isabelle her life—settled in a place she'd called home since she was a child and happy about it.

He shook his head at the clichéd thought that "home" was more a "who" than a "what."

Home. That word again, a word that always brought him back to thoughts of Jules. He'd once thought that home meant Diane, but he realized now that that had always been just for show.

He spent most of that evening in the hotel, ordering from room service, content to watch a stupid American comedy dubbed in French. He thought of Jules—probably already playing at the club—and wished he could have been in Paris to hear it. He pulled out his phone and dialed Jules's cell. There was no answer, of course, but Jason didn't care.

"Jules," he said, "we need to talk. Tomorrow, after I get back. It's important." Then he added, "I hope it went well tonight. Je t'aime."

CHAPTER 17

JASON SMILED as he turned the key in the lock of the apartment door. Not quite two months, and Rosalie's flat already felt more like home than his apartment in Philly ever had. He'd no doubt as to why.

The early-morning ride on the TGV had been uneventful, but he'd used the downtime to do some serious thinking about how he would handle his return to the States. A great deal depended on Jules's answer: if Jules was willing to move to the States and live with him, Jason would stay at the firm; if not, Jason would quit his job and move to Paris. Either way, Jason would tell his friends and colleagues about Jules; he had nothing to hide but his own happiness. He'd come to the conclusion that what he called himself—gay or bi—didn't matter. The only thing that mattered was that he would be with Jules for however long Jules cared to have him—a lifetime, if he had his way.

"Jules?" he called as he dropped his bag in the hallway. There was no answer, but the apartment smelled of cheese and leeks. *Quiche*, he thought happily. No doubt Jules had decided to run out at the last minute to pick something up to serve with it.

He threw his wallet onto the table and checked his phone for messages—Jules hadn't texted him. Shoving the phone back in his pocket, he opened one of the large windows in the living room and sat down on the couch. Early March, and he smelled spring in the air. He wished he could stay to see more than just the stirrings of it, but he knew that wouldn't be possible. Not this year, at least.

We'll see what next year brings. He'd come back to Paris again soon, to live or to visit. But either way, he'd do so with Jules at his side.

God, but it felt good to face the future with something other than uncertainty! He thought of the way that he'd ceded all control to Jules two nights before, and it made him grin. He wasn't sure how he felt about performing on the piano again, but he knew that if he chose to, it wouldn't be as painful.

With time, who knows? It was a start.

The front doorbell rang, and Jason got to his feet. *He must have forgotten his key.* Jason chuckled to himself as he walked down the hallway. *Good thing I got back early, or he'd be sitting out there, waiting for another half hour.*

He unlocked the door and opened it, his face bright with anticipation. "I can't leave you alone, can I, gosse?" he said, but the face that greeted him was not Jules's.

"What?" said the woman who stood there, looking startled.

"Diane?" He stared at her. His mind couldn't quite grasp seeing her here, in this place.

She smiled. "Jason." She always called him that, never Jaz. She said it was juvenile. "The door to the building was open—I hope you don't mind. I let myself in."

"What are you doing here?" he asked, her words barely registering.

"Is that any way to greet your fiancée?" The tentative quality of her voice belied her smile.

"I—I—come in, Diane," he stammered, with an awkward gesture toward the living room.

She followed him into the apartment. "I hope you don't mind my showing up here unannounced."

"Listen, Diane," he began. Damn, but he *hated* feeling unsure of himself; he'd made it his goal to spend his life entirely in control. That is, until he'd met Jules. This time, though, the thought of Jules warmed him.

She walked past him into the living room, where sunlight streamed in through the windows from the courtyard.

"Diane," he began again, "there's something you should—"

"I don't care. I don't care what you've been doing since you left. I've missed you." She chewed on her lower lip, appearing ill at ease herself. "I tried calling you so many times…. I wanted to apologize, but I was afraid you wouldn't see me. I talked to Rosie, and she promised to tell you that I called. But when I didn't hear back, I realized that I couldn't do this over the phone—that I owed it to you to talk face-to-face. So I decided to fly over here and surprise you. I figured we could spend some time together. Getting to know each other again. And what better place to rekindle what we had than in the City of Love?"

He saw remorse and pain in her eyes—disappointment, too, that he didn't appreciate how much effort it had taken her to hop on a plane and come all the way to Paris. "Thanks," he said, unsure of how to react. "But—"

"I hurt you. What I did was wrong. But I was so angry…." Her blue eyes filled with tears.

"I know. We both fucked up."

"Brad meant nothing to me, I swear. I think I *wanted* you to find me with him. I realize that now. I can't believe how cruel I was."

Brad. *So that was his name*. Jason really didn't want to know. It still hurt like hell.

"It's done, Diane. It's over. We both fucked up. I don't blame you." The neatly set table with fresh flowers in the bud vase caught his eye. He hadn't noticed until now.

Sweet Jules. He missed me. God, I missed him.

She walked up behind him and put her arms around his chest, but he could only sigh.

"I really appreciate your coming here," he said, putting his hands over hers and lifting them off as he turned to face her once more. "It means a lot to me."

Their eyes met. "But it's not enough, is it?" she said slowly. Her forced smile faded with comprehension. She'd seen the finality of it all in his eyes.

"I've met someone, Diane." He took her hands in his and tried not to smile at the thought of Jules. He knew he should *want* to hurt her—he *had* wanted to hurt her, once—but he hadn't the heart for it now.

For a moment she was silent. Then she said in a quiet voice, "Rosie warned me. She told me that you'd moved on." She squeezed his hands. "I didn't believe her. I told myself that you loved me—that you *still* love me."

"Diane, I…." *Dammit! Why the hell can't I say anything? There are so many things I've wanted to say to her….* "I really think—" he began again, but his words were cut short by her lips on his.

She pulled him closer, combing her fingers through his hair. He inhaled the familiar scent of her perfume and, for a moment, was transported back to when they had first met, when he'd been fascinated by her, captivated by her beauty, and excited by her zest for life. The fragrance was inextricably connected to those early heart-pounding impressions of her, and he clasped his arms around her in spite of himself. He barely registered the sound of the front door opening.

Jules reached the living room with his hands full of shopping bags. "Jaz…." The name died on his lips.

Jason jerked out of the kiss, stared at Jules in growing shock, and practically shoved Diane away. "Jules," he began as his heart nearly stopped, "this isn't what—"

But Jules was already leaving. He'd dropped the bags in the hallway and run out of the apartment.

"Jules!" Jason shouted after him.

Jason turned back to Diane. The look of shock on her face was plain. There was no need for an explanation; she'd clearly put the pieces together. Without another word, he ran out of the apartment after Jules. The door slammed behind him.

WHEN JASON emerged from the apartment building, he didn't see Jules but decided that he must have headed for the boulevard, so he took off down the street. It was cold without his jacket, but he didn't care. He rounded the corner onto boulevard Saint-Michel and saw Jules two blocks away, running toward the Métro station.

Jason shouted, but Jules either couldn't hear him or was ignoring him. "Jules!" Jason shouted again, reaching the light at the corner. The traffic was heavy, so by the time he got to the other side of the street, Jules had disappeared into the subway.

"Shit!" Jason swore as he felt in his pocket for his wallet and realized that he only had his cell phone. He had no money or fare card to get through the turnstiles. The station lobby was empty except for the woman in the ticket booth, and he barely hesitated before vaulting over the entrance reserved for the disabled, hoping that the clerk hadn't noticed.

There were two platforms. *Which way?* The sound of a train approaching made the decision for him—he could always run back up the stairs if he saw Jules on the other side of the tracks, but he wouldn't let him get on a train.

Oh God. Jules... you've got *to let me explain!*

He reached the platform just as the train doors closed. Panting, he leaned over, palms on his thighs, struggling to catch his breath and ready to scream in frustration. In that moment, he caught sight of Jules through the train windows, standing on the opposite platform.

"Jules!" he yelled, but the noise of the train drowned his voice out. Another train—heading in the direction of Les Halles—was arriving. He raced back up the steps and across the tracks as the train stopped and passengers boarded. Then he ran down to the other platform.

The doors had already closed by the time he reached the bottom of the stairs. Jason was helpless to do anything but watch the train pull out of the station. As it picked up speed, he saw Jules through the window of the last car. Their eyes met for an instant, and Jason could see that Jules's face was streaked with tears.

"Jules!" he yelled again. But Jules looked away. Then the train was gone and he was standing alone on the quay as the air surged around him. "Oh God, Jules," he whispered as his eyes burned with tears.

JULES WATCHED Jason through the window of the train. He saw the look of pain on Jason's face, and it pained him as well. He considered calling Jason with the cell phone in his pocket. As if on cue, it vibrated a moment later, and he opened it to see Jason's name on the display.

No. He remembered Jason and Diane embracing. It hadn't been a casual greeting, not the bises. Jason had been kissing her—a real kiss, passionate and demanding. Jules's chest tightened painfully. *He said he wanted to tell you something*, he thought as he pressed the power button to shut off the phone.

Now he understood why Jason hadn't told him the other night. *He's going back to her. He couldn't tell me over the phone; he wanted to tell me face-to-face. He said it was important.*

His chest hurt. The pain was crushing. He forced himself to slow his breathing. He didn't want Jason to see him like this. He didn't want Jason to see him at all—he didn't want Jason to have to explain or feel guilty. Why make him suffer more? He'd known it would end; he just hadn't expected it to end like this.

He knew Jason loved him; he'd believed him when he'd said it. *But there are many different kinds of love.* Jason had never intended to start a relationship with another man, and now he would go back to his life, his work, and his future wife. That was the way things were meant to be.

It was only for a short time. It's been a wonderful seven weeks. Best of my life. He brushed away his tears.

He climbed the stairs from the subway and headed down a narrow street. He'd go back to the apartment and get his things after he was sure Jason had left the country.

JASON CAUGHT the next train to Les Halles, but Jules was nowhere to be seen. From that enormous station, Jules could have gone to a hundred different places. Even so, Jason spent the better part of two hours wandering up and down the moving walkways, the stench of urine and stale cigarettes a perfect complement to his growing sense of despair. Finally, knowing he would not find Jules and not willing to risk exiting the station and having to jump the turnstile again, he took the train back to Luxembourg, back to the apartment.

Diane had left. For that, Jason was more than thankful. What else could he have told her, anyhow? He'd made his decision about the future; he would not look back to the past. Their relationship had ended years before, and he simply hadn't realized it until now.

She'd left a note on the table.

Jason,

I should have realized that you'd moved on. It's time for me to do the same. I wish you only happiness.

Diane

In spite of everything—in spite of the dread that pressed against his heart, in spite of the tears that still wet his cheeks, in spite of the grief and the guilt he felt at hurting Jules—in spite of it all, the edges of his mouth moved upward in a bittersweet smile.

CHAPTER 18

"THANKS, SERENA." Jason looked up at his legal assistant and managed a smile. "Oh, and I'll need the pleadings file for the Cleveland case," he added. "No rush, just when you get a chance. Discovery's due in two weeks, and I don't think we've gotten all the documents from the client yet."

"Of course, sir."

"Jason," he corrected her. "We've been through this before. You've been working for me too long to call me 'sir.'" Truth was, hearing her call him that made him feel old.

"Jason," she repeated. "Can I get you anything while I'm at lunch? You look tired."

"Thanks," Jason answered. "I'm fine. Nothing a little sleep and a few Excedrin won't cure."

"Jet lag still?"

"Nah," Jason said, "but it's been a long week." He knew only too well that he couldn't blame his insomnia on jet lag—certainly not nearly two months after returning to Philadelphia. Damn, but he was exhausted; he hadn't slept well since he'd gotten back from Paris, and the constant throbbing over his right eye wasn't helping either.

Or maybe you're acting like a brokenhearted teenager.

"I bet you wish you were back in Paris about now," Serena said. "Was it as wonderful as they say?"

"It was wonderful," Jason replied. "Thanks for asking."

Well, it was *wonderful, while it lasted.*

Scott poked his head into Jason's office. "Jaz Man," he said with a grin.

"I'll be back with the pleadings file, Jason." Serena slipped out of the door as Scott walked inside.

"Thanks," Jason called after her.

"Nice," Scott noted, watching Serena leave. "'Jason,' huh? So why do you get all the gorgeous legal assistants while I get stuck with Joan?"

Jason chuckled. "Because Joan is the best paralegal we've got, and your wife is as sharp as they come. Alli's not about to let you out of her grasp; she knows how your eyes wander."

"Yeah," he said, slipping into the chair in front of Jason's desk.

"Alli's also sexy as hell, you big idiot."

"Yeah," Scott repeated as his face broke into a wide grin. For all his talk, Jason knew Scott loved his wife. He loved to say that he read the menu but ate at home. "But we were talking about you, Jaz Man." He picked a pen off Jason's desk and began to twirl it in his fingers.

"*You* were talking." Jason shook his head. "I'm just along for the ride."

"So, why not Serena?"

"You're joking, right?" Jason knew Scott wasn't joking, but he went on anyhow. "You of all people should know that dating a coworker isn't a good idea. How many cases have we handled where it blew up in our clients' faces?"

"It doesn't have to be Serena," Scott insisted. "But hell, it's been months since you and Diane called it quits. And since you got back from Paris, you've been hanging around this place until midnight every night. Even a taskmaster like me knows that's seriously twisted."

"I've got a lot of work to catch up on."

"Like hell. You've always had a lot of work. But these days… Jaz, you look like shit."

"Drop it, Scotty," Jason warned. "I'm not interested in dating right now. Maybe in a while…."

"In a while you'll be dead, man," Scott countered, narrowing his eyes with suspicion.

"Hopefully that'll be a really *long* while." Jason shuffled a bunch of papers from one side of his desk to the other and tried to think of a way to get rid of Scott.

"You met someone in Paris, didn't you?" Scott leaned over the desk with a half smirk.

They'd been through this a dozen times before. "I didn't—"

"You're lying, Jaz Man. I know that look."

"Whatever I did in Paris stays there," Jason cautioned.

"So what's she like? I bet she was beautiful."

Jason stared blankly at the file in front of him. "Beautiful," he repeated softly.

"Shit! I was right." Scott was gloating now. "You *did* leave your heart there. That explains it." There was a ring of triumph in his voice. "Broke your heart, didn't she?"

"Fine, asshole," Jason countered with a menacing scowl.

"I *knew* it!"

"You don't *know* anything, Scotty," Jason retorted. "Now get the hell out of here and let me get some work done so I don't have to stay as late tonight."

"So it was a romantic winter fling, huh? Damn! I'm jealous."

Jason got up, walked over to the door, and held it open. "Out!" he ordered, the edges of his mouth turning up. It was hard to be mad at Scott—it always had been. The guy was too good a friend.

"How about joining me and Alli for drinks after work Thursday? Eight o'clock. My treat."

"As if," laughed Jason. "You'll be too drunk to pay, anyhow."

"Then you'll come?" Scott's face brightened.

"Sure," Jason answered with a theatrical sigh. "Branson's?"

"Yeah. And you damn well better be there by eight, or I'll drag you!"

"Yes, sir," Jason replied with a mock salute.

Scott turned and walked down the hallway and waved back to Jason. Jason watched him leave and took a deep breath, sitting back down again at his desk. The guy was right, of course. It was time to get out and start living his life again. He'd spent too many sleepless nights thinking about Jules.

It wouldn't have worked anyhow. He knew full well he was rationalizing the constant ache in his chest. He was so damn tired that he'd even considered calling his doctor to get something to help him sleep. *It's a good thing. At least you feel* something. After Diane, he'd been numb. But this thing with Jules hurt far more than he had ever expected.

Jason had spent his last two days in Paris hanging out in all the places he thought Jules might go, even taking detours through the Jardins du Luxembourg a half-dozen times in hopes of finding him. He'd gone to the Loup-Garou, he'd called Henri (who swore up and down that he hadn't heard from Jules), and he'd even contacted the agent who had been working to book the trio into the Paris jazz scene. His last attempt before boarding the flight home had been to Jules's mother—a difficult conversation in which she swore at him repeatedly for having Guy's custody changed to his uncle. Finally, with weary resignation, Jason had left Paris with the firm conviction that Jules did not want to be found.

Since returning to Philadelphia, Jason had tried Jules's number countless times with nothing to show for it, and had given up only when he heard a message that the line had been disconnected. He'd called Henri, but Henri's answer was always the same—Jules didn't want to speak to him, even when Jason explained to Henri that there'd been a misunderstanding and that he only wanted five minutes with Jules.

And then that last call two weeks ago—the memory of which pained Jason like a fresh wound. The words still played over and over in his mind; he would never forget them. "He told me to tell you that it's over," Henri said. "He said that it never would have worked with you two. He said to let him go—that you both need to move on."

Jason figured by now, Jules had retrieved his violin and belongings. He'd probably left the key. A few times Jason had been tempted to fly back to Paris and install himself as a permanent fixture at the Loup-Garou and wait for Jules to come. In the end, though, he'd come to the conclusion that Jules had done the only sensible thing—he'd cut his ties and let Jason go back home.

Damn brat. Even now, Jason could imagine the curve of Jules's lips and the enticing smell of his hair. He recalled the feel of Jules's cheek between his shoulder blades as they slept, and it made his shoulders tense with need.

"Shit." He'd snapped the pencil he was holding in two. A drink or three would be a good thing, and Thursday wasn't going to be soon enough. He would leave work early today—get out for a change.

Jules was right. It's time to move on.

EACH TIME he'd tried to leave the office, the thought of another night alone in his apartment was so unappealing that he'd turned back to his work. In the end, his "early" evening had him arriving at his apartment at ten o'clock, and he'd pretty much given up the idea of going out. He stripped out of his suit and pulled on a pair of worn sweatpants, then dug in the fridge for a beer. Lying on the couch minutes later, he picked up the remote and turned on the radio. Coltrane. "A Love Supreme."

"Shit," he muttered as he threw the remote against the wall. The sounds of the saxophone washed over him, and he closed his eyes. Fine. He'd mope. Then he would get over Jules once and for all and….

It's not that easy, old man, and you know it.

Nearly every night since he'd left rue d'Assas, it had been the same: three beers, the vague sensation of sleep or something like it, wake up and run, go to work and—bingo—back home again.

"Jaz," Rosalie had said when he'd called her the day his flight left, "I'm *so* sorry. Maybe he'll realize that you two need to talk—that you can work through this misunderstanding."

"A love supreme, a love supreme, a love supreme…." The words filtered out of the speakers, intoned over the sound of the piano.

Some misunderstanding. Face it—you knew when you left that that'd be the end of it. He *knew it too.*

Funny how the twenty-two-year-old seemed to understand reality better than the thirty-four-year-old. But that was one of the reasons he'd fallen for Jules.

I miss him. He'd gotten over Diane. He'd get over this too. Wouldn't he?

"Fuck this." He was tired—tired of hiding who and what he was. It was time to start living again, to figure out how to move forward without Jules.

Taking in a deep breath, he went back into his room and dressed in a black silk shirt and a pair of jeans—Rosalie's design. A quick assessment of his reflection in the mirror revealed growing shadows under his green eyes and a slimmer frame than he remembered. Still, the man in the mirror was passable. And what did it matter, anyhow? He was hardly looking for the love of his life, right?

THE FRONT door of the club beckoned, but he sat in his car in the parking lot, hesitating. The Door was high-end, a place where men could meet men. He knew some of the women at the office came here to dance and ogle, confident that they wouldn't get hit on. Except that was precisely what *he* wanted tonight. The need to be with another person had grown to a fever pitch in the past week. He was tired of imagining Jules as he jerked off in the shower, for all the good it did to quell his need.

Time to move on, Greene.

It wasn't the first bar he'd tried since the night of Jules's message—the straight bars had been his first line of attack. But instead of watching the women, he found his attention drawn to the men there. So he'd come here instead, hoping at least for a distraction and, with a little luck, someone with whom to spend the night. The thought both frightened and excited him.

At last finding the courage to walk over to the door, Jason smiled at the bouncer, who let him in with an appreciative nod. For a Tuesday night, the club was surprisingly busy with an assortment of men—some dressed conservatively, having come directly from the office, others in more provocative clothes. Men in black leather gyrated to the music, while others populated the small round tables scattered around the dance floor.

Jason headed straight for the bar, too wound up to face anyone without the relaxing heat of alcohol in his system. He ordered his usual scotch and soda and downed it without delay, feeling the burn in his throat.

"New here?" the bartender asked with a sympathetic smile.

"Yeah." Jason handed the man his empty glass and indicated he wanted another. "Is it always this busy on a weeknight?"

"Usually. Most of the guys here work hard—play hard too." Jason followed the bartender's gaze to the dance floor, where several men had their shirts open, hands on each other's skin. It looked more like sex than dancing.

"Shit." Jason chuckled. "Serious play."

The bartender studied Jason for a moment, then asked, "New to the scene, huh?"

"That obvious?"

"Yeah." The bartender handed Jason his drink. "But you'll find that's a good thing. Fresh meat is more interesting."

Jason fought the urge to squirm. The thought of being fresh meat unnerved him. *Shit.* This was going to be a lot more difficult than he'd thought. He tossed back his second drink in record time and was about to ask for another when he felt someone's hand on his and started.

"New here?" came the smooth voice at his side. He turned to see a wiry dark-haired man seated on the stool next to him.

Jason extracted his hand from the other man's grasp and frowned. "You could say that." He was unsure how much he wanted to share with the newcomer. He'd never been comfortable with people who didn't respect his personal space, but he reasoned that in a place like this, some unwanted physical contact was to be expected.

"I'm Tom," the man drawled, reaching out to touch him again.

Jason's back stiffened, and he pulled his hand away once more. "Nice to meet you, Tom." He picked up his refilled drink and got off the barstool. Hopefully Tom would get the message that he wasn't interested. He looked around the room for an empty table where he could drink his scotch in peace. No such luck.

"I didn't catch your name." He felt the man's hand on his shoulder this time and turned around.

"I didn't offer it," he snapped, at the end of his patience.

"Honey," Tom said indignantly, "you may be pretty, but even pretty boys need to learn—"

Jason grabbed his wrist and twisted it behind his back.

"Shit," Tom hissed. "Don't get your panties in a wad. I'm just trying to be friendly!"

"I think the gentleman's made himself pretty clear, Tom," said a voice behind Jason. "And by the looks of him, I'm guessing he could throw a damn good punch."

Jason's unwelcome shadow snorted and scowled at the newcomer but left quickly, disappearing into the sea of humanity on the dance floor.

"Thanks," Jason said, relieved to be rid of Tom. "I really didn't want to beat the shit out of him."

"My pleasure," his rescuer replied with a smile, "although I'd have enjoyed watching that. Sam Ryan," he said more formally, holding out his hand. He was tall—an inch or two taller than Jason and perhaps a few years younger.

"Jason Greene. Have we met before?"

"I get that sometimes."

For a moment neither man spoke. Then Jason, eager to dispel the uncomfortable silence, asked, "Is it always so intense in this place?"

"Here? Nah. But Tom gets his ass thrown out of here pretty regularly. He's irritating but relatively harmless."

"I gathered."

"Care to join me?" Sam pointed to a table that had just been vacated.

"Sure."

Sam gestured to one of the waiters for a refill, then turned back to Jason with a compassionate quirk of his lips.

"I know," Jason laughed, "I look like a first-timer."

"I wasn't going to say that. Are you?" Sam's deep blue eyes were warm, friendly. Inviting.

"You could say that." Jason took his measure of Sam: rugged jaw, strong nose, undeniably handsome. Jason frowned as he tried to place Sam's face, and Sam appeared to do the same.

Another silence passed between them, and then Sam exclaimed, "The Turlington case!"

Jason laughed, recognition washing over him. "You sat first chair. Damn! I remember you now—you beat the shit out of me on cross."

"Your client's manager was lying, you know." Sam grinned from ear to ear.

"Like hell," Jason shot back playfully, thinking that the tiny lines at the edges of Sam's lips looked surprisingly sexy.

"Jury wouldn't have bought it either," Sam pointed out as he brushed a thick blond curl from his forehead.

"Yeah." In the end, they'd settled the case before the jury rendered its verdict. "Glad we never had to find out."

"Funny," Sam said as he took a swig of his beer, "I didn't expect to see you in a place like this."

"Do I look that out of place?"

"No," Sam answered. "But last I heard, you were engaged to some gorgeous PR executive over at Dillon and Associates."

"Right." Jason lifted his beer and studied it. "That was then—before I walked in on her and a colleague."

"That bad? I mean, I'd understand how that could put you off of women for a while, but still…."

Jason chuckled. "No. That's not how I ended up here. That's a *much* longer story."

"Share?"

Jason shook his head. "Not ready for that. Not yet."

"Sorry." Sam appeared shamefaced. "I didn't mean to push you where you didn't want to go."

"S'okay. No offense taken. I'm ready to move on."

They chatted for some time about the trial, then discussed their work more generally. Jason realized he'd been drinking far too quickly and made a conscious effort to slow down and nurse his drink. The familiar territory of the courtroom made for easy conversation, and when Jason glanced down at his watch a while later, he noted with some surprise that it was after midnight. Seeing Jason look at his watch, Sam contemplated his beer and studied Jason's expression, assessing him.

"You wanna get out of here?" he suggested after a slight hesitation. "My place is a few blocks away. Walking distance."

Jason considered the offer. *This* is *what you want, isn't it?*

"Look, Jason," Sam said, "if you want to hang here, that's fine too. No pressure."

"Nah. I'm good."

"No pressure, really," Sam repeated. "We do whatever you want… nothing more."

"Thanks, man." Sam's relaxed manner had put Jason at ease, and he couldn't deny that he was interested.

They paid their tabs, exited the bar together into the warm night, and walked the few blocks to Sam's building, a sleek high-rise with a parking deck below. As they took the elevator up to the fifteenth floor, Sam looked at Jason and asked, "You sure you're all right with this, Jason?"

"Sure," Jason replied. "And please, call me Jaz."

"Jaz. Like the music?"

"Something like that."

They reached the door of Sam's apartment, which was a study in chrome and black leather seating. Here and there, brightly colored modern canvases hung on the white walls. "Nice paintings," Jason commented.

"Thanks. A friend of mine painted them." Jason noticed Sam's expression falter with the words—it was an expression now familiar to Jason, one of loss and grief. Not as raw as the one he'd seen on his own face, but unmistakable nonetheless.

A moment of silence passed between them until Sam offered, "Beer?"

"No, thanks." Jason stepped closer to Sam with determination. "I had something else in mind."

Sam's eyes widened in pleasant surprise as Jason brushed tentative fingers over his lips, then boldly claimed them for his own. Sam responded in kind, seeking Jason's tongue.

Jason moaned, his need to feel the warmth of another body against his own so great that he could barely stand it. And Sam smelled so damn *good*: masculine, with a hint of musk that made Jason's cock harden in his jeans. It had been too long. He pushed Sam against the wall, pulling Sam's shirt out of his pants and reaching underneath to feel the hard expanse of his chest.

Now Sam too struggled with Jason's clothes, tugging the dark T-shirt over his head and licking at the hard nipples that greeted his lust-filled eyes. "Damn, Jason," he hissed, "you've got me so hard I can't even—" But Jason's mouth was on his again, probing, tasting.

Sam was nothing like Jules; his body was broad where Jules's had been lean and lithe. He pushed the memory of Jules's body away and began to enjoy the pleasure of threading his fingers through Sam's hair while he felt the tantalizing heat of Sam's tongue on his nipples. For the first time since he'd returned to Philadelphia, Jason felt *alive*.

"Bed?" murmured Sam, his lips against Jason's ear.

"Hell yes!" A moment later, he was lying on top of Sam in a king-size bed. Sam was now shirtless as well. Jason bit at Sam's neck, then traced a line downward, tasting and licking circles over the muscles of his chest. He continued to explore with his tongue as he reached for the waist of Sam's pants and unfastened them.

"Shit." Sam groaned as Jason freed his erection from the fabric, pausing for a moment to take in the width of it and inhale the telltale masculine aroma. He then went to work on his own jeans, pulling them off until they lay against each other, skin to skin.

He reached his arms under Sam's muscled body, grabbing his ass and squeezing it. The skin there was soft, but he found himself remembering Jules's skin and the sweet curve where back met ass, the way Jules smelled, the sound of his voice….

"You okay?"

Jason realized his shoulders were tense and that he'd pulled away. "Shit, Sam," he said, frowning. "I…." He sat up on the edge of the bed and rubbed his face.

He felt a strong hand on his shoulder. “Let’s stop,” Sam said.

“God!” Jason nearly shouted as he stood up and looked back at Sam. “I’m the world’s biggest asshole.”

Sam laughed. “Nah. You’re just not ready, that’s all.”

“I can’t believe you’re so calm about this,” Jason replied with a frustrated shake of his head. “I mean… I *wanted* this. Shit, I wanted *you.*”

“Same here” came the easygoing reply. “But you can feel it too, can’t you? You’re not ready for this. Not yet.”

“I’m so sorry, man.” Jason knew his apology was woefully inadequate.

“Don’t be.” Sam got up and pulled his pants back on. “Here.” He tossed Jason his jeans. “Let’s go sit in the living room. How’s a beer sound?”

“Great.” Jason followed Sam out of the bedroom. The buzz of the scotch had faded, and he was feeling pretty raw.

“Have a seat.” Sam pointed to the leather couch. Jason sat down, leaning against the cushions. Sam returned a moment later with two beers and handed him one.

“Thanks.” Jason took a grateful pull on the bottle. The beer felt good against his dry throat. “I’m really….” Why was this all so difficult? He should have just stayed at home. Now he felt like the world’s biggest heel.

“Don’t,” Sam warned with a charming grin. “Look, Jason, I’ve been where you are. I know what it’s like to lose someone.” Blue eyes glittered in the semidarkness with those words, and the fine lines around Sam’s mouth seemed at once more pronounced.

Jason said nothing but took another swig from the bottle. Sam’s expression and his choice of words made Jason wonder what kind of loss Sam spoke of. The look of grief in Sam’s eyes shimmered, then quickly vanished. “You loved him, didn’t you?”

“That obvious?” The familiar ache clutched at Jason’s chest, and he ran his hand through his hair, doing his best to get a grip on his emotions.

“Wish to hell it wasn’t, Jaz. I like you.”

"Feeling's mutual." Jason traced the line of Sam's jaw with his thumb and drew a deep breath.

Sam smiled. "Want to talk about it?"

Jason shifted on the couch and stared down at his beer as though it held all of the secrets of the universe. "His name's Jules," he said after a moment's hesitation. "I met him in Paris about four months ago." He wasn't sure why he was even talking about this with a man he barely knew, but there was something of a kindred spirit in Sam that made him feel like he could open up about Jules.

"Paris in winter?"

Jason shook his head and snorted. "Paris anytime is great, and I needed to get away from here. After what happened with Diane, I mean." Sam nodded. "I heard Jules play in a jazz club. He's barely twenty-two. Came on to me, and before I knew what the hell I was doing…." Jason exhaled. "I was ready to give it all up for him."

"What happened?" Sam asked with obvious interest.

"I was running away from things here. Diane kept calling—I kept avoiding her. She showed up and…. I should have stopped her sooner," Jason continued after a long pause. It still hurt so much to remember. "I was just so… overwhelmed. She kissed me and—"

"And he saw it," Sam finished.

Jason nodded. "I chased after him." He tensed his jaw with the pain of the memory and turned back to Sam. "It was my fault. If I'd told him how I felt from the get-go instead of waiting so long, maybe he would have believed it. But after he saw me with her, he never gave me a chance to explain." He sighed. "Two weeks ago his friend gave me the message that it was over—that he didn't want to see me anymore. That I should move on. Helluva great job I'm doing with that, don't you think?"

"I think you need to give it time. Who knows, maybe he'll realize…." Sam rested his hand companionably on Jason's shoulder.

"Not likely." Jason pursed his lips. "Thanks for listening, though." He pulled on his shirt, then went to find his shoes.

"I hope things work out." Sam got to his feet. "But if they don't, give me a call. Hell, even if they *do* work out, a guy can't have too many friends."

"Thanks, Sam." Jason managed a tight smile. "I appreciate the ear."

"Nothing to thank me for. Just don't forget I'm here if you need to talk."

"Thanks." Jason leaned in and planted a chaste kiss on Sam's cheek. "Night," he said as he walked out of the apartment a minute later.

"Night, Jaz."

Jason headed toward the elevator, glancing back to see Sam close the door behind him. He sighed.

CHAPTER 19

SLEEP WAS elusive after Jason arrived back at his own place, and after it finally found him, the morning came far too quickly. Bleary-eyed at the insistent buzzing of his five o'clock alarm, he decided to forgo his morning run in favor of another hour spent tossing and turning. He finally gave up on sleep and took a quick shower—he was too tired to even attempt to placate his body's traitorous erection—and he was on his way to the office, with a quick stop at Starbucks for a venti café au lait to quell his growling stomach.

As usual, the office was nearly empty at seven in the morning. Piles of paper sat on his desk, poised for his review. He hated discovery; poring over the stacks of documents, reviewing them for information he was not required to provide to opposing counsel, was monotonous, mind-numbing work. A bright-eyed newbie associate would have been a better choice for the task, but the tedium would help him focus on something other than his personal life. For that, he was grateful.

It was nearly ten o'clock when his assistant buzzed him to let him know he had a delivery. More documents. He'd been waiting for the Cleveland client's FedEx package—if it were more than just a boxful, he would have no choice but to enlist some help. He barely looked up when, a few minutes later, Serena entered and set a vase of yellow roses on his desk.

"For me?"

"Your name's on the card," she replied. Despite her obvious curiosity, she said nothing more and walked back out. He had no doubt that the identity of the sender of the roses would be the hot topic of office gossip for the remainder of the day.

"Thanks, Serena," he called after her. Then, waiting until the door was closed, he pulled the small card from the envelope with his name.

A guy really can't have too many friends. I hope I can count you as one of mine.—Sam

Jason sighed and ran a hand through his hair. He'd call Sam later and ask him if he'd like to have dinner next week. The guy had been nothing but a mensch about it all, and he knew the entire sordid tale. He still felt like a jerk after what had happened; he hoped he could make up for the night before. With a sad smile, he took the card and stuck it in his desk drawer.

No need to give Scotty more ammunition. I'll get enough flak over the roses!

IT WAS nearly one o'clock when his office phone rang—his direct-dial number. He'd been slowly working his way through an indulgent Philly cheesesteak he knew he'd regret later when he saw the caller ID. "Hey, Rosie," he said as he picked up the receiver.

"Jaz" came his sister's voice. "How're you doing? It's been weeks since you've called. I was worried."

"I'm great," he lied.

"Like hell you are. You sound horrible. Did you hear from Jules?"

"Yes." Jason willed his voice not to break. He heard the sharp intake of her breath and was glad he didn't have to repeat the entire depressing saga from the beginning—once in twenty-four hours was definitely his limit. He kept it simple. "He said it was over. That it's time I moved on."

"I'm sorry."

"Thanks. I appreciate it." A deep breath, then: "So what's up? You usually don't call me from Milan during the week. Is everything all right with you and Stefano?"

"Stefano's great," she answered. "But I'm not in Europe. I had some business in New York, and I thought I'd try to catch up with you over the weekend."

"I'd love to see you." He brightened somewhat. He *needed* to see her. Rosie would work her magic on him, drag him out of his funk. Lord knew he was coming up short in the magic department right about now.

"I'm staying at the Plaza. You up for some jazz this Friday night?"

"Sure," he answered. "I can hop a train and meet you. D'you have somewhere in mind?"

"McCoy Tyner's playing at the Blue Note. I took the liberty of snagging us a few tickets before it sells out. Ten-thirty show all right?"

"Sounds great." Jason knew his tone was a bit less enthusiastic as her mention of the club reminded him of Jules. "I can make it down there by ten or so."

"That'll work," she replied. "If you want, we can grab a drink after the show. My appointment with the buyer from Neiman Marcus isn't until Saturday afternoon, so I can sleep in."

"Neiman? That's great, Rosie!"

"Yeah. I've been thinking of expanding our line, maybe looking at manufacturing a prêt-a-porter collection for the States. They seem really interested."

"I knew you'd get your foot in the door if you tried."

"Thanks," she said. "I'll tell you all about it when I see you. Ten o'clock Friday night, then?"

"You got it. Love you, Rosie."

"Back at you, bro." She kissed the telephone, and he laughed in spite of himself.

"Thanks," he said.

"For what?"

"For being you. I really needed to hear your voice."

"I can't wait to see you, Jaz," she answered. "Take care of yourself, and I'll see you in a few days."

"Later, Rosie."

He set the receiver down and sighed. The Blue Note. He'd planned to show Jules the place sometime.

Things change. Life moves on. Just be glad you had the time together, and let it go.

THE REST of the week flew by in a flurry of depositions and frantic calls from clients. Drinks with Scott and Allison went a long way toward helping him feel human again; that, and his surprising conversation with Sam, when he called to invite him out to dinner the next week. Jason had already come to think of Sam as a friend. Maybe later—much later, he now realized—there might be more.

By the time he arrived at Penn Station on Friday, it was seven thirty, and he was more than happy to have left Philadelphia and his work behind. It was a warm early-summer evening. The smell of the city this time of year was actually a pleasant, familiar one—metallic, but with a hint of the sweet scent of late-flowering trees and flowers. Jason decided to walk down to the Blue Note from Penn Station, having arrived with more than enough time to meet Rosalie. The walk did him a world of good, and he made a slight detour to stop in Washington Square Park and just sit for a while. It was really nothing like Paris, he thought wistfully, although it held its own charm.

Even though it was dark, the park was alive with people. He watched old men playing chess next to young kids skateboarding over the concrete. Surprisingly, the couples who strolled by hand in hand didn't elicit the same pain as they might have weeks before; it felt more like an ache now, a longing. Dull, although ever-present. Manageable. Here and there, students sat cross-legged on the grass, laptops glowing like giant fireflies in darkened corners of the park. Jason closed his eyes for a few minutes and pictured himself back in the Jardins du Luxembourg. The sounds were similar, but his imagination would not cooperate. Finally, with a quick glance at his watch, he stood back up and headed over to West Third Street to meet his sister.

There were already people queued up outside the Blue Note—tourists who hadn't had the foresight to purchase tickets online. "Greene," he told the girl at the front, who pulled an envelope from behind her and handed it to him. "Thanks," he said, heading inside the darkened room of the club.

Most of the tables in the narrow seating area were already taken. Smoking was now prohibited in New York clubs and restaurants, but the place had a dim, hazy feel to it, as if it still housed the souls of all the musicians and patrons who had frequented the small venue over the years. The band hadn't yet begun its set, and without the lights on the stage, it was hard to make out faces in the darkness. Jason looked around several times, grinning when he saw Rosalie's unmistakable profile as she stood up and waved at him from the back of the room. He waved back at her and made his way through the gauntlet of tables poised to attack him in the murky darkness.

"Jaz," she cried as she threw her arms around him and squeezed him tightly. "I'm so glad you came. I missed you!"

That was when he noticed someone else sitting at her table.

"Jules?"

His heart nearly stopped when he saw Jules there, and for a split second he wondered if he weren't imagining things. He thought his chest might burst as Jules stood up tentatively, obviously worried about how Jason would react to his being there. Jules's hands trembled, and his face was pale and drawn. He'd lost weight, and there were shadows visible under his brown eyes, even in the dim light of the club. His cheeks were flushed, his expression hesitant.

Without another thought, Jason strode over to him and took him in his arms. "Oh God, Jules…. I tried to find you… I wanted to tell you…." He knew he wasn't making much sense, but he didn't care.

Rosalie smiled smugly. "I found him at the apartment." She looked at them with obvious delight. "I went back to Paris after you left—I figured he'd be back to get his stuff once he knew you were gone. Took me a while to get it through his thick skull that you weren't back together with Diane. Even longer to get him on an airplane."

"Jaz." Jules appeared unsure of what to say. "I know you're probably angry. I told Rosie that you wouldn't want to see me."

"You idiot," Jason said, still holding him in a crushing embrace, "you're about the best thing I've *ever* seen." He kissed the top of Jules's head and lingered there, inhaling his beguiling fragrance. He felt the tension in that lean body ease.

"I'm so sorry, Jaz," Jules whispered against his chest. "When I saw you with that woman, I just—"

"It was my fault." Jason pulled away just enough to see Jules's face. "I should have told her to leave, but I felt like such a jerk already for calling off our engagement, and I didn't want to make it any worse."

"But… then why…." Confusion surged in Jules's eyes. "You said you needed to talk to me about… something important. I thought it was about *her*…."

"Jules, *no*! I wanted to talk to you… to ask you if you'd come back to the States with me. To live with me."

Jules stared at him as though he hadn't heard correctly.

"Gosse," laughed Jason, ruffling Jules's dark hair and then meeting his eyes once again. "I was going to tell you that I wanted to be with you. Here or in Paris—I didn't care."

Jules's lips parted in surprise, and he glanced back at Rosalie. She only grinned and said, "I told you, I know my brother."

"I looked everywhere for you. Hell, I'd have flown back in a heartbeat if I'd known where to find you." Jason was dizzy being so close to Jules; it all felt so unreal—dreamlike, really—to be in this place with Jules.

"You would have?" Jules said it as though he didn't believe Jason's words—as though he, too, were in a dream.

"Damn straight." Jason cupped Jules's face. "If I hadn't told Scotty I'd be back, I'd have stayed in Paris and looked for you some more."

"I didn't want you to find me." Jules looked ashamed. "Henri told me you were looking for me, so I stayed away from the club until after you'd gone home."

With his thumb, Jason brushed away a tear he found on Jules's cheek. "Stupid fool." Jason's words were harsh, but his tone was tender, and his voice cracked as he spoke. "When I was in Grenoble alone, I realized how much I missed you. I understood then that I couldn't come home to Philly if you weren't coming with me. And"—he laughed shakily—"if you said you wouldn't come, I was prepared to stay in Paris with you."

"In Paris? You'd give up your job a—and everything?"

Jason nodded.

"You really mean it, don't you?" Jules said in awe, his lips parted in silence for a long moment. "When your sister invited me to come with her to New York, I thought she was crazy. I thought that even if she was right—even if you hadn't gotten back together with Diane—that there wasn't much of a future for… for *us*."

"He took more than a little convincing," Rosalie put in with a roll of her eyes. "I told him that if I was wrong, he'd still have a great time—that I'd show him around town."

"Thanks, Rosie." Jason felt overwhelmed. "You're the best."

"I know." She smirked and then winked at Jules. "And now it's time for me to leave you two lovebirds alone." She shook her head when they both tried to protest. "Nope," she insisted. "I'll see you back at the hotel in the morning." She handed Jason a room key. "I booked Jules the room next to mine, so you'll still get to see me plenty."

"I can't thank you enough, Rosie," Jules declared fervently as he kissed her on the cheek.

"Remember, gosse," she said, borrowing Jason's term of endearment and wagging a finger at Jules, "just treat my brother nice, don't go running off, and I'll be happy."

"I will, Rosie. And I promise I won't run."

Jason took Jules's hand in his and held it tightly. He had no intention of letting Jules go a second time, even if it meant that he never let Jules out of his sight again.

Rosalie planted a kiss on her brother's cheek before leaving with another cheery wave. The band was just getting ready for their set, and Jason flagged down a waiter. "Champagne. French." The waiter nodded and flashed a knowing smile.

Jason gallantly gestured for Jules to sit, making Jules giggle, and they sat with their hands clasped tightly under the table. Jason longed to be alone with Jules, but he could wait—he'd always imagined the two of them in this place, and he was determined to enjoy this as much as he would enjoy their physical reunion later on.

For the longest time, neither of them spoke, each content to know the other was there. “How long can you stay?” Jason asked at last.

“We’ve got our next gig in three weeks,” Jules told Jason.

Jason grinned.

“You were right, Jaz.” Jason heard the excitement in Jules’s voice. “The Milan gig was the beginning of much more. We’re booked almost every week starting in June.”

“Three weeks, huh?” It wasn’t going to be enough, and he knew it. There was no way he would send Jules back to Paris alone.

“I could cancel some shows if you’d like,” offered Jules.

“Not on your life,” Jason shot back. “You’ve wanted this for too long. And you’re *damn* good on top of it. You deserve to be busy.”

“I’d rather be with you.” Jules fidgeted in his seat and looked uncomfortable.

“Who’s to say that I won’t be with you?” Jason brushed his fingers over Jules’s lips. “There’s nothing going on here that can’t go on without me.”

“But—”

“Shhh,” Jason said. “We’ll figure it out. I told you. Here or Paris—it doesn’t matter to me.”

The waiter brought the Champagne and showed the bottle to Jason for his approval before popping the top and pouring two glasses. “Santé!” Jason smiled, touching Jules’s glass with his own.

“To Rosalie,” Jules toasted. “A woman who knows how to take charge.”

“To Rosalie,” Jason repeated, and they both sipped the bubbly gold liquid. When the music started, Jason put his glass back down on the table and reached around Jules’s shoulder to pull him closer. “Je t’aime, gosse,” he whispered in his ear.

Jules’s face lit up and he sighed audibly, leaning in toward Jason. “Je t’aime aussi, Jaz.”

CHAPTER 20

IT WAS three in the morning when the taxi dropped Jason and Jules off in front of the Plaza Hotel. They'd stayed at the Blue Note until the band had finished its last set. The music had been wonderful, but for Jason it couldn't compare to the look of sheer rapture on Jules's face as he'd taken in the music and the venerable club. He couldn't remember ever having enjoyed an evening out as much, although as the night progressed, he found himself more and more distracted by Jules's presence at his side. By the time they stepped out of the taxi, he felt as though he were about to burst from his own pent-up need.

"Want to walk a little?" He took Jules's hand. In spite of his physical desire—or perhaps because of it—he wanted to step back a bit and just enjoy Jules's company. Then, when they returned to the hotel, he'd be able to do more than just jump Jules; he'd be able to appreciate making love.

Jules nodded and squeezed Jason's hand. The edge of the park was lit with the line of streetlamps of Central Park South, and even at such a late hour, they were not alone. Now and then a taxi barreled by. The distant sounds of honking horns and an intermittent car alarm could be heard over the gentle breeze.

"I walked around the park today," Jules said wistfully as he and Jason sat down on a bench under the leafy branches of a large tree. When Jason wrapped his arm around Jules's shoulders, the city seemed to disappear. "It's beautiful. It reminds me a little of the Bois du Boulogne in Paris."

"You miss Paris, don't you?" asked Jason.

"Ouais. New York's great, but…."

"I miss it too." Jason leaned over to kiss Jules on the top of his head.

"I like it when you do that," Jules said. "It makes me feel safe."

"I'm glad." Jason's shoulders tensed as he spoke.

"You seem uncomfortable with that," Jules pointed out.

"You can see right through me, can't you?" *You always could.*

"I don't think of you as my father, Jaz."

Shit. "How do you do that?"

"Do what?"

"Cut right through the crap to the truth."

Jules giggled. "It's easy with you. I'm not sure why. I mean, I can usually guess what other people are thinking. But with you, it's always right there when I look. I guess I just see past all the layers."

"Have I told you lately how much I love you, gosse?"

"Nah," Jules replied. "Why don't you tell me again?"

"I love you, gosse." Jason claimed Jules's lips. His mouth tasted of Champagne, and Jason moaned as their tongues met in a silent dance.

"I don't think of you like a father," Jules repeated after he'd pulled away for a breath. "Anything but." He smirked and stroked Jason's hair before he traced his fingers underneath Jason's ear. Jason gasped. "But you care about me, and you want me to be happy. It's something I've never had before."

"God, I missed you," Jason whispered as he drew Jules closer and looked out over his head at the park. "I kept telling myself that I'd get over you—that it was better this way. I didn't want to hold you back."

"Really? Because you've done just the opposite. You've helped me trust my music. Even David and Henri are playing better now. They show up on time for practices. Most days, that is."

Jason chuckled and looked into Jules's face. "I've got a few people that I'd like you to meet in Philadelphia. A few of my law school buddies do entertainment law. We might be able to book you some gigs in the US if you're interested."

"Are you kidding?" Jules laughed. "David and Henri would love it!"

"What about you?" Jason rubbed a thumb over Jules's cheek. "Would you love it?"

"Only if you'd come with me," Jules replied with an evil grin. "You could be our manager. Shit, with you around, nobody'd try to take advantage of us! You're downright scary when you're in lawyer mode, you know."

"You got it." Jason stood up from the bench and held out his hand to Jules. "Now come with me."

"Where are we going?"

"Hotel room," Jason replied. "Unless you want me to pick you up and drag you there. I've had enough of walking."

Jules appeared to consider the idea. "I might enjoy that, you know. Remember, I like being punished."

"Careful what you ask for." Jason playfully swatted Jules on the ass.

Jules smirked again, then sidled over to Jason and kissed him. He pushed his tongue into Jason's mouth and glided it over his teeth suggestively.

"Shit, Jules. If we don't get back to the hotel room, I'm going to have to take you right here, behind a fucking tree!"

JASON STOOD naked in the bathroom of their hotel room, assessing himself in the mirror as he washed his face. The eyes that stared back at him were tired but undeniably content.

The bathroom door opened behind him, and two graceful arms encircled his bare chest. Jules, too, had shed his clothing, and his warm body felt like a revelation after so many months apart.

Jason smiled at Jules's reflection. "I'm tired of waiting." Jules wore a look of unadulterated mischief. He ghosted his hand over Jason's abdomen, feeling the muscles there and dipping lower to the thick thatch of reddish-brown curls to clasp Jason's erection.

"Fuck," Jason groaned in English.

"That's the idea." Jules rubbed the top of Jason's cock until a bit of precome wet his fingers. He used the moisture to lubricate his hand and fisted Jason until he trembled.

"Feels so good." Jason groaned and leaned back into the embrace. "But I want you on the bed, gosse, where I can feel *all* of your body." He eased Jules's hand off his erection, led him toward the bed, and pulled him onto the mattress so that they lay facing each other on their sides.

Jason charted a course from Jules's shoulder over his waist and hip. "It scares the shit out of me how much I love you," he whispered in French.

"I won't leave you ever again. Je te le promets." It was a promise Jason had no reason to doubt. "Je t'aime."

Jason pushed Jules onto his back. The shape of Jules's body was much like the curve of a violin: graceful and elegant. Jason caressed the smooth skin starting from a point under each arm and following the slight inward line toward his waist.

Everything changes now. The thought no longer frightened him, he realized as he smiled to himself and kissed Jules.

"You're daydreaming." Jules laughed as he pulled Jason close so that their chests touched.

"I was thinking about you." Jason felt embarrassed to have been caught in his reverie.

"I like that. But I'd like it even better if you'd kiss me."

Jason obliged without complaint, cradling Jules's head. Then, moving back so that he kneeled between Jules's legs, he began to lick at the familiar, mouthwatering cock. He breathed in its aroma, savoring the slightly bitter, heady taste and wanting more. After licking at the underside of the hard width, he took it as deep inside his mouth as he could without gagging, then sucked hard. *Sing for me*, he thought when he heard Jules's strangled moans.

When he reached under Jules to cup the taut ass in his hands, Jules's body rose to meet his mouth. Jason was suddenly reminded of the music he'd first heard, months before, in the dark and smoky Paris nightclub: it drew him in and wrapped him in warmth, just as he did Jules. The plaintive quality of Jules's music was present in every muscle beneath Jason's hands, in the way he tasted, in the low growls and gasps that culminated in a crescendo of desire. Jason knew he could never get that music out of his head; he certainly could never get Jules out of his thoughts.

"Jaz.... Oh shit, Jaz!" Jules convulsed beneath Jason, shooting his release into Jason's hungry mouth.

"I love you," Jason said as Jules's body shook with the aftershocks. "Toujours. Always, Jules."

Jules's breath stuttered, his brown eyes still glazed with pleasure. "Please," he whispered as he handed Jason the bottle of lube. "I want to feel you inside of me. I thought I was going to die, waiting for this. I've wanted you so much."

"Hell yes." Jason poured some of the liquid into his palm and warmed it, then trailed a finger back behind Jules's balls to the tight opening beyond.

"No," Jules begged. "I don't want to wait."

"I don't want to hurt you."

"You won't" was his reply, and Jason knew Jules wasn't just talking about physical pain. "Just go slow."

He rolled a condom over his aching cock, lubed himself well, then pressed his swollen tip against Jules's hole, slicking the entrance and fighting the urge to push forward into that warm place.

"Please," Jules whimpered.

The beat of Jason's heart was like a frenetic drum, the sound of his moans like the low, slow vibrations of an upright bass, the drone beneath the song that ran through his body. He pressed inside and, hearing Jules gasp, looked up to see an expression of pain that melted into one of pleasure. Reassured, he pressed onward, Jules's body opening completely to him until he found himself wondering where he ended and Jules began. "You're beautiful," he murmured as he remembered the first time they had kissed.

"Please… Jaz…," Jules begged again, and Jason began to move with deliberation, finally settling into a rhythm he felt in both of their bodies. He'd always wondered about the inspiration for Jules's music but had grown to understand the place where that passion was born. He'd never visited that place within himself, not until he'd met Jules.

This is what music is… what my heart is… and my soul.

He understood the depth of Jules's sensuality and why it had so drawn him, right from the start: it made him feel alive and human, full of faults, but accepting of them nonetheless. That was Jules's gift.

By now Jules's body had reawakened, and Jason reached between them to take Jules's cock in his hand, timing his movements to match each driving stroke of his own desire.

"Jaz… plus fort… je t'en prie!"

The muscles in Jason's thighs burned as he thrust harder. Warmth radiated upward from his belly, and he tried to keep his eyes open for as long as he could. Soon it became too much for him, and he succumbed to the intensity of his orgasm and Jules spilled into his shaking hand. He shivered and rolled onto his side, clasping Jules to his chest, holding him tenderly.

"Toujours, Jaz," Jules repeated in a rough whisper. "Always."

Three Years Later

THE CROWD applauded the second encore enthusiastically. The Blue Note was nearly full to capacity, in spite of the fact that it was a weeknight. Jules stood and smiled at David and Henri, who grinned back at him. Their last set had been the best of the evening. Some of the patrons were already leaving the club, although many stopped first to compliment the trio on their performance. By the time he'd wiped the rosin off the strings and tucked the violin away in its case, only a dozen or so people remained.

"Bonsoir, Jules!" called Henri, who was following David out of the club. David waved. "We'll catch up with you tomorrow."

"Bonsoir!" Jules called after them. He turned back toward the tables and had only taken a few steps when a strong pair of arms encircled him.

"You were great, as always." Jason claimed a quick kiss.

"Thanks, Jaz." Jules's neck and shoulder muscles relaxed as he leaned back into the embrace. "You ready to go home?"

"You know I am." Jason smiled, but there was a trace of sadness in his eyes.

"You're sad." Jules kissed Jason's cheek.

"You can still read me like a book," sighed Jason.

They'd be flying back to an empty apartment this time—the first time they would not be returning home to Guy's indomitable presence. The kid had turned out to be much like his older brother: strong, intelligent, and self-sufficient. Not only had Guy excelled in high school, he'd gained entry to an accounting program at a prestigious university near Montpellier.

"He'll be back home over winter break," Jules reminded him, then yawned in spite of himself. He took Jason's hand. "I'll miss him too."

THEY ARRIVED back at Charles de Gaulle Airport two days later to sunshine and a clear blue sky.

Damn, Jason thought as they waited to claim their bags and go through customs, *it's good to be home.*

As the taxi made its way into Paris, Jason leaned against the door and gazed out the window. The familiar spires of Sacré-Cœur rose white over the city.

"Something on your mind?" Jules kissed Jason's cheek.

"Just thinking," Jason replied.

"About?"

"About you." Jason looked at the man who sat beside him. Jules looked back at him, and Jason saw the Jules he'd fallen in love with.

Jason turned and put his arm around Jules's shoulders, pulling his body closer. Gone were all the vestiges of the boy Jules used to be—the lean body had filled out nicely. Jules's chest was now more powerfully muscled, and he'd grown an inch since they had met three years before. His face, too, was more mature; his voice was deeper—but these things only served to make him more attractive to Jason. He saw their future now far more clearly than before; he could see them growing old together.

"And?" Jules laid his head on Jason's shoulder.

"You're still cute when you're irritating, you know."

"And I still know it" came the coy reply.

"Gosse."

"And?" Jules repeated with a wide grin.

"And I love you, gosse." He laughed softly.

"I knew that too." Jules smiled and leaned up to kiss him.

SHIRA ANTHONY was a professional opera singer in her last incarnation, performing roles in such operas as *Tosca*, *Pagliacci*, and *La Traviata*, among others. She's given up TV for evenings spent with her laptop, and she never goes anywhere without a pile of unread M/M romance on her Kindle.

Shira is married with two children and two insane dogs, and when she's not writing, she is usually in a courtroom trying to make the world safer for children. When she's not working, she can be found aboard a 35' catamaran at the Carolina coast with her favorite sexy captain at the wheel.

Shira's Blue Notes Series of classical music themed gay romances was named one of Scattered Thoughts and Rogue Word's "Best Series of 2012," and *The Melody Thief* was named one of the "Best Novels in a Series of 2012." *The Melody Thief* also received an honorable mention, "One Perfect Score" at the 2012 Rainbow Awards.

Shira can be found on:
Facebook: https://www.facebook.com/shira.anthony
Goodreads:
http://www.goodreads.com/author/show/4641776.Shira_Anthony
Twitter: @WriterShira
Website: http://www.shiraanthony.com
E-mail: shiraanthony@hotmail.com

The Blue Notes Series by SHIRA ANTHONY

http://www.dreamspinnerpress.com

The Blue Notes Series by SHIRA ANTHONY

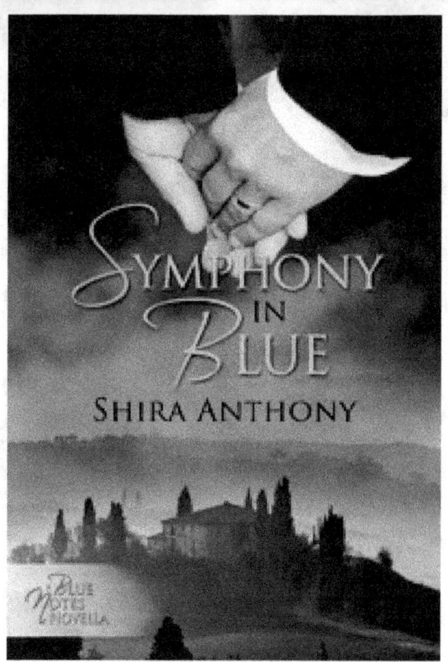

http://www.dreamspinnerpress.com

SHIRA ANTHONY & VENONA KEYES

http://www.dreamspinnerpress.com

SHIRA ANTHONY & EM LYNLEY

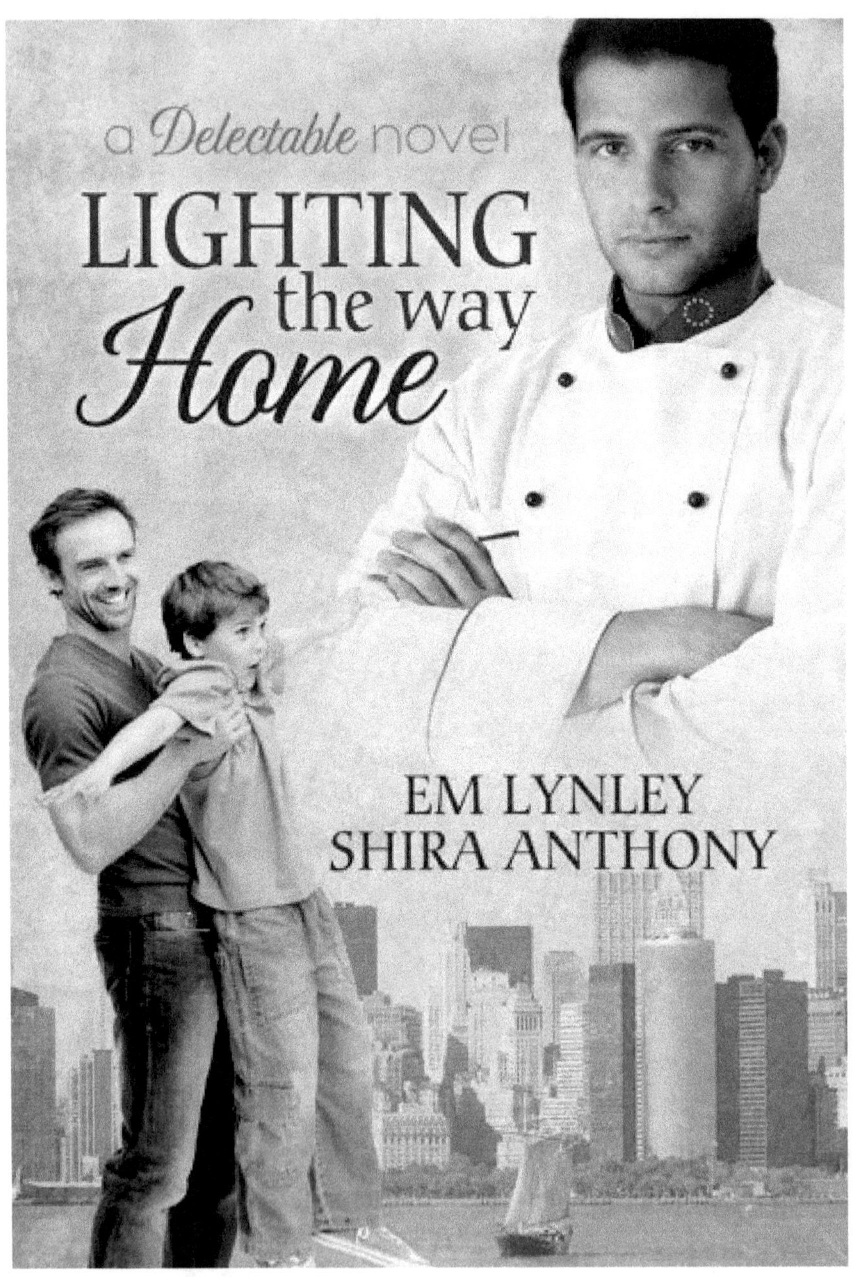

http://www.dreamspinnerpress.com

Novellas from SHIRA ANTHONY

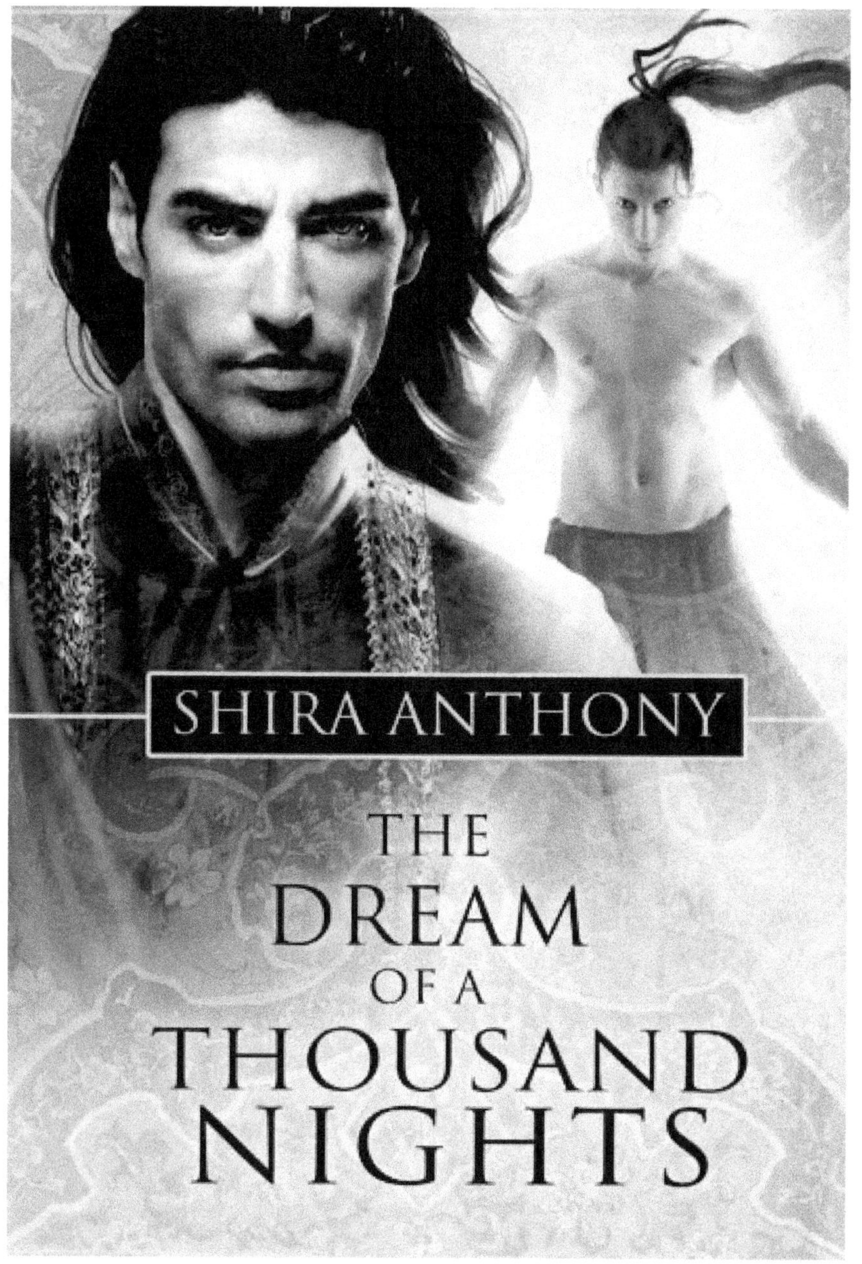

http://www.dreamspinnerpress.com

Also from Dreamspinner Press

http://www.dreamspinnerpress.com

Also from DREAMSPINNER PRESS

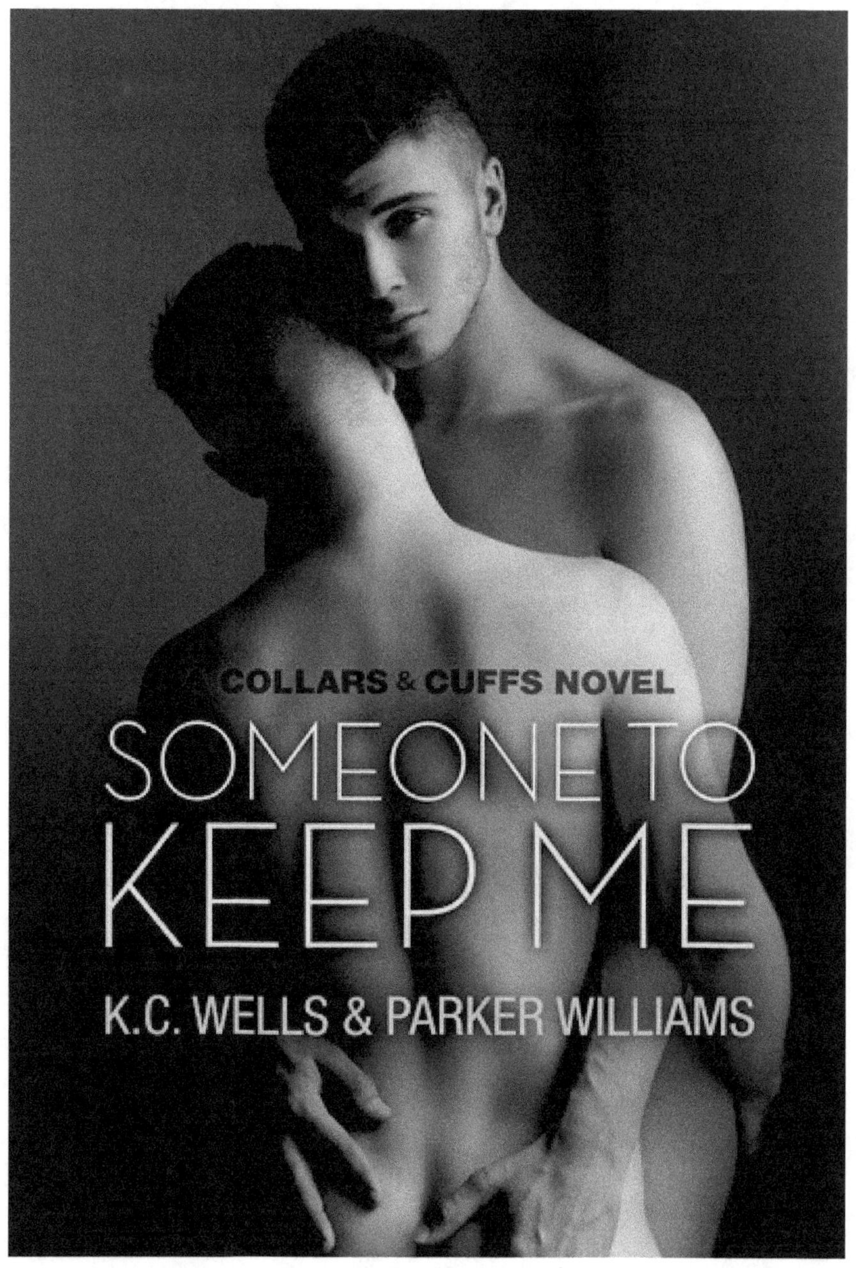

http://www.dreamspinnerpress.com

www.ingramcontent.com/pod-product-compliance
Lightning Source LLC
LaVergne TN
LVHW050621100826
845148LV00011B/1673

* 9 7 8 1 6 2 7 9 8 3 8 2 2 *